"Been there." He nudged closer. "Done that." His belt buckle nudged her abdomen. "More than eager to do it again." He swooped.

She met him halfway. Her mouth demanded more than merely a simple kiss. She asked for heat, but not without offering it in return.

She scorched him, and he reveled in it. He set his hands free, and they filled themselves with the trim, supple back, her narrow waist, the gentle flair of her hips. Pulling those hips firmly against his seemed the most natural of movements.

"What's that?" He traced one finger around a shape in her hip pocket.

"Front-door key," she managed while kissing his throat.

He dipped his fingers into the pocket. "Do you mind?"

"Not at all." If a woman could purr, she did.

He slipped the key from her pocket and worked it into the lock. Whitney's shoulders had been pressed against the door. If he hadn't had his arms around her when it opened she would have fallen into the house.

"I saved you," he pointed out.

"Oh." For a New Yorker, she gave a more than credible Southern Belle sigh. "My hero."

Who would have thought, he thought as he kissed her again, that fooling around with Whitney Sheridan could be so much fun? Humorous, even.

When she deepened the kiss, he forgot about fun, forgot about humor. In truth, he nearly forgot his own name. All he knew was that at any moment he might disappear inside her and never find his way out again. Never even try. And that was fine with him.

BOOK YOUR PLACE ON OUR WEBSITE
AND MAKE THE
READING CONNECTION!

We've created a customized website just for our very special readers, where you can get the inside scoop on everything that's going on with Zebra, Pinnacle and Kensington books.

When you come online, you'll have the exciting opportunity to:

- View covers of upcoming books
- Read sample chapters
- Learn about our future publishing schedule (listed by publication month *and author*)
- Find out when your favorite authors will be visiting a city near you
- Search for and order backlist books from our online catalog
- Check out author bios and background information
- Send e-mail to your favorite authors
- Meet the Kensington staff online
- Join us in weekly chats with authors, readers and other guests
- Get writing guidelines
- AND MUCH MORE!

Visit our website at
http://www.kensingtonbooks.com

ALL THE ROOMS OF MY HEART

Janis Reams Hudson

ZEBRA BOOKS
Kensington Publishing Corp.
http://www.kensingtonbooks.com

ZEBRA BOOKS are published by

Kensington Publishing Corp.
850 Third Avenue
New York, NY 10022

All Kensington titles, imprints and distributed lines are available at special quantity discounts for bulk purchases for sales promotion, premiums, fund-raising, educational or institutional use.

Special book excerpts or customized printings can also be created to fit specific needs. For details, write or phone the office of the Kensington Special Sales Manager: Kensington Publishing Corp., 850 Third Avenue, New York, NY 10022. Attn. Special Sales Department. Phone: 1-800-221-2647.

Zebra and the Z logo Reg. U.S. Pat. & TM Off.

First Printing: January 2004
10 9 8 7 6 5 4 3 2 1

Printed in the United States of America

In addition to being a love story about a man and a woman, this book is also about a woman's love for her aunt. Aunts are such special people for those who are blessed enough to have them. During the course of one's life an aunt can be and often is many things: surrogate mother, pseudo-grandmother, best friend, teacher, confidant, personal cheerleader. As a side benefit, many of them are also the producers of all those wonderful cousins. This book is lovingly dedicated to all my aunts, great-aunts, step-aunts, and aunts-in-law, including . . .

the dearly departed and sorely missed:

> *Blossom Smith, who took me into her home one summer*
> *Joy Allison, who always made me feel special*
> *Betty Brown, whose smile could light up a room*
> *Jewell Huckaby, who was, indeed, a jewel*
> *Phyllis Adams, whose laughter was contagious*
> *Rose Helms, always so cheerful*
> *Great-Aunt Madge Miller, whom I was never lucky*
>   *enough to meet*
> *Great-Aunt Mintie Beaver; I never got to meet her, either*

the ones, praise God, who are still with us:

> *Davy Cooper, my second mother*
> *Maxine Smith, eldest, and so dear*

Patsy Brown, youngest, my dinner buddy
Betty Adams, the caretaker
Jerri Adams, the mah jong player
Gladys Reams, wherever you are
Marie Brown, my newest aunt

and my adopted auntie:

Lorraine Stone, "Auntie," fellow writer, of the kind
and generous spirit

In case I haven't said it lately, I love you all.

And to Fluffy and Kiko, who will always have rooms in
my heart.

Prologue

To the uninitiated, the control room of World News Network might have resembled something akin to utter chaos. A mad, crowded scramble of voices and bodies, monitors flashing, decisions being made, orders being snapped. A hive of activity that never stopped. To Whitney Sheridan, it was home. It might be chaos, but it was a controlled chaos, with everyone doing his or her job. Whitney's job was to oversee it all and make sure that the three-hour news broadcast she produced hit the air as professionally and flawlessly as possible with the latest news and information for their viewers. Hopefully before their competition got the story.

She was damn good at her job. Even people who didn't like her admitted it.

No one knew her well, outside of work. Whitney kept to herself, didn't socialize with her coworkers if she could avoid it. She was smart, she was tough, and she was driven. When she walked through a room the air fairly snapped with the tense, wound-up energy in her.

And at five foot four, with smooth, short hair the color of dark mink, eyes the color of rich coffee, and a flawless complexion, she was damn fine to look at, too. Or so her male coworkers thought to themselves as she stepped into the control room.

The truth was, she was overworked, stressed out, and wired. She was obsessive about her job and knew it. She had no personal life to speak of and didn't want one. Her job was demanding, and so was she. That's the way she liked it.

The control room and the studio it overlooked were her home.

In the control room, two rows of chairs were lined up back to back, no more than a narrow walkway separating them, each row facing a wall of waist-to-ceiling monitors. Beneath the monitors sat the switchers, control panels, computers, and graphics generators that supplied the bells and whistles to what might otherwise be nothing more than talking heads in the studio.

Thumbing an antacid tablet from the roll in her pocket, Whitney popped it into her mouth and chewed. She walked between the rows of chairs and took the two steps up to her station. From there she could oversee the entire control room and, via the glass wall at the end of the room, the studio below them. It was another hive of activity, with cameras ringing the anchor desk, stagehands and copy editors running around in the background.

They were just coming out of a break when the call came in from Afghanistan.

"Whit." From the seat next to hers, her assistant, Sandy, gave her a nudge. "Farley on one for you. Says it's urgent."

Farley always said it was urgent, Whitney thought. But, then, he and his crew were in Afghanistan, so it probably was. And, to be fair, Farley, as the crew's field producer, was good. Damn good. The problem was, he was a glory hound, and sometimes took unnecessary chances with the lives of his crew, with the truth, with whatever hampered him on any given story.

Oh, he'd never crossed the line, but he had teetered on it more than once. Whitney gritted her teeth and hoped this wouldn't be the time he stepped over.

She straightened her headset and pushed the button to connect her to Afghanistan. "What have you got, Farley?"

"I've got hot shit, Sheridan. Some warlord just attacked Afghan and coalition forces. We've got casualties and everything. We're ready to go live and feed a B-roll with voice-over."

Whitney covered her mouthpiece and called out, "Do we have the feed from—where are you, Farley?"

"Just south of Kohst."

"Kohst," Whitney called out. "Farley's feed from Kohst."

"Monitor three," the director called back.

"John's ready?" she asked Farley of the reporter with his crew.

"He's ready."

"All right. Stand by." She pushed another button on the console so she could speak directly into the ear of the anchors in the studio. "We've got breaking news. We're going live to John Standish in Afghanistan, where new fighting has broken out."

Five seconds later Karen, one of the co-anchors at the news desk in the studio, wrapped up her story and announced that there was breaking news to report. Then, like the professional she was, she neatly turned to her co-anchor, Ben, who gave the lead-in to John.

It all went as smooth as a choreographed and much rehearsed dance routine. Or as smooth as any report on war and killing could go. With one eye Whitney checked the monitors and noted with grim pleasure that none of their competitors had the story yet.

John finished explaining where he was and what was happening, then gave the cue for the B-roll footage that his cameraman had shot earlier. John did the voice-over.

The video was excellent and graphic, and barely thirty minutes old. And then that line, the one Farley liked to tease, loomed large.

Whitney punched back to Farley on her headset. "Farley?"

"Yeah, great stuff, huh? And you ain't seen nothin' yet."

"I'm not going to see any American faces, am I?"

"Just wait for it, Whit. It'll be great."

"Don't you dare," she hissed. "You son of a bitch, if some mother in Iowa is sitting down to supper and sees her son—cut it," she bellowed across the control room. "Cut the damn footage, *now.*"

She punched back into Ben's earpiece in the studio. "We seem to have lost our satellite feed. We'll return to John Standish in Afghanistan as soon as we reestablish contact. To repeat, an Afghan warlord in the Kohst province opened fire moments ago on Afghan and coalition forces."

As she spoke, her words were repeated from Ben's mouth, live on camera in the studio. She finished the recap, aware of the sudden tension in the control room.

"Go to break," she ordered the director as soon as the recap was over. She punched back in to Farley on location. "You sorry son of a bitch."

"You dumped out? Goddamn you, Sheridan, I'll have your ass for this."

"And you'll choke on it, you bastard. How *dare* you show the face and name of a dying U.S. soldier on live television?"

"It's news!"

"It's unconscionable, you bastard. You want to explain to his mother why she just saw her son die, live and in color, on television? When I get through with you they won't even hire you to produce a ham sandwich." She flicked the switch on her console and disconnected him. With her other hand she reached into her pocket for another antacid tablet.

"Whit," her assistant said hesitantly, "the boss is on line one."

"Of course he is," she muttered. She rolled her shoulders to ease the tension, knowing the movement was in vain. Tension had been her middle name for years.

She punched into line one. "Don't say it."

"You didn't know that was on the video?" her boss asked. She could practically hear his teeth grinding.

"Of course I didn't," she snapped. "I'm not taking another feed from that bastard without viewing it personally first."

"Wish you'd thought of that five minutes ago," he growled.

"Yeah, well, I wouldn't let the asshole cover a fashion show, but what do I know?"

"Are you criticizing my decision to send him out?"

"Me? Criticize you? You mean you couldn't tell?"

"No need to get nasty, Whitney."

"Then get off my back and let me do my job."

"We'll talk about your attitude at the end of your show."

"My attitude?" she cried. "How 'bout we talk about replacing Farley?"

"That, too."

With a snarl of frustration, Whitney unplugged from the boss and turned back to the control room just as the commercial break ended and the studio went live again. Her attitude, her ass! She dared her boss to jump down her throat about her attitude. They both knew she was the best damn producer in the business. He wasn't about to fire her for mouthing off to him. That was, as he'd said before, part of her so-called charm.

"Maggie," she barked to the nearest editor. "Get that B-roll from Afghanistan edited—without that poor guy's face and name—and put that story together on tape for replay."

"Whit," Sandy said again. "You've got another call."

"It better by damn be important, and it better not be Farley."

"No, it's some lawyer from Texas. He says it's personal."

Whitney frowned. "I don't know any lawyer from Texas." But her aunt lived there. With a sudden sinking sensation in the pit of her stomach, she took the call and turned away for privacy.

"Ms. Sheridan, my name is Harry Winslow."

"What can I do for you, Mr. Winslow?"

"I'm calling about your aunt, Claudia Henderson. I'm afraid I have bad news, Ms. Sheridan."

No. Oh God, no. "What's happened?" she managed.

"There is no good way to say this. Ms. Henderson had a heart attack during the night. She apparently died in her sleep."

With those simple, devastating words, the bottom fell out of Whitney Sheridan's world.

Chapter One

They came from all over the Texas Panhandle and beyond to bid a final farewell to Claudia Henderson. They were teachers and politicians, bankers, farmers and ranchers, craftsmen, waitresses, mechanics, housewives, doctors, lawyers, and, according to rumor, one genuine Indian chief. Old people, children, and every age in between. But of the nearly one hundred fifty mourners at the graveside service, only one was related to the deceased.

She stood alone amid the crowd, slender and sophisticated in her trim black suit and sensible pumps, her face pale, eyes red-rimmed but dry. A few recognized her from old photos Miz Henderson had shown off proudly. Others guessed, correctly, at her identity, as Miz Henderson had spoken often of her one and only niece.

Whitney heard the whispered questions and speculation buzz around her like the lazy drone of bees and paid no heed. She stared with burning eyes at the dark rose–colored casket, shiny with brass fittings, sitting on a stand over the gaping hole in the ground. Guilt lodged as a huge lump in her throat. How many times in recent years could she have come for a visit, written a letter, picked up the phone?

Oh, she had called Aunt Claudia now and then, had sent her a card at Christmas, her birthday. But she hadn't visited, hadn't invited Claudia to come to New York, in more than three years.

How sad, she thought now. How foolish, and self-ish.

The drone of the minister's voice ended, and a woman next to him began singing "Amazing Grace." What Whitney thought of as the funeral song. There must be a rule somewhere that you had to have that damn song at every funeral. She hated that damn song.

She gritted her teeth and thought of something else. The house. She would have to face Aunt Claudia's house today, the memories there. She had flown into Amarillo last night and stayed at a hotel. This morning she'd gotten up at dawn and driven her rental car east across the Texas Panhandle to this tiny town of Washita, a stone's throw from the Oklahoma line.

Harry Winslow, Aunt Claudia's attorney, had met her at the funeral home in time for the ride behind the hearse to the cemetery. He seemed a competent man. She assumed he was, otherwise Aunt Claudia wouldn't have hired him. She was relieved to know at least one person here.

There were others, people she thought she recognized from her childhood summers spent in Washita with Aunt Claudia, but she doubted they would remember her. And that was fine. She was here to see her aunt buried and take care of whatever estate details might require her attention. Then she would go back to New York, back to WNN, where she belonged. A day or two, she thought, should be enough time to settle everything.

The song that reminded her so much of death finally ended. She knew what came next. They'd told her at the funeral home that her aunt had left specific instructions for the service.

As planned, the funeral-home director and two helpers removed the huge spray of gladiolas and carnations from the casket. The banner across the arrangement said "Beloved Aunt." They were from Whitney.

After moving the flowers, they opened the casket. Whitney sucked in a breath and locked her gaze on the patch of sky visible between the top of the open casket and the edge of the awning erected to protect at least a few of the mourners from the hot Texas sun. She couldn't look. Not yet.

She couldn't not look.

Aunt Claudia.

Whoever said the dead looked peaceful—at least when the funeral director got through with them—was full of shit. She didn't look peaceful. She looked . . . gone. Not there. Nothing there but the shell that used to house one of the sweetest, most loving women on earth.

Then the file-by started, as a line formed and the mourners filed by the casket, paying their final respects. Some just glanced down and hurried past. Others slowed and looked. Many cried. Some spoke softly, words of good-bye. Then they came to Whitney, one by one, to express their sorrow for her loss, to say nice things about Aunt Claudia, to tell her that if she needed anything, anything at all, they were there for her.

Like each part of the funeral ritual, this was meant to comfort. It made her want to run. But she stayed, and thanked each person, because Aunt Claudia would have expected her to. Aunt Claudia was always big on good manners and proper etiquette.

The limo ride back to the funeral home took less than ten minutes. Whitney bit her tongue on the ridiculousness of a limo for such a short ride because, according to Winslow, Aunt Claudia had planned it all herself and left written instructions to be followed in the event of her death.

Whitney had to bless her aunt for not arranging for the traditional gathering-back-at-the-house routine that followed so many funerals. She had spared Whitney that nightmare and asked that any such gathering be held at her church.

"Tell me about this trust she set up," Whitney said.

The attorney folded his hands on his lap. "It's a living, revocable trust, and you are named her successor trustee."

"In English?"

"She placed everything she owned in the trust, kept the right to change her mind at any time, and named you, as her only living relative, the person to control the trust should she become unable to make her own decisions, or in the event of her death."

Whitney looked at him sharply. "Was she sick?"

"No, no." He shook his head and patted her hand. "It was nothing like that. She simply wanted all her affairs in order after she retired from teaching. So she placed the house, car, her portfolio—"

"Portfolio?"

"—and her shop—"

"What shop?"

"—in the trust, so you wouldn't have to sell everything to pay inheritance taxes. I gather you were unaware of the existence of Claudia's Attic."

"Of course I know she had an attic. She used to let me play up there when I was a kid. Hot and dusty and full of junk."

"Yes, well, that's not the attic I meant. She has a business, on Main Street, called Claudia's Attic. They take in handcrafted goods, mostly needlework, and sell it on consignment. She was so proud of that shop." His eyes took on a faraway look that made Whitney wonder just how good a friend he'd been to her aunt. He was years too young for Claudia, but these days, who cared?

"At any rate," he said, blinking himself back to the present, "we can go over all of the details tomorrow at your convenience. Just call me at my office and let me know when."

"Tomorrow is Sunday," she reminded him.

"That's not a problem. Your aunt was very special to me. An hour or so on a Sunday is little enough for me to give her."

They rode in silence until the limo reached Main and turned toward the funeral parlor.

"If you don't stay long at the church," Winslow said, "no one will mind, my dear." He patted her hand, much as she suspected a grandfather would. Which came close to amusing Whitney, since the man was maybe ten years older than she was.

"I'll stick it out for a while," she said. Good manners, she thought. Proper etiquette. Respect for her aunt.

So she stuck it out, the food, the condolences, the memories people wanted to share with her, with each other. A dozen women had brought every imaginable kind of food to the family recreation room in the basement of the First Southern Baptist Church across the street from the funeral parlor.

The room was long and low, with short windows high on three walls and two rows of support posts marching between long folding tables. Two tables had been pushed up against one wall and nearly groaned under the weight of the food. There were casseroles, a baked ham, a rump roast, an entire roasted turkey. Three different potato salads, tossed salad, three-bean salad, pea salad, seven-layer salad. Carrot sticks, celery sticks, baked beans, mashed potatoes. Iced tea, coffee, and lemonade.

And those were merely the things Whitney could identify at a glance.

There were not, thank God, as many people here as there had been at the cemetery, but the room was packed.

"I know you spoke with dozens of people at the cemetery," Winslow said, "but a few of your aunt's closest friends wanted to meet you. I'll just introduce you to them, if that's all right."

Good manners, she thought. Proper etiquette. She could do this. Steeling herself, she forced a small smile. "Certainly."

"Ah." Winslow held out an arm toward the woman approaching them. "Whitney, this is your aunt's next-door neighbor, Betty Roberts."

Whitney would have shaken the woman's hand, but never got the chance before she was enveloped in grandmotherly arms and a cloud of floral perfume.

"Oh, honey," the woman said. "I'm so sorry about Claudia. She was one of my dearest friends. I can only imagine how difficult this must be for you. You probably don't remember, but she used to bring you over to my house when you stayed with her all those years ago."

"Of course I remember you, Mrs. Roberts." And a fond memory it was, Whitney thought with a painful sense of nostalgia. "You always gave me lemonade and oatmeal cookies."

"Oh." Betty Roberts clapped her hands over her face as her eyes teared up. "Oh, my dear, how sweet of you to remember."

What was she supposed to say to that, Whitney wondered. She had never been any good at small talk, had no idea how to deal with other people's emotions. Containing her own was enough of a problem.

"There she is." Two women who looked as alike as two peas in a pod spoke in unison as they swooped down on Whitney, side by side, each with one arm out, looking, together, like a giant gray-headed, friendly bird of prey.

"We so wanted to meet you under happier circumstances," said the one on the right.

"Claudia talked about you all the time," the other one said. "She was so proud of you."

"And she loved you so much," the first one said.

And I loved her, Whitney thought, but the words were locked somewhere in her throat.

"Whitney," the attorney said, "this is Mavis"—he motioned toward the first woman—"and her sister Avis. They were dear friends of your aunt's."

"If you need anything while you're in town," the second one said, "anything at all, all you have to do is ask."

"Thank you," Whitney managed.

"Oh my goodness." The first one—Mavis?—said. "Here's Dorothy. Dorothy Gonzales. We, the three of us, played cards once a month with your aunt."

"Bridge Thursday, we call it," Avis said. "The second Thursday of every month."

Dorothy approached, dabbing a tissue to the corner of her eye. "We're going to miss her so much. But what am I saying? We can't possibly miss her more than you will, can we? I just can't believe she's gone."

Dorothy dabbed at her eyes again, then sniffed and looked around. "Oh, look, here's our dear Adam. Adam, you must come meet Claudia's Whitney."

"Dear Adam" was six feet two inches of sun-streaked bronze male whose condolences, when he spoke them, did not reach his eyes. Whitney could feel the animosity shooting from his deep blue eyes. But apparently no one else did.

"Adam," the attorney told her, "is doing some work on your aunt's house."

"What kind of work?" Whitney asked.

"Repairs," Adam said. "Some remodeling. I'd just gotten started. You'll have to let me know what you want to do about it."

"What do you mean?"

He gave a negligent shrug. "The house is pretty

much a wreck right now. Walls torn down, cabinets ripped out, that sort of thing. I'll stop by tomorrow and we'll talk about it."

Whitney was not used to letting other people call the shots for her. "I'll call you. Are you in the phone book?" She didn't know what his problem was, but she wasn't about to simply obey his instructions.

"We'll talk tomorrow," was all he said. "Ladies, Harry." He nodded to the four older women and Winslow.

As she watched him walk away, Whitney knew she had never been so summarily dismissed in her life. He obviously had a problem with her. She didn't have a clue what it could be and was too numb to worry about it.

The next hour was a blur of food and introductions, condolences and hugs from strangers. She wanted, desperately, to be alone, to curl up in a tight ball in some dark corner and will this crippling ache deep inside that kept gnawing its way through the numbness to go away.

But first came good manners, proper etiquette, and potato salad.

It was late afternoon by the time Whitney pulled her rental car up in the driveway of her aunt's two-story Victorian home at the east end of Main at the edge of town. She parked beneath the portico rather than driving around back to the garage. She didn't know if her aunt still owned that old Cadillac she used to drive, and she wasn't ready to find out. It was enough of a shock to see the once white house sporting a coat of yellow paint with white trim.

The new color threw her. She didn't know what she thought of it. Did it mean that the inside of the house would be different, too? Memories were all Whitney had left. What if they weren't there?

She left her suitcase in the car and climbed the side steps to the porch that ran the length of the front of the house. Maybe later she would find the energy to carry in her bag and unpack, but for now it seemed enough to simply face the house and the memories it held.

Even the porch held memories, despite its change of color since Whitney last saw it. The yellow looked softer, more inviting than the stark white it had been during her childhood summer visits. But the white color had never put her off. She had sat out here on hot summer evenings with her aunt and watched the cars go by as people came and went from town.

Whitney stared down at the swing that hung from chains in front of the living room window. She didn't need to close her eyes to see herself sitting there, eight years old, her aunt leaning close to show her again how to embroider a French knot on a linen table scarf.

A lump the size of a golf ball swelled in her throat. How could she hurt so much, when she hadn't even opened the front door yet?

"Come on, Whit," she muttered to herself. "Get it over with." Steeling herself, she used the key the attorney had given her and opened the front door.

Chapter Two

Instead of a houseful of memories, she was instead met with . . . drop clothes, chaos, and a hole in the floor.

The wall separating the entryway from the living room had been torn out, leaving a gaping scar in the floor and ceiling. A glance to her left told her the formal dining room was now an office. To her right, in the living room, tarps, drop cloths, and a couple of old sheets covered the furniture, which had been shoved away from the walls to the center of the room.

It was, in a word, a mess. With a crushing sense of disappointment, she wondered what she had been expecting. To open the door and be greeted with her happy childhood memories?

Despite the drop cloths, however, Whitney knew that if she closed her eyes she would be able to see the room as it had been years ago in her childhood. The camelback sofa had been yellow, with a ruffle around the bottom. There had been a big rocking chair that creaked with every rock to and fro, covered in a stiff, nubby fabric that used to hurt the backs of her legs when she sat in it while wearing shorts.

Whitney shook her head and closed the door behind her to keep out the heat and hold in the air-conditioned coolness. She hadn't thought of that scratchy old rocker in years. It had been a dark, dull green with curved wooden arms. She wondered if that tall shape across the room was it.

In one respect she felt cheated that the interior of the house was such an unfamiliar mess when she had expected to be greeted with fond, poignant memories. Reliving the memories might have been painful, but they were all she had.

On the other hand, the relief she felt at not yet having to face those memories, or any more of her past, left her weak. It also left her feeling guilty.

She pushed herself away from the door and crossed to the kitchen. It, thankfully, was still in one piece, although the brief glance she spared it told her a little remodeling would not be amiss.

Upstairs she bypassed the room that had been "hers" during her childhood. Whether it looked the same or had been turned into storage, she wasn't ready to face it.

Next came her aunt's room. No way was Whitney ready to look in there yet. She kept her sights on the spare room at the end of the hall.

This would do. A twin bed, sewing machine, ironing board, desk, small television. Yes, this would do just fine for the few days she would have to stay in town.

After hauling her luggage in from the car she unpacked and settled into the spare room, with the television murmuring in the background. Whitney was constitutionally unable to go more than a few hours without watching a newscast. Any newscast.

She changed into her nightshirt, crawled into the narrow bed, and stared at the television. And stared, and stared. The sun set, the hours crept by, and still she stared, wide awake, dry-eyed, numb. Not until the sun rose again, heralding Sunday morning, did she force herself to turn off the television, because she knew that as long as it was on she would not sleep.

The last time she checked the digital clock on the small desk across the room it read nine-thirty a.m.

At one p.m. Sunday Adam Burkett pulled into Miz Henderson's driveway at the end of Main. He didn't get very far. The New York niece had parked her rental car—at least, he assumed it was hers—right smack in the middle of the driveway so he couldn't get around without tearing up the lawn or taking down a fence, and not far enough up to let him get out of the damn street. Even nudging up against her rear bumper, which nearly made him spill his coffee, he had to leave his tailgate hanging out over the gutter.

Damned rude, inconsiderate . . . He'd told her he'd be over today. He supposed this could be her way of telling him she didn't want to talk to him, but if it was, that was too damn bad. As far as he was concerned this was still Miz Henderson's house, and he'd promised to do the work she had wanted. He tucked his project notebook under his arm and grabbed his coffee. He wasn't in the mood to let some stuck-up snob from New York get in his way. Just because she hadn't cared enough about her own aunt to come see her in years and years didn't mean others hadn't loved Miz Henderson, Adam included.

He would have rung the doorbell, but it didn't work; it was one of the things he was supposed to fix. He opened the storm door and, with the side of his fist, pounded on the heavy front door. And pounded. And pounded.

He got no answer.

He might have chalked the lack of an answer up to more big-city snobbery, but it had been less than a week since he had knocked on this very door and gotten no answer, and when he had let himself in, found Miz Henderson in her bed, dead. He did not want a repeat, but he couldn't bring himself to simply walk away.

She could have gone to church with someone, he supposed, but that didn't seem likely. She hadn't been overly friendly with anyone yesterday. Besides, she'd had plenty of time to get home by now.

He was going to have to check on her. He didn't see any way around it. First, however, he pounded on the door one more time. "Ms. Sheridan? Ms. Sheridan! Can you hear me?"

Just as he reached for the knob, the door flew open.

"*What!*" Whitney Sheridan scowled up at him, her hair a nasty snarl around her face. She didn't look so smooth and sophisticated now, with dark circles hanging beneath puffy eyes. "Jesus H. Christ," she snapped. "What the hell's the matter with you? South America can hear you."

Adam let out a breath. "You're all right." And, damn, was she ever, he thought. She wore a thin T-shirt that barely covered the tops of her thighs, and not a single thing more, except a pair of panties. Her attire left everything, and nothing, to his imagination. And just then his imagination decided to kick into full throttle and present him a picture of Whitney Sheridan stark naked.

Hellfire, he didn't even like the woman. What was the matter with him?

But, then, he supposed he didn't have to like her to be attracted to a body like hers. He'd just have to get over it.

"Not by a long shot," she muttered in answer to his comment. Then her eyes lit. "But I'm about to be." Without so much as a please-may-I, she reached out and took his cup of coffee.

"Hey."

She held the cup beneath her nose and inhaled slowly. Her eyes slid shut; the furrows across her brow smoothed away. Her lips curved upward. "Oh, yes, there is a God."

"Help yourself," he offered dryly.

She blinked up at him. "Thanks." She took a small sip, closed her eyes again and moaned, then took a deep gulp. "Oh, that's good."

"I'll tell my mother." He nudged her back from the door and stepped into the house without waiting for an invitation. "She'll thank you."

"Please," she said, taking another sip as she closed the door and turned to follow him. "Come in."

"I just did." He glanced around on his way toward the kitchen. "I guess the place is kind of a mess."

"Kind of," she muttered behind him.

The woman obviously wasn't much of a morning person. Since the cup of coffee she'd taken from him had been only half full, it seemed a safe bet that it wouldn't be enough to get her going. He tossed his notebook down on the kitchen counter and headed straight for Miz Henderson's coffeemaker next to the sink.

The coffee was helping Whitney wake up, even though waking up was the last thing she wanted. Okay, next to the last. The last thing she wanted was this man in this house at this hour.

"What are you doing?" she demanded.

"I lost my coffee." He opened a cabinet and pulled out a can of coffee and a package of filters. With every movement, the T-shirt tucked into his worn jeans pulled taut across broad shoulders. "I'm making more."

Whitney frowned. "You seem to know your way around."

"I've been here a time or two. Your aunt and I were friends."

She took another sip. The coffee was cooling off. "A little young for her, weren't you?"

By the way he turned, slowly, deliberately, one eyebrow arched higher than the other, that cool, even icy expression in those blue eyes, Whitney knew she should have kept her mouth shut.

"She didn't know you very well, did she," he stated.

Whitney ran a hand through her hair, wishing desperately that she had simply stayed in bed. "Don't you mean I didn't know her?"

"That's a given." He filled the carafe and poured the water into the reservoir. "But what I meant was, she always talked about how nice and sweet you were. She never mentioned you had a disgusting side."

Whitney lowered her head and stared into the cup she'd taken from him. "I had that coming."

"Yes, you did."

"I'm sorry." She shook her head. "I'm not usually so rude."

"If you say so."

"But then again," she added, irritated with herself almost as much as she was with him, "I'm not usually met with so much hostility from a stranger who knows nothing about me."

"I know enough." He reached over and flipped open the notebook before her. "Let's get down to business. These are the repairs and renovations your aunt hired me to do."

Whitney thumbed the edges of the pages. "It's pretty thick."

"Miz Claudia liked a lot of detail."

That much, Whitney thought, was obvious by the sheer number of pages filled with her aunt's handwritten notes.

"If you'll look over the projects and sign off on them, you can get on with whatever other business you have and go home while I finish up around here. I'll get in touch when everything's finished."

Slowly Whitney turned her head and looked up at him. "In your dreams, mister."

"Yeah," he said, sounding not at all pleased about it. His gaze stroked down her T-shirt, her bare legs, and back up. "Probably."

"Oh, good grief." Whitney rolled her eyes. "If you dream about every pair of bare legs you see, your nights must be pretty busy."

The humorous, suggestive reply that sprang to Adam's lips surprised him. He swallowed it quickly.

He had no desire to be humorous or suggestive. With this woman it was strictly business, and the sooner begun, the sooner concluded.

"Do you want to look at the projects?" he asked.

"Of course. Overall, it looks to me like major renovation."

Adam nodded. "You're right. Many of the projects are small, but when you add them all together, it's a whole-house face-lift. The projects are in the order she wanted them done."

"Starting with the living room."

"That's right."

She ran her finger down the list of things to be done in the front room.

Adam knew the list by heart. Repair molding above front window; clean fireplace; paint ceiling, walls, mantle, window sills; new carpet and pad . . .

The doorbell rang, startling Whitney into jerking.

Adam took a step back from the counter and leaned sideways to see around the corner toward the front door. "It's Harry."

"Who?"

"Harry Winslow."

She stared at Adam blankly, then her eyes widened. "The attorney?" She looked down at her T-shirt and bare legs. "Stall him. I've got to get dressed." And she shoved past him and ran up the stairs.

Adam frowned after her, wondering if he should feel flattered or insulted that she hadn't worried about getting dressed for him, only for Harry.

In the end, he told himself, it didn't matter. He made his way to the front door and ushered Harry Winslow into the house.

* * *

"Mr. Winslow." Whitney rushed down the stairs, trying to catch her breath. She had washed her face, dragged a comb through her hair and thrown on slacks, a knit shell top, and leather sandals in record time. "I'm sorry to keep you waiting."

"It's no problem." The lawyer raised a coffee cup in her direction. "Think nothing of it."

"I see Mr. Burkett has already poured you a cup. I'll get one, too, and we can sit in the office. You," she added to Adam as she poured herself a cup of coffee and thumbed an antacid from the roll in her pocket, "can make yourself scarce for a while or come back later."

"Oh, I'll hang around. I need to check the measurements on these kitchen cabinets."

It figured, Whitney thought. The man couldn't take a hint and get lost.

Then again, she did need to go over the work outlined in his notebook, and she was bound to have questions. Whatever Aunt Claudia had agreed to, Burkett could easily have changed to suit himself. Whitney would have to make certain she wasn't being cheated and that his work was acceptable.

All in all, it was probably best that he hang around. But did he have to be such a pig about it?

With a slight sniff of disdain for Burkett, Whitney led Harry Winslow to her aunt's office.

The paperwork of death was, to Whitney, horrendous. It seemed designed specifically to make the surviving family members long to share in the eternal rest of their dearly departed.

Harry chuckled in sympathy. "Are you getting writer's cramp?"

"Hey," Whitney said. "If you can explain all this for what must be the zillionth time for you, the least I can do is sign my name. This living trust is all so much easier to deal with than a will, I can't believe it. Are you sure it's legal?"

Harry laughed. "Of course it's legal."

"I wish my parents had done this," she told him as she signed yet another form. "Mother didn't have many assets, but it took more than a year for her four-oh-one K to get through probate and the IRS."

"That's rough," Harry offered.

"It was, but when Daddy died it was more than two years before his estate was settled. Even then, there wasn't enough cash to pay the probate on the house and cars, so I had to sell everything to pay the government."

"Well, you won't have to worry about any of that with your aunt's estate. Once you sign these papers and stop by the bank and sign a signature card there, everything is yours and is at your disposal."

The words—meant, she was sure, to ease her worries—sent an odd shiver down her spine, as if Aunt Claudia herself had just passed behind her. It was a friendly sort of feeling, but left Whitney sad. She would much rather have her aunt than a house, a car, a shop, even a portfolio.

Before she could become too maudlin Harry pushed another form beneath her pen, and someone knocked on the front door. She glanced out the front window.

On the front porch stood Betty Roberts from the house next door—the woman of the wonderful oatmeal cookies and lemonade of Whitney's childhood—with a smile on her face and a casserole dish in her hands.

Whitney thought she had been handling herself pretty well, considering she didn't like company, was no good at all at socializing, and was operating on less than four hours' sleep. She hadn't insulted Harry at all, and Adam only a little, but Adam deserved it for waking her up.

But what was she supposed to do with a smiling neighbor? With food?

Give her a room filled with snarling editors, tense reporters, primping anchors, and half a dozen different types of techs, and Whitney could not only hold her own but command control.

But a casserole-bearing neighbor filled her with dismay, uncertainty, and dread. In Whitney's experience, people bearing gifts usually wanted something in return. Nobody gave something for nothing in her world.

With a heavy swallow she excused herself to Harry and went to the door, thumbing another antacid. On her way she was nearly trampled by Adam Burkett.

"Sorry," he muttered. "I thought you weren't coming."

"Thanks," she said rather ungraciously, "but I've got it."

Adam stepped back, tipped an imaginary hat, and made his way back to the kitchen. It had been all he could do to keep from bowing and saying, "Yes, your highness."

He wouldn't have put it past her to leave Betty standing out there on the porch.

The speed with which she grabbed the casserole from Betty and sent the woman on her way did nothing to raise Adam's opinion of her. When she carried the casserole to the kitchen he turned his back and unnecessarily measured the width of the windowsill.

It was another hour before Harry gave Whitney a final handshake along with yet another reminder for her to go to the bank the next day with the proper forms so she could sign a signature card and have access to her aunt's accounts. As if she might starve to death or something equally dramatic if she couldn't immediately get her hands on Aunt Claudia's cash.

Harry was a nice man and seemed to be a capable attorney, but he was definitely a worrywart. She was relieved to send him on his way.

She closed the door behind him and leaned back against it with a sigh. The neighbor with her casserole and the attorney with his paperwork were taken care of. Two down, one to go. She still had the carpenter to deal with.

He wasn't in the kitchen. After a brief search she determined that he wasn't anywhere on the ground floor. She didn't relish the idea of his being upstairs with her underwear. He didn't have any business being up there in the bedrooms, especially not before she had given approval for the work in his notebook.

Before she could work herself up into a full head

of steam she happened to glance out a back window and spotted him in the backyard. Pruning a tree?

"I know trees are wood," she said upon joining him a moment later, "but isn't that stretching the duties of a carpenter a bit far?"

"Just taking care of this dead limb," Adam said. "It broke in the storm we had last week. I meant to get right to it, but somehow it kept getting pushed to the back burner. Funny how we mean to do something but keep putting it off because we think there's always time."

"Since I don't want to be accused of putting things off," she said, "I'll be inside going through your list."

She didn't watch to see what he did with the tree limb, but he followed her into the house within minutes. She took his notebook to the breakfast table on the other side of the kitchen bar area and sat down.

Her experience with home repairs and remodeling was limited. If anything went wrong, her landlord took care of it. But she'd heard her coworkers talk, and therefore knew that the prices Adam Burkett was charging her aunt were dirt cheap compared to what the same jobs would cost in New York. Try as she might, she could not fault the rates. If Adam held to them. In her experience the final bill was always higher than the estimate.

"How much of this work was my aunt's idea?" she asked.

He leaned back in the chair across from her. "That depends on what you mean."

"Explain."

He gave a negligent shrug. "If you mean was it her idea to repair the molding along the ceiling above the front window, no. She wanted to give the room a face-lift, but she hadn't noticed that piece was cracked. Overall, she told me what she wanted done or what she was unhappy with and I helped her figure out what to do about it. Now you're going to ask me if I took advantage of her."

Whitney pursed her lips and shook her head. "Of course I'm not."

"Why not?"

"Because if you did, you wouldn't tell me the truth, so what would be the point?"

"True enough," he said. "But I will tell you that your aunt was a good friend of mine. I've known her all my life."

"Were you one of her students?"

"I was. Fourth grade. You were half right earlier. I loved her. Just not the way you meant."

"I apologized for that."

"You did."

"You don't like me very much," she said.

His eyes narrowed. "Not particularly. Do you want to go over this stuff now?"

Whitney arched her brow. At least he seemed honest about his feelings. "Yes," she said. "Let's get it done."

She read again the details of what was to be done to the living room—or rather, what had already begun—along with the prices being charged. Paint and carpet samples were included with the information. She could find no quarrel with any of it, until a piece of flowered paper fell to her lap.

"What's this?"

"A wallpaper sample."

"For what?" It was without a doubt the gaudiest,

most hideous, flowery wallpaper Whitney had ever seen. "A French bordello?"

Adam let out a grunt. "You don't like it?"

"I hope you haven't already bought it."

"It's for the wall around the fireplace. Your aunt picked it out."

"Is that supposed to make it better?"

He shrugged and crossed his arms over his chest as he leaned back in his chair. "Maybe."

"Look," Whitney said. "I don't owe you any explanations, but it so happens I loved my aunt very much."

"You had a damn funny way of showing it."

"How I did or did not show it was between my aunt and me. Try to focus, here, Burkett. This work is no longer being done for her. It's being done to make the house more saleable, and to honor her agreement with you."

"Don't do me any favors. You don't owe me anything. I can finish the living room and stop right there."

"You could," Whitney acknowledged with a nod. "Except you've already agreed to the other jobs, and you don't seem the type to back out on a deal."

He eyed her for a long moment before speaking. "So now you know what type of person I am?"

"I know what kind of person my aunt was, and her attorney says she liked you. That says a lot."

"Am I supposed to say thank you?"

Whitney tilted her head, deciding this conversation couldn't be avoided any longer, so she jumped in. "You don't like me very much. I don't know why, but that's your privilege. I don't need you to like me,

I don't even mind your occasional rudeness. Until it starts interfering with getting this work done."

"Sister," he said with a drawl. "I haven't even begun to be rude to you."

"Well, aren't I the lucky one, then," she said.

"I haven't been near as rude to you as you were to Betty earlier."

Whitney stared at him blankly. "I beg your pardon?"

"You all but told her thanks for the food, now get lost because I've got more important things to do than talk to a woman who was one of my aunt's closest friends. Tough nuts, sister."

Whitney stared, aghast. "I said no such thing."

"Not with your words, but your manner said it all. You might not believe this, or care, but Betty's hurting, too. She might have a need to connect with someone her best friend cared about."

"Mr. Burkett," Whitney said carefully. "I don't care if you don't like me. But I'll be damned if I'll put up with your treating me like a child and taking me to task for how I do or don't treat people. If you're planning to ever do it again, tell me now and we'll sever our business ties here and now and you can be on your way."

He acknowledged her with a nod. "We can sever our ties right now if you prefer. Regardless, you're right, I have no business telling you what to do."

"If that was an apology, it's accepted."

He opened his mouth to speak, but Whitney held up her hand to stop what she knew would be a denial.

"If it wasn't an apology," she said, "that's fine. As I said, I don't care if you don't like me. Just don't get the idea you can tell me what to do. If you want to finish this job, then let's get to it."

"You're not curious about why I don't like you?" he asked. "No, never mind," he added quickly. "You won't be around long enough for it to matter, right? So why don't we get to work."

Whitney stared at him a moment, wondering if it was worth her time and energy to argue with him, to get him to reveal why he more than disliked her. But as he'd said, she wouldn't be around long enough for it to matter. Besides, she just flat didn't care what he thought.

She held up the scrap of ugly wallpaper. "Forget this. The rest of the walls are going to be white?"

"Slightly off-white. Eggshell."

"I think eggshell sounds like the perfect color for the fireplace wall, too."

"All right." He made a notation on the list of things to be done in the living room. "Anything else?"

"I don't see any notes on the carpet." She got up and walked the few feet to the living room and studied the thick-pile carpeting. "This looks pretty new."

"About two years."

"Fine. You won't damage it, get paint on it or anything?"

"Aw, gee, you spoil all my fun."

Whitney wanted to smile at that, but couldn't. She was still a little sore over his accusation about how she had treated Betty from next door.

Had she done that? Been rude? Practically pushed her off the porch? She had the sinking feeling that she had done exactly that, and it didn't sit well with her. She resumed her seat without looking at him, popped another antacid tablet into her mouth, and flipped the page in his notebook to the next project. Her stomach chose that precise moment to growl.

The irritating man across the table from her chuckled. "I guess you haven't eaten."

"Since you woke me up when you pounded on my door, I guess not."

He shrugged. "You've got a casserole. I hear Betty's a good cook."

Whitney smirked. "I take that to mean you're hungry."

"Watch out," he told her. "You're on the verge of being nice. Don't spoil things now."

The decision, which went unvoiced, was nonetheless unanimous. The lasagna from Betty Roberts was delicious. Afterward Whitney and Adam took out the list of repairs again and got back to work.

They spent the next hour going over one project after another, walking through the house as they went so Whitney could see the problems that needed to be fixed. She found nothing she disagreed with, other than that hideous wallpaper for the living room.

Adam was mildly surprised and intensely relieved. He had expected her to nitpick, or demand different repairs or colors or something. He had expected, he admitted, the worst. She had, for the most part, disappointed him.

But when he left, he still had a substantial job to do on Miz Henderson's house. Aside from the money, he wanted to do the work for Miz Henderson. He wanted her house to look the way she had wanted it. Now that he knew her niece wasn't going to stand in his way, he could do this one last thing for the woman who had meant so much to him for most of his life.

"All right, then." He closed the notebook and held out his hand. "We have a deal?"

She shook his hand. "We have a deal. The only thing you haven't provided is a timetable. How long do you anticipate taking to complete everything?"

"If I get back to work tomorrow and nothing else comes up—"

"What do you mean, if nothing else comes up?"

"I have other clients. Sometimes things come up that have to be taken care of right away. Your aunt said it wouldn't be a problem for her if I had to go take care of another job here and there in between jobs here."

"It could be a problem for me," she told him. "I can't stay away from work indefinitely. How long if you don't stop to work for someone else?"

"You don't need to be here for me to get the work done," he said.

"I beg to differ."

He shrugged. "That's up to you, but it's really not necessary. I know what I'm doing."

"Then answer my question. How long?"

"If I don't run into any problems, three or four weeks."

"What kinds of problems would slow you down?"

"Lots of things."

"Name a few," she insisted.

"Peeling off the wallpaper in the upstairs bathroom and finding a dozen layers of older paper underneath it. Old wiring that has to be replaced. That sort of thing."

She sat a moment and counted up all her unused vacation and sick days and decided she had more than enough. "All right. A month to six weeks. I can stay that long."

"I'm telling you, you don't have to be here. You don't want to be here. The work is going to be noisy and dusty and damned inconvenient to live around, and when I get to the kitchen you won't even be able to cook."

"That's not your problem. I'm not familiar with your work, but the quality of it will help determine the selling price of the house. It would be irresponsible of me to leave when I should be here supervising the work."

"Suit yourself." Adam nearly patted himself on the back for not sneering. Did she think he couldn't do the work without her looking over his damn shoulder? Well, to hell with her. If she wanted to hang around Washita for a month or more, what did he care? Besides, he didn't think she would last two weeks before she hightailed it back to New York City.

"I'll see you in the morning then," he said. "Around eight-thirty."

To her credit, she didn't blanch, as he'd thought she would, seeing as how she'd slept until after one p.m. today. But that might have been a slight tic he saw at the corner of her eye, and it did his heart good.

"That's fine," was all she said.

* * *

"Why didn't you invite that poor girl?"

Adam stared at his mother, trying to figure out who she was talking about. "What poor girl?"

"Claudia's niece. That poor girl."

Adam rolled his eyes. "First of all, I doubt she's poor, and she's not a girl. Second, why would I invite her?" They often had guests at their weekly family cookout in his parents' backyard, but usually not strangers.

"Why wouldn't you?" his mother demanded. "She's a stranger in town, all alone. Alone in the world, from what I hear, having just buried her only living relative. I'm sure she could use a friend or two."

Adam smirked. "Yeah, but who wants to befriend a barracuda?"

Fifty-seven-year-old Mary Burkett pinched her youngest son on the arm.

"Ow!"

"Shame on you," she told him. "I taught you better manners than that."

Adam hung his head; his shoulders drooped. "Yes, ma'am."

"Yes, ma'am," she mimicked. Then she laughed outright. "You faker. Go give her a call and invite her over."

Adam shook his head. His mother had obviously made up her mind that Whitney Sheridan would join the Burkett family cookout. He'd seen that look in his mother's eyes before. She hadn't earned the nickname "The General" by failing to get her way, no matter how gently or lovingly her orders were issued.

"Dad," he called toward the den where his father

was finishing the Sunday paper. "She's picking on me."

"'Bout time you got home to take your share."

"Oh, you two." More than a full head shorter than her husband and son, Mary propped her hands on her ample hips and *tsk*ed. "One of you needs to mow the backyard before everyone else gets here."

"You can do that, can't you, son?" Teddy asked hopefully.

"Sure, Dad. I'll mow the yard and you can talk to the New York lady."

"Me? I don't know her. I wouldn't know what to say to her."

Mary fanned her hand in front of her face. "My, my. I feel a trip coming on. I think I'll go spend a couple of weeks in Phoenix with my cousin."

"All right." Teddy tossed the paper aside and rose from his easy chair. "I'll mow, son. You get Miz Henderson's niece here in time for burgers." Teddy Burkett would mow to the moon and back if it would keep his wife from leaving him home without her for even one night. He would never survive two weeks on his own, and he was a brave enough man to admit it.

Chapter Three

As soon as Adam left her house Whitney was finally able to take a shower. She was sorely tempted to go back to bed, since she'd gotten only a few hours of sleep the night before, but it was mid-afternoon already. If she slept now, she would probably be awake all night again.

There was plenty for her to do. So much, in fact, that she wasn't sure where to begin. She had to go through all of her aunt's belongings and decide what to do with them. The very idea of such a task weighed heavily on her.

Maybe a walk would shore her up enough to be able to face the task. She pocketed the house keys and a fresh roll of antacids and headed out the front door. The June sun was warm, but not too hot with the steady breeze to keep the temperature feeling pleasant. She took the sidewalk along Main Street and walked into the heart of Washita.

She wanted to see Claudia's Attic, the shop her aunt owned, but it would be closed today, Harry had told her, and he hadn't had a key to give her. She would be able to get a key tomorrow from the manager. That meant that if she wanted to see the store today she would be reduced to peering through the window like a looky-loo. Since she didn't care to draw attention or speculation to herself, she would refrain from peeking through windows.

But that didn't mean she couldn't walk by and get a good look from the sidewalk.

Main Street looked vaguely familiar to her, although as a child she hadn't paid it that much attention. Except for the Dairy Boy. They had the greatest hot dogs on earth, and Sno-Kones that could freeze your back teeth and turn the lower half of your face an interesting flavor-matching color for hours and hours.

There had been a café, too, where Aunt Claudia had taken her a time or two. Whitney remembered that her bare legs had stuck to the vinyl booth where they'd sat. She had giggled over the sucking sound when she had pulled her skin free.

At the far end of town there had been a feed store where she and Aunt Claudia had bought a flat of flowers one year to plant in front of the porch.

A dozen other memories surfaced as she neared what had been the Mecca of her childhood, only to find that here, too, things had changed. It wasn't Dairy Boy any more, but now bore a sign naming it Dairy Mart.

Her breath hitched in her chest. Good grief, she wasn't getting emotional about a hot dog, was she?

Suddenly Whitney realized that rather than strolling easily down the street, she'd been walking fast and hard, as if rushing to get back to the control room before the commercial break was over. She took a deep breath and let it out slowly, vowing to at least act as if she were relaxed.

Walking on, she passed a hardware store, grocery,

flower shop, and a dozen other businesses. In the middle of town sat what appeared to be the only bank, the First Washita Savings and Loan. And there on the corner, at the edge of the bank parking lot, sat Claudia's Attic.

Slowly, Whitney stopped and stood across the street from her aunt's business.

Were it not for the sign and the small paved parking lot where a lawn should be, one might assume it to be simply another of the old, early twentieth-century homes that decorated Main and trailed down several side streets. The covered porch surrounding the two-story, white frame house looked cool and inviting, the only spot of shade on that southwest corner of the intersection.

CLAUDIA'S ATTIC. The ten-foot-long sign, painted to look as if it were done in counted cross-stitch, stretched across the porch roof in the clean, bright colors of red, white, and blue. Very attractive, but then Aunt Claudia had always had a good eye.

The store had wide front windows filled with merchandise. Whitney decided to finish her walk down Main, then return on the other side of the street. That would take her directly to the small parking lot in front of Claudia's Attic.

She turned away and reminded herself to walk slowly, like a normal person. This wasn't a power walk, merely a stroll down Main to clear her head.

She thumbed an antacid tablet from the roll in her pocket and popped it into her mouth.

It didn't take long for the far west end of Main Street to come into view. The entire town was barely a mile long, marked by the feed store at the west end and Aunt Claudia's house on the east.

A block before the edge of town sat the Good Eats Café. Whitney wasn't sure she remembered the name, but one glance into the plate-glass window sent memories flashing through her mind. A glass of iced tea nearly as tall as she was. A waitress with orange hair and green-tinted glasses, snapping a wad of pink bubble gum between big white teeth.

The café door swung open, and an overhead bell just inside jingled. A laughing woman around Whitney's age came out with two young boys.

"Come on, Mom," one of the boys said with a definite whine in his voice. "You said we could go out to Kevin's and ride horses."

"I said we could go soon." The woman hitched her purse strap over her shoulder and turned to face the boys in the doorway. "I didn't mean today. If you want a clean uniform for tomorrow's game, we have to do laundry today."

"We could do laundry after we get home from riding."

"Oh, you mean after you go to bed? Come on, get out of the doorway before Miss Ada accuses us of trying to air-condition Main Street."

The younger boy, about six or seven, glanced at Whitney, ducked his head and snickered.

The woman turned to see whom he was looking at and spotted Whitney, barely five feet away. "Oh. Hi."

Whitney gave a nod and a slight smile. "Hello."

The woman's eyes widened. "You're Whitney."

Whitney cocked her head. "Do I know you?"

The woman laughed. "Oh, yeah, you're Whitney, all right. I always envied the way you could arch one eyebrow that way. It's so intimidating."

"I beg your pardon?"

"Mom," the eight-year-old whined.

"You two get in the car. I'll be along in a minute." She put a hand to the back of each boy and nudged them toward a blue SUV parked at the curb. Then she turned back to Whitney. "I'm sorry. There's no reason for you to remember me. What were we, maybe ten, eleven, the last time we saw each other?"

A picture teased the back of Whitney's mind. She looked closer at the woman before her, letting her image meld with the one in her head. "Janey?"

"Oh Lord, I had no idea you would remember me." Janey opened her arms wide and wrapped them around Whitney's shoulders. "I'm so sorry about Miz Henderson. You must be devastated. We were there yesterday at the funeral, all of us, but I didn't want to bother you then, you had so many people around you." One more squeeze, and she stepped back. "Your aunt was so wonderful. Everybody loved her. Just everybody. How long will you be in town? I'd love a good long visit if you have time before you head back to New York."

"New York? How did you know that?"

"Heavens!" Janey laughed and waved her hand in the air. "Your aunt was so proud of you, she talked about you all the time. Had everybody in town watching WNN when you went to work there, looking for your name on the credits. Around here, you're practically famous."

More than a little stunned, Whitney swallowed hard. For a brief instant she thought she felt a burning behind her eyes, but then it disappeared. "I had no idea."

Janey laughed again, then sobered. "Will you be in town long?"

"It looks that way. About a month, at least, while the house is being worked on."

"Ah, renovations. Adam Burkett, right?"

"What, is he the only carpenter in town?"

"Pretty near," Janey said cheerfully. "He's certainly the most popular. I mean, he's the last of the Burkett boys, the only one who's still single. And you've got him for a month? Whew." Grinning, she blew on her fingertips and shook her hand as if to cool it. "If it was me, and if I wasn't married, I wouldn't care that he's five years younger than me. And if you tell anyone I said that I'll deny it with my dying breath."

Whitney pursed her lips, remembering lazing beneath the tree in her aunt's backyard and listening to Janey talk a blue streak in the summer afternoon heat, with a glass of Betty Roberts's lemonade sweating in her hand.

"As far as I'm concerned," she told Janey, "he's all yours. He doesn't like me, and it's mutual."

"Oh, pooh." Janey waved her hand before her face. "But if you're going to be here for a month, then maybe you'll have time to get together. I work at the bank during the week, but maybe you'd like to come to one of the boys' softball games. It seems like we have one almost every night. Miz Henderson used to come all the time. She got a real kick out of it. Maybe you will, too. Why don't I give you a call? I assume you're staying at her house."

"Yes, I am."

Janey reached out and squeezed Whitney's arm. "It's so good to see you again after all these years. I'll call you. I can't wait to hear about life in the big city."

Whitney smiled, as she knew was expected of her,

but inside, confusion and uncertainty reigned. Seeing a childhood friend left her feeling disoriented.
The prospect of getting together with her and talking filled her with apprehension.

Imagine that. The woman not so secretly known
as the Dragon Lady in certain national newsroom
circles could be intimidated by the Texas version of
a soccer—or in this case, a softball—mom. If word
got out, Whitney's credibility in the WNN control
room would go up in smoke.

But, really, she thought as Janey backed away from
the curb and waved good-bye, what did she know
about getting together with a friend for a visit? Her
own social life . . . well, hell, she didn't have a social
life. Everything she did, everyone she associated
with, had to do with her job. If she couldn't talk
about work with someone who knew what she
meant, what was there to talk about, and with
whom?

God, she was pathetic.

Shaking her head at herself, she crossed the street
and started back down Main to get a closer look at
Claudia's Attic. By the time she reached it she decided she didn't care if people saw her peeking. She
turned up the sidewalk to the front porch, similar to
Aunt Claudia's porch at home, with potted flowers,
wicker chairs, and a swing, and peered in the windows.

The window displays were attractive and full without being too fussy. Colorful quilts, throw pillows with
homey sayings stitched into them, decorative doilies,
hand-painted flowerpots, and other artsy-craftsy
things, all attractive, all apparently handmade.

Beyond the window displays, Whitney could see

shelves of merchandise and supplies for the do-it-
yourself crowd, most of which she couldn't begin to
identify. For her, a torn hem in her skirt meant a trip
to the dry cleaners to have it repaired.

Overall the shop was neat and clean and attractive. Aunt Claudia must have taken great pride in it,
and justifiably so. From the balance sheet the attorney had shown Whitney, it appeared that the shop
did a brisk business.

"See something you like?"

Adam Burkett's voice from Main Street behind
her made Whitney jump back from the window.
With a hand to her heart—to keep it from leaping
out of her chest—she slowly turned toward him. He
sat behind the wheel of his pickup, idling at the corner, and leaned toward the open passenger window
of the cab.

Whitney leaned a shoulder against a porch col-
umn and crossed one foot in front of the other.
"Maybe," she called.

After checking in his rearview mirror, Adam
backed down the street until he had room to turn
into the parking lot. He pulled in and parked ten
feet from the porch where Whitney stood.

He propped his elbow in his open window. "I
didn't think you went in for frou-frous and frilly stuff
like that."

Whitney lowered herself to sit on the top step of
the porch. If he thought she was going to come
hang off his car window to talk to him, like some
high-school cheerleader all gaga over the star foot-
ball player, he had another think coming.

"I wouldn't think," she said easily, "that you knew
me well enough to make a judgment like that."

"Well, now." He swung open his door and climbed out, then came and sat next to her on the steps. "You're right about that. There's somebody else who doesn't know you very well—not at all, actually—and she wants to remedy that."

"And who might that be?"

"My mother," he said with half a grin. "Every Sunday evening we cook hamburgers in my parents' backyard. I've been sent to persuade you to join us today."

Whitney stared at him a moment, not sure she heard him correctly. "Pardon?"

"Hamburgers. Cookout. Backyard? It's a pretty simple concept."

"Why should that have anything to do with me?"

"It has to do with you," he told her, "because my mother, also known as the General, with good reason, thinks you shouldn't be sitting all alone in that great big house with nothing but old memories for company."

"Your mother said that?"

Adam frowned. His mother hadn't said that, hadn't said anything like it. But the words, the sympathetic thought, couldn't have originated from him. He didn't even like this woman, much less care whether or not she had anyone to keep her company on a Sunday night.

"That's what she meant," he finally said. "What she said was, 'Go get that poor girl.'"

"And of course, you said, 'Yes, ma'am'?"

"Of course. We don't call her the General for nothing."

She reached over and patted his arm. "Tell your

mother the general thank-you, but I wouldn't dream of intruding on a family get-together."

"You won't be intruding. You'll be saving my life. I'm hungry. I can't go home without you."

She laughed. "I'm sure the situation isn't quite that dire."

"That's because you don't know the General. She'll make life miserable for Dad and me for a week."

"Your dad? How did he get dragged into this?"

"He has to live with her. He had the choice of coming to get you or mowing the yard. If I fail to get you there, she'll be after him for days for not coming for you himself. Me, I'll just be the family failure."

"I promise to feel sorry for you for days and days."

"You're all heart. Come on. Have a hamburger, meet the family. You might actually enjoy yourself."

She shook her head and smiled, unsure why she was going to the trouble to explain herself. Normally she would simply say no and be done. "I'm not big on family gatherings."

He shot her a look from the corner of his eye, then looked out toward Main. "There's an understatement."

"What's that supposed to mean?" she demanded.

"Come to the house with me and maybe I'll tell you."

"Huh. You think I really want to know bad enough to spend an evening with a guy who's already told me several times he doesn't like me? When I have to spend nearly every day for the next month with him as it is? Do I look like a glutton for punishment?"

Again came that look from the corner of his eye,

this time raking her from head to toe. "You don't look like any kind of glutton."

Now what, she wondered, was that supposed to mean?

"Come on." He stood and extended his hand toward her. "If you don't come meet my mother, she'll just turn up on your doorstep at the most inconvenient moment possible. Believe me, she's a master at it."

"Shame on you for talking about your own mother that way." But despite her better judgment, she found herself accepting his hand and rising to her feet. Because his hand, hard and callused though it was, felt so good to her, she quickly turned it loose. Then, like a trained puppy with no will but to appease, she followed him down the steps and climbed into the cab of his pickup.

The Burkett house sat on a quiet tree-lined street three blocks north of Main on the west end of town. It was a small redbrick house with a narrow driveway leading to a single-car detached garage situated at the back of the property. Said driveway was currently occupied by two pickups, an SUV, and a small sedan. With much grumbling about driveway hogs, Adam was reduced to parking in the street.

"Why did you look at me? I'm not parked in your driveway," Whitney protested.

"No, but you're hogging yours."

"Pardon?"

"Do us both a favor and pull your car farther into the driveway before I get there in the morning so I don't have to leave my tail hanging out in the street."

Whitney frowned. "All you had to do was say something."

"I just did. Now, stop stalling and get out."

"I'm not stalling." But she was, and it surprised her. Her own self-perception was that of a strong, tough-minded woman who worked hard and demanded her fair due. That didn't sound much like someone afraid to meet a man's family. She reached for the door handle. "Let's go."

Whitney was no stranger to families. She'd had one of her own until fairly recently, and she'd been around the families of her friends growing up. She understood family dynamics, so she figured it should be easy to get a handle on what the individual members of the Burkett gang were all about.

As they rounded the back corner of the house and stopped at the edge of the backyard, the sun was already sinking below the treetops, putting the yard in cooling shade. The grass was thick and green, with borders of colorful flowers along the edges of the lawn.

There was a redwood picnic table and a folding card table set up near the small back porch, and at the end of the driveway stood a single-car garage, complete with a narrow wooden staircase leading the way up to a small apartment above it.

"That's where I live." Adam pointed toward the apartment.

She nearly snorted. First, as if she wanted to know where he lived. That would be the day. Second, he was nearly thirty years old and lived in his mommy's backyard. How sweet.

But she said nothing. As much as she was wishing she had never come, she had accepted the invitation and was a guest at his mother's home. She would be polite.

"How convenient," was all she said.

He grinned. "Sure is."

A few feet away from the foot of the stairs leading to Adam's apartment stood a shiny black Weber grill, with smoke wafting up from it. A man stood at the grill, hands on his hips and a toddler, a little girl of around two, wrapped around one leg, while he stared at the grill. In one fist he held a long-handled spatula. Next to the grill, a foil-covered plate sat on a TV tray doing duty as a table, presumably waiting for the coals to be just right.

The man's graying hair and lean jaw pegged him as Adam's father. That, and the big chef's apron that read "Dad" across the chest. Someone had taken a marker and, above the word "Dad" added the word "Grand."

"That's Dad," Adam told her. "That wiggling little growth on his leg is Crissy, my brother Brian's youngest."

Near the back fence stood an old but functional swing set, currently in use by three young boys. Or, more accurately, it was in use by one young boy, while the other two fought over who got to go down the slide next.

"Those," Adam told her, "would be the monsters. The oldest is Will. He's seven. He's Crissy's brother. The other two, Kenny and Barry, six and four, belong to my oldest brother, Dan."

The back screen door creaked open and slapped shut as a stream of people emerged from the house. The two men were easily identified as Adam's brothers, both older than he.

"Brian and Dan," Adam comfirmed.

Three women came out with them, issuing orders as to where the men should place the bowls and plates and utensils they carried.

Two of the women were near the ages of the two men. "The first woman is Debbie, Dan's wife. The other is Cindy. She claims Brian, though God knows why."

It was the older woman who held Whitney's attention. Whitney didn't need to be told that this was Mary Burkett, Adam's general. But he said it, anyway.

"That's Mom."

"I think I figured that out."

The woman was small and round and lovely, with lines of love and laughter on her face. A face whose masculine version graced her son Adam.

And she was indeed the general of the clan. She was also the Madonna, the mother, the grandmother, the nurturer. She dispensed orders and hugs with equal frequency. The orders were gentle, disguised as requests. The hugs were fierce and loving.

Watching Mary Burkett with her family made Whitney's heart hurt.

"There they are," the woman cried upon spotting Adam and Whitney at the edge of the yard. She set a bowl of coleslaw on the picnic table and headed toward them, wiping her hands on her apron. "You're Whitney. Welcome, honey, welcome."

The next thing Whitney knew, she was enveloped in warm, slightly and pleasantly plump arms and a sweet cloud of baby-powder fragrance.

"Thank you for inviting me," Whitney managed once Mrs. Burkett set her free.

"We're so glad you came. There's no need at all for you to spend the evening alone, you poor dear." She slipped an arm around Whitney's waist and took her around the yard, introducing her to everyone as though she was some highly honored guest.

Whitney stiffened her spine and vowed to bear the attention gracefully. Good manners, after all. Proper etiquette.

If only she could remember why she had ever agreed to this.

But as it turned out, the evening wasn't so bad. The food was great, and no one treated her like an outsider. They treated her, instead, as one of the gang, as it were.

Teddy, Adam's father, offered her seconds on the potato salad.

"Oh, please, no thank you. If I eat any more, I'll burst."

Mr. Burkett laughed. He set the bowl down. "You used to come stay with Claudia when you were little, didn't you?"

"Yes, during the summers."

"Is it okay that I asked? I don't mean to upset you."

Whitney shook her head. "It's all right. Were you friends with her?"

"We've known Claudia since our oldest hit fourth grade and got her for his teacher."

"She was a terrific teacher," Mrs. Burkett said.

"Just terrific. Students and parents and fellow teachers alike thought so."

"Are you sure you don't want more potato salad?" Mr. Burkett offered.

And so it went. Compliments about Aunt Claudia followed by offers of food. And underneath it all, subtle offers of friendship.

Whitney appreciated the compliments, politely refused the offers of seconds, and gave little to no attention to the overtures for friendship. She wasn't here to make friends. All she had to do was get through the evening, then tomorrow, then the next day. She didn't need friends for that. Even if she were willing—and she wasn't—to invest her emotions in other people, she wouldn't be around long enough to make it worth the effort. Hadn't Adam said that very thing to her earlier?

While it irked her to agree with him on anything, she had to admit he was right. She wouldn't be around any longer than necessary.

The last of the homemade ice cream was nothing more than a small blob here and there on the table or a young boy's shirt when Whitney finally felt she could safely leave without offending anyone. Adam, the rat, had long since deserted her and, along with his brothers, was buried from head to waist beneath the hood of one of the vehicles in the driveway with a string of drop lights running from the house to the car.

"Again, thank you so much for having me," Whitney told Mrs. Burkett.

"We're just so glad you came. I hope you'll feel free to come back whenever you feel like company."

Whitney couldn't imagine imposing on someone that way. "How gracious of you to offer."

"Nonsense. I've been where you are, honey, having to sort through a loved one's belongings and decide what to do with everything. It's a terribly difficult thing to have to do."

"I know," Whitney said. "I've had to do it before, with both of my parents."

"Both of them?" The sympathy in the little general's eyes touched Whitney more than she'd thought possible. "You poor thing."

"Thank you." Was that the right thing to say to being called a poor thing? Whitney wasn't sure, but nothing better came to mind.

"I don't suppose Claudia left instructions on what she wanted done with her personal belongings."

"No," Whitney said. "She didn't."

"Well, after you've gone through everything and decided what you want to keep, you let me know and I'll help you take care of the rest."

"Oh, Mrs. Burkett, I couldn't impose on you that way."

"It's no imposition at all." Mrs. Burkett patted her hand. "Claudia was such a dear. I do know that she would want her china tea set to go to Betty, her neighbor, unless you want it for yourself."

"I wouldn't have known that. Thank you. Do you know of anyone else who might want something of hers? What about you?"

"Oh no, honey, not me. Claudia and I were pretty good friends, but we weren't that close. I would imagine that her bridge partners would each want something of hers, but I wouldn't have any idea what."

"Bridge partners." Whitney frowned, remembering what she'd heard at the church the day before, following the graveside services. "The twins, right?"

"That's right. Avis and Mavis, and Dorothy Gonzales."

"Can you think of anyone else?"

"Well, she was terribly close to Miss Ella, over at Shady Oaks."

The name Shady Oaks tickled something in the back of Whitney's mind. "The nursing home?"

"That's right. Miss Ella lives there now. Claudia used to go there a few times a week to visit. Miss Ella liked to have Claudia read to her. If there was something of Claudia's that was small, or something to hang on the wall, Miss Ella might like to have it."

"I'll see what I can come up with."

"You poor dear, you've got your work cut out for you. But I guess you've got some time. Adam says you're staying until he finishes the work on the house?"

"Does he?" Whitney smiled to take any sting out of her response, but answering with a question instead of an answer seemed the most polite way of signaling that she preferred not to provide personal information about her plans. Besides, it seemed prudent to avoid explaining that she intended to stay in town the entire month because she didn't trust Mary Burkett's son to do the work to her satisfaction.

In fact, the only prudent thing Whitney could think to do just then was make her excuses and leave. She hadn't intended to stay for hours, but it was now well past dark, and the children were starting to nod off. Having had little sleep the night before herself, Whitney knew just how they felt.

"Mrs. Burkett," she began.

"Mary, please, honey. Call me Mary. I imagine you've had a long day. Whenever you're ready to leave, you just say the word and I'll go round up that youngest son of mine to see you home."

"There's no need to bother him," Whitney told her. "It's such a nice night, I think I'd like to walk."

"All that way?" Mary said in protest.

Whitney couldn't help but laugh. "In New York, it would be the equivalent of a couple of blocks. I'll be fine."

"I'm sure you will." Mary pushed to her feet and smiled. "But there's no need for you to walk alone."

Whitney would have protested that she didn't need company, but Mary Burkett, the General, was already rounding the house to find her youngest son where he worked on the car with his brothers.

Whitney decided not to wait around. She made a quick farewell to Adam's father and sisters-in-law. Unless she wanted to traipse through the Burketts' home she would have to walk down the driveway as she left, which meant passing Adam. She could tell him good night at that time.

Adam's mother hadn't raised any fools. He knew how long it took to eat ice cream, which he and his brothers had forgone. And he had a good idea how long Whitney would sit still for his mother's probing or advice or whatever it was that his mother wanted to accomplish with Whitney. The thought of that little scene almost made him wish he could be a fly on the wall and watch.

Almost, but not quite. The General was way too good at spotting flies and swatting them, and who knew what that New York woman might do.

He could guess one thing she might do, and that was slip away from here and head home as soon as she could. He was mildly surprised that she had actually stayed long enough to eat. He was even more surprised that she had been so civil to a bunch of strangers. She'd sure been nicer tonight to his family than she'd been to poor Betty earlier, or even the people at the church after the funeral yesterday. Not that she'd been exactly rude at the church, but she'd sure been standoffish.

Figuring that Whitney had probably reached her limit of civility, Adam left his brothers and washed up in his mother's kitchen. He caught up with Whitney as she left the backyard and stepped onto the driveway. His mother was giving his brothers the third degree about Adam's whereabouts.

"I'm right here," he said.

His brothers, who couldn't have cared less about where he was, barely grunted at his announcement. His mother beamed. Whitney Sheridan frowned.

"You ready to go?" he asked Whitney.

"I wouldn't want to take you away from your family," Whitney said. "I thought I'd walk. It's not far."

"No," he agreed, "it's not far, and it's a nice night. Come on, then, I'll walk you home."

"There's no need for that," she protested. "It's not as if I can't find my way."

She might as well have said that it wasn't as if she wanted his company. The devil his mother had always sworn was inside him silently chuckled at the idea.

"Of course you can find your way," Adam's mother said, placing one hand on Whitney's arm and the other on Adam's. "But Adam wouldn't be much of a gentleman if he didn't walk you home."

"And we all know what a gentleman I am," Adam asserted.

"Of course you are," his mother said. She leaned close to Whitney and whispered loudly, "He really is, you know."

Whitney gave a crooked smile. "And you're not a bit prejudiced, are you."

"The General, prejudiced?" Adam protested. "Of course not. She's merely astute. Perceptive. Brilliant."

"Go on," his mother urged with a squeeze of his arm. "Don't stop now."

"I could go on for hours," he claimed. "But our guest is ready to go home." He leaned down and kissed his mother on the cheek. "Catch ya later, beautiful."

"What do you think?" Teddy Burkett stood beside his wife and watched as their youngest son turned down the sidewalk with Claudia Henderson's niece.

"That's one troubled young woman," Mary said. In the glow of the streetlight at the corner she could plainly see the way Whitney walked in a way that left no chance that she and Adam might accidently touch. "She seems like a good person, but there's a lot of baggage there."

Teddy slipped his arm around his wife's shoulders

and turned her back toward the yard. "You figure that out by the way she ate her burger?"

"No, silly." She pinched his side. "It was the way she held her ear of corn."

The evening air was too humid to be considered refreshing, but it was cool and not uncomfortable, just slightly below skin temperature. And even though the town was filled with streetlights, a million stars twinkled overhead. Whitney was surprised by a strong desire to drive out into the country, away from all the lights, and simply stare up at the night sky.

"Curb ahead."

The sound of Adam's voice broke the spell. With a frown of irritation, she shot him a glare. "What?"

"Curb." He motioned to the end of the sidewalk at the cross street a few feet away. "You were staring up at the sky so hard I was afraid you wouldn't notice. Imagine what my mother would say to me if you broke your ankle or conked your head or skinned your knee."

"I'm sure she'd never let you live it down. If you turn around and go home now, you won't have to know whether or not I fall down and hurt myself. Which I assure you is not likely, but if it happens it certainly won't be your fault. Unless you trip me or knock me down. And if you did either of those, I hate to admit to something so childish, but I would feel compelled to tell your mommy on you."

"No, please, not that."

Whitney laughed, albeit reluctantly. Dammit, she didn't want to laugh with this man. After they crossed the side street and stepped up onto the Main Street sidewalk again, she let out a loud sigh.

"All right," she said. "I give in. Why don't you like me?"

Keeping his stride short enough to match hers, Adam tucked his fingers into the back pockets of his jeans. "You want me to like you?"

"I don't care," she answered honestly. "I'm just curious, that's all. Earlier today you thought I should know. So I'm asking."

Adam didn't know what to make of this woman. He'd never met anyone so carelessly, even brutally, honest before. He believed she really meant it when she said she didn't care whether or not he liked her. She hadn't said it to be rude, but merely as a matter of fact. How was he supposed to understand a woman like this?

Maybe that was it. Maybe he wasn't supposed to understand her. Maybe all he had to do was be as honest with her as she was being with him.

"All right," he finally said. "I don't like the way you've treated your aunt in recent years."

Whitney stopped walking and gaped. "I beg your pardon?"

"And," he added, drawing the word out, "I don't like that lady-of-the-manor tone you use now and then, like you're talking to a servant. A stupid one."

"Well, for heaven's sake. You think I have time to care that you might take the tone of my voice wrong? And what business is it of yours how Aunt Claudia and I got along? And we got along just fine, thank you very damn much."

She took off as if she were shot out of a cannon. Not running, but it was a near thing, to Adam's way of thinking. He had to stretch his legs to catch up with her.

A blue sedan sped past with a toot of its horn. One of the Harmon twins, no doubt. Or maybe their dad. Adam waved.

"Hit a sore spot, did I?" he asked when he reached Whitney's side.

"Aunt Claudia and I got along wonderfully," she told him, her nose so high in the air that she'd have been in danger of drowning if it had been raining.

"I'm sure you did, by long distance." Adam did not try to keep the edge out of his voice. He'd seen the longing in Miz Henderson's eyes too many times to temper his anger now. "She loved you. Adored you. Worshiped the ground you walked on. Yet you couldn't take the time to come see her, not once in how many years? Not even for one damn weekend?"

Whitney's stomach tightened. With anger. With regret. With shame. "I don't need you to tell me when I did or didn't see my aunt. When I should or shouldn't have seen her. Just because we didn't live in each other's pocket, the way you and your family do, doesn't mean I didn't love her."

"You should have come to see her," he said tightly.

"You think I didn't want to?" she demanded.

"Big high-powered news producer like you, you could have found a way. You just didn't want to bother, did you?"

"A lot you know." She lengthened her stride, hoping he would take the hint and leave her alone. "You don't know anything about me."

He had no trouble keeping up with her with those mile-long legs of his. "I know plenty about you. She talked about you all the time. But even if she hadn't, I know your type."

"Oh, so now I'm a type, am I?" With a toss of her head, she stretched her legs even farther.

"City girl," he said with a sneer in his voice. "Snob. Too busy moving and shaking the world to spend any of your precious time in small-town America. Especially someplace like the Texas Panhandle. What is it you people call this part of the country? Fly-over country. Because that's all it's good for, flying over on your way from one coast to the other. Well, wake up, city girl. There's a whole big world out here, and when somebody loves you it shouldn't matter where they live or how far away they are, you damn well have a responsibility to go see them once in a while."

Whitney stopped and whirled, jabbed the forefinger of her right hand into his chest. It was like stabbing a brick. "Look, buster. You were friends with my aunt. That's great. Friend enough to stick your nose into her family business. Fine. But that doesn't make you my friend and doesn't give you the right to criticize how I run my life or relate to my family. So *back off.*"

A few feet away, in the street, a car rolled to a stop. "Evening, folks. Everything all right here?"

At the sight of the police car at the curb and the friendly, freckled face peering out of the driver's side window, Whitney was left nearly speechless. Nearly, but not quite.

"Officer, this man is bothering me."

"Oh, for crying out loud." Adam threw his hands in the air and rolled his eyes.

The young cop frowned. "Adam? What's going on?"

"You know each other," Whitney said in disgust. "That figures." She whirled on her heel and stomped off toward her aunt's house.

The cop let out a low whistle. "Boy howdy, Adam. That looks like one pissed-off lady to me."

Adam rubbed his hand over the spot on his chest where she had drilled her finger into him. "Yeah."

"The way you're rubbing your chest, I'd say she must have hit a sore spot."

"Offhand," Adam said quietly, "I'd say I did."

Chapter Four

Maybe, Whitney thought, she might have been a little hasty in leaving the Burketts' and getting rid of Adam. The house seemed especially filled with memories tonight.

It started when she went to the kitchen for a drink of water and allowed herself to look around for the first time. That was when she saw the framed cross-stitch she had made the summer she was eleven. It was done in the same greens and oranges that decorated her aunt's kitchen, and across the center in big, bold letters, each one made up of dozens, maybe hundreds of tiny cross-stitches, it said "Aunt Claudia's Kitchen."

Aunt Claudia had been so pleased and proud, she had framed it and hung it on the wall beside the refrigerator. All these years later, it still hung there in that same spot. The glass that covered the design was spotless, and there wasn't a speck of dust on the oak frame. It had been well cared for.

Whitney couldn't help but smile at the memory of the Band-Aids Aunt Claudia had been forced to supply for Whitney's pricked fingers to keep her from bleeding on the fabric or the thread.

She had worked so hard on that piece. Had

wanted so badly to please her favorite—her only—aunt. What a wonderful summer that had been. It had been one of their last together.

The ache in her chest moved up to her throat and lodged there. Half of her wanted to play the coward and get a room at the motel for the night, away from these memories. The other half of her wanted to wallow in the memories, to fall into them and weep for the aunt she loved, for the parents she'd lost, for the lonely, brittle person she had become. For the lost little girl who lived inside her.

The tears would be a relief, but she knew they wouldn't come. Regardless of what had happened in her life, and plenty had, she had not shed a tear since the day she had buried her mother ten years ago. When her father had died two years later Whitney had been too devastated to cry.

If she was to be denied the release of tears, she decided, then the least she could do was get the hell out of the kitchen with its cross-stitched memories.

The living room was no help. Everything there was under tarps and old sheets, leaving her to guess. She didn't have the energy to guess, and saw no purpose in trying.

She climbed the stairs, and there, on the wall, where she had passed a half dozen times or more since her arrival, hung another memory. She must have been blind not to have noticed it. Perhaps deliberately blind?

It was a white paper doily, with a red heart made of construction paper pasted to the center of it. Letters of gold glitter spelled out "Be My Valentine."

Dear God. She'd been eight when she made that.

She didn't remember Aunt Claudia having framed and hung it on the wall. She'd had no idea her aunt had kept that silly thing all these years.

The lump in her throat grew larger.

Enough memories for one night. She made a beeline for the guest room, where she was staying. She didn't bother turning on the light in the room. Not out of any fear of running into any more sweet yet painful memories, of course. Whitney Sheridan wasn't afraid of anything. Emotions didn't bother her. They never controlled her or got in her way.

"Ouch!" Emotions might not get in her way, but she couldn't say the same for the chair at the desk. It had no trouble getting in the way of her shin in the dark.

After a restless night with little sleep, Whitney felt as if every nerve in her body was wound as tight as it would go. She made sure to be up before Adam arrived, but now she had to face him, and doing so was going to ruin her appetite for sure. Maybe, she thought, breakfast would taste better if it was cooked by someone other than herself. And in some kitchen other than one filled with memories she wasn't ready to face again so soon

The Good Eats Café sounded like the perfect answer. When Adam arrived, she grabbed her purse and made for the door. As she passed him, a flash of the dream she'd had during the night and had since forgotten shot through her mind and left her reeling.

Something about tangled sheets, sweating muscles, labored breathing, and a fire inside her veins that threatened to burn her alive with pleasure. And all of it in the arms of Adam Burkett.

Oh, Good God. She'd *dreamed* about him? She'd had an erotic dream about Adam Burkett?

She definitely needed to get out more.

"You're leaving?" he asked.

"I'm leaving." The sooner the better, before the heat rising in her cheeks aroused his curiosity.

Oh, damn. Why did she have to think the word *arouse* in conjunction with him?

"I thought you wanted to supervise my work," he taunted.

"Oh, I'll be back to look things over. I'm sure you can manage on your own for a while." *So I can get out of here and catch my breath. Get my head back on straight.*

"By the way," he said as she reached for the door. "Thanks for leaving me in an awkward situation with the cops last night."

"I'm sure you managed to talk your way out of any trouble. He was probably a friend of yours."

"Of course." He grinned widely.

Whitney curled her lip and left for breakfast.

The morning was so humid that by the time she made the walk down Main to the café, Whitney felt decidedly damp. The cool air conditioning inside the café was more than welcome. A bell over the door jingled an announcement of her arrival.

There were just over half a dozen customers scattered across the room. Whitney took a seat in a booth against the far wall, putting her back toward the front window and the Washita version of rush-hour traffic. Which meant a car, or more often a pickup, every few minutes.

At the table she'd chosen there was a menu tucked between the napkin holder and the salt and pepper shakers next to the wall. She plucked it up and began reading.

An older woman came from behind a swinging door and climbed onto a stool to man the cash register. She gave Whitney the once-over and a nod.

"Franki!" the woman bellowed. "Get your buns out here. You've got a customer."

From the kitchen on the other side of that swinging door came the reply. "Don't get your support hose in a twist."

If Whitney had had a mouthful of water, she would have choked on it, or spewed it across the table. As the two women, one still unseen, continued their testy banter, she felt a smile tug at her mouth.

These two women either genuinely detested each other or had great mutual respect and affection. Whitney guessed the latter.

She knew how it felt to have a friend like that, someone you were so comfortable with, who understood you inside and out, knew all your secrets, and liked you anyway. She had been that close at one time to a coworker. Until Connie had taken a job in London.

Whitney had been devastated. She couldn't blame Connie for moving to the other side of the damn ocean. The opportunity had been too good to pass up. But did she have to breeze out the door without a backward glance, as if Whitney had meant less than nothing to her?

Old news. Whitney shook the memories away. She hated looking back. There was nothing in her past but heartache.

The kitchen door behind the counter finally swung open, and a woman in her mid-twenties rushed out, a large, heavy tray held over one shoulder. "Be right with you," she called to Whitney. Then, to the woman at the cash register, she muttered loud enough for everyone in the place to hear, "Is your butt nailed to that chair? You coulda got her some water."

"Now, none of your sass," the older woman said as the younger stopped at a table and unloaded plates piled high with pancakes and waffles. "That there is Claudia Henderson's niece, come all the way from New York City to say good-bye and take care of business."

If she thought it would do her any good, Whitney might have considered holding the menu up in front of her face. But since everyone was already staring at her, she decided to give a slight, short nod to the room in general.

"Way to go, Ada May," the waitress said tartly. "Embarrass the fire outta the customers. That'll keep 'em coming back."

"Just stating fact," Ada shot back. "Besides, she looks like she can take care of herself just fine. Can't you, young lady?"

"I do all right," Whitney said, not having to raise her voice to have it carry to everyone in the room.

"Of course you do," the woman called back. "And you're smart enough to know that I don't mean anything I say."

Whitney's lips twitched. "I got that."

* * *

A dish such as *huevos rancheros* was probably never intended by its originator to be served with biscuits and gravy, but that was the way it came at Good Eats, which, Whitney learned during the course of her meal, was owned by Ada May Puckett, the woman at the cash register.

A dish such as *huevos rancheros* was also never intended to enter Whitney Sheridan's stomach, if the burning ache now attacking her was anything to go by. She was chewing an antacid tablet by the time she reached the door.

Outside the humidity hit her like a wall. She felt as if she were trying to breathe through a wet towel. A thick, hot, Turkish towel.

She didn't remember the humidity from her childhood summers here. But, then, she supposed kids never noticed stuff like that. She didn't remember snow being cold, either, and these days it damn sure was. Cold and messy and a pain in the ass. At least she didn't have to worry about that today.

Traffic, what there had been of it, had thinned some while she'd been in the café. She paid it little mind as she walked east in the morning sun toward the shop her aunt had owned.

There was a green Buick parked in the small front parking lot. As Whitney crossed the street she noticed the CLOSED sign in the front window had been turned to read OPEN.

She dug through her memory and came up with the name Harry had given her for the manager. Carla. Carla Bowers. According to Harry, Carla had been with the store since it opened three years earlier.

Three years, Whitney thought as she neared the porch. Aunt Claudia had owned this place for three years and never mentioned it.

It hurt, Whitney admitted. Her aunt must have poured her heart and soul into this shop, getting it up and running, making it thrive the way Harry and the balance sheet indicated it did. Yet Aunt Claudia had not felt compelled to share any of that with Whitney.

Of course, Whitney hadn't exactly invited confidences in recent years. Confidences indicated closeness, and Whitney had worked deliberately to keep that closeness at bay. Because if it hurt to have been left in the dark about Claudia's Attic, it hurt even more to be close to someone, as, one way or another, they always left you. Always. If you weren't too close, the theory was that their leaving wouldn't hurt as badly.

So much for theories, Whitney thought, feeling the pain of her aunt's death clear down to her soul. She knew that pain would be with her always, because she still felt the years-old pain of her parents' deaths as if they had been torn from her life just yesterday.

"Suck it up, girl," she told herself. There was pain, yes. But she refused to let it rule her. With stiff determination, she climbed the steps onto the porch and pushed open the door to Claudia's Attic and stepped inside.

Perhaps if she hadn't let her mind wander she might have been in a better frame of mind, one more conducive to appreciating the pretty, the delicate, the handmade. As things stood, everything seemed a little too fussy for her tastes. Never mind that many things on display reminded her of her childhood. These days, she readily admitted, at least to herself, she had no taste in anything other than a good newscast. Not since she'd been a teenager.

Why, she wondered, had she decided that teenagers didn't need to spend their summers with their aunts? And why, oh, why, had her parents let her stay home instead of sending her to Texas that first year, and the next, and all the years after that?

From a back room somewhere a pleasant voice called out, "I'll be right with you!"

"Take your time," Whitney called back.

Barely a minute went by before a fiftyish woman with short salt-and-pepper hair and a name badge that read CARLA entered the room.

"Oh, Miss Sheridan," she said upon spying Whitney. "I'm so glad you had time to come in today."

Whitney vaguely remembered being introduced to her at the church after the funeral. "I have to admit," she said. "I had no idea my aunt owned a shop until Harry told me."

"It was her pride and joy, and I've always felt privileged to work here."

A pretty little speech, Whitney thought. The woman was laying it on a little thick, but it was still pretty.

"I think Claudia was waiting to tell you about the shop until you had time to come out. She wanted to show it to you, to surprise you."

"She did that," Whitney murmured.

"The coffee's probably ready by now, if you'd like some. Or I could heat water for tea."

"Coffee's fine," Whitney said. "Black, no sugar."

"It's back here, in the kitchen." She motioned for Whitney to follow her. "Claudia wanted to put in two or three small tables and serve sandwiches or salads or something for lunch out on the porch during nice weather. Just last week she started investigating the requirements we'd have to meet. You know, all the proper licenses and permits and whatnot. It looked like it was going to be a big hassle, but she wanted to do it. And listen to me, running off at the mouth like I had good sense. Here's your coffee. I hope you like it strong."

The woman was nervous, Whitney thought. It was understandable. Whitney was the new owner, the new boss. Carla's livelihood now depended on whatever Whitney decided to do.

As a rule, Whitney generally didn't expend much energy reassuring new employees. To her way of thinking, they would figure out for themselves soon enough what kind of person she was. They would come to like her, or not. As long as they did the job they were hired to do and didn't cause trouble, Whitney really didn't care whether they liked her or not.

But this wasn't the newsroom, it was a craft shop, a gift shop, a consignment shop. It wasn't New York, but the Texas Panhandle. And Carla wasn't some nervous intern too eager to please, or a hungry graduate fresh out of journalism school, ready to cut Whitney's throat and take her job the first chance that arose.

Whitney blew the steam away from her mug and took a sip. "The coffee's fine. Thank you." She took another sip. "The way I understand it, you more or less run the shop, don't you?"

Carla smiled, and there was no small amount of pride in the expression. "I'm the manager, yes. Claudia loved the shop, but she didn't want to have to be here all day every day, so she made me her manager."

"So you have to be here all day, every day."

"Pretty much, but I enjoy it. And we have other help."

"Tell me about them," Whitney said.

"All right. Well, counting me, we have two full-time employees and one part-time. The part-timer is Maggie Brooks. She's retired from the bank. Sandy McLain is our other full-timer. She'll be in a little later. Among other things, she's our Internet wiz. She's building our Web site so we can sell merchandise online. That was Claudia's idea."

Carla went on to explain that there were two distinct types of merchandise for sale in Claudia's Attic. First came the craft items for the do-it-yourselfers—materials, threads, needles, yarns, glues, painting supplies, all the different items needed to pursue various crafts that were of interest mostly to women. The second type of merchandise consisted of finished items—quilts, wall hangings, aprons, paintings, ceramics. Whatever type of handmade items Claudia thought her customers might like.

"By 'her customers' I assume you mean the local people here in Washita," Whitney said.

"At first, yes," Carla agreed. "But as these things go, word started to spread and people started coming from farther and farther away. The other side of the county, the Panhandle, the state. We even get people in from Oklahoma and Kansas and Colorado. That's why Claudia wanted to try the Web site."

Whitney shook her head in puzzlement. "I'm sorry, but I don't get it. I mean no disrespect to anyone, but aren't these craft supplies, and even the finished products like the quilts, fairly common items? Why would people drive from another town, let alone another state, to shop here?"

"Quality." Carla said the word with a sharp nod of confidence. "The supplies are the same brands you can get in any good craft shop, but we have the most liberal return policy you can imagine. As for the finished products, we take only the best. We sell them on consignment, so all we're out is the space for display, but people know that when they come here they'll find only the best-made handcrafted items available. Look at it this way," she added. "There are a dozen places other than WNN to get the news, yet millions of people tune it in every night. Why not some other channel? Because of style, content. Quality."

Whitney couldn't help but smile. "You make a good sales pitch. And you forgot personality as a big draw."

Carla laughed. "Sometimes I get carried away. Do you know yet what you're going to do with it all?"

Whitney shrugged. "I didn't even know about the shop until Saturday afternoon, so it's all come as a surprise to me. Still, my job is in New York, so I suppose I'll have to sell the shop. It doesn't seem practical to keep it under the circumstances."

* * *

Whitney spent nearly an hour at the shop, letting Carla show her around and meeting Sandy McLain when she came in to work. After assuring them both that she had no intention of shutting the shop down and pitching them out into the nearest unemployment line, she went next door to the bank and signed the appropriate paperwork per Harry's instructions, then walked the short distance back to the house.

Because Adam was working in the living room, she circled the house and entered via the back door. The sound of hammering pounded out a counterbeat to the twangy country music blasting from Adam's boom box.

He glanced over his shoulder and gave her a nod. "Come back to check on me?"

Whitney sniffed. "Believe it or not, my world does not revolve around you. I have other things to do."

"Aw, shucks." He wiggled his hips in time to the music. "I thought you wanted to watch me."

"Watch you what? Dance around like an idiot?"

"Hey, I'll have you know I'm a good dancer."

"I'm so pleased for you." She headed for the stairs, berating herself for getting dragged into such an inane conversation.

"I could teach you," he offered.

"To dance? What makes you think I don't know how?"

"Do you?"

Halfway up the stairs she paused and looked down. How could a man look so damned appealing in jeans and a tool belt? His shirt was dirty and damp with sweat; his hair fell down onto his forehead.

Maybe it was the way that sweat-dampened shirt

and those dusty jeans draped and hugged his hard, curved muscles. Or the way the light made his blue eyes shimmer.

Shimmer, for crying out loud.

She shook her head. A man's eyes couldn't shimmer. She was losing her mind. "Since we won't be dancing together," she told him, "it really doesn't matter, does it?"

"Man," he said, shaking his head. "I'll bet you're a barrel of laughs at a party."

"What's that supposed to mean?"

"Nothing." He shook his head again and turned back to his work. "Not a damned thing."

With another sniff, Whitney continued up the stairs and did her best to dismiss him from her mind. As a distraction, the work she had yet to begin was a doozie, she thought as she once again faced the fact that she had to go through her aunt's belongings and decide what to do with them. Furniture, clothing, jewelry, shoes, linens, knick-knacks, pots and pans and dishes and all the other kitchen and household stuff a person accumulates over the course of a lifetime.

Good God, Whitney thought. When she died, some poor stranger was going to get stuck with having to go through her things. A sobering thought. Some stranger going through her underwear.

It didn't bear thinking about.

Neither, if she had a choice, did going through her aunt's things. She didn't even know where to start.

The smart thing, or perhaps the easiest and certainly the most self-serving, would be to go through every room in the house and set aside everything she wanted to keep for herself.

Wait. Sort everything into categories: keep, put in a garage or yard sale, have appraised and sell separately, give to the Salvation Army or Goodwill or whatever agencies served the needy in this area.

Simply making the decision to categorize everything made her feel more sure of herself. She was so sure of herself, in fact, that she decided to think about it a little more and refine her categories while finishing off Betty's lasagna.

She wasn't procrastinating, she assured herself. There were plenty of things to go through in the kitchen, weren't there? She had to eat, didn't she? And if she made a pitcher of iced tea maybe they could keep the peace in this house a little better.

Adam had his back to her when she went downstairs, and that was fine with her. She made a pitcher of tea, then heated the last of the lasagna. There was plenty for two. With a sigh, she went to the living room and invited Adam to join her.

He looked hesitant.

"I made tea."

"You'll want to watch out doing stuff like that."

"Why?" she asked.

"Because I might actually start to like you."

"Oh no, not that," she protested.

"It could happen," he warned.

"I'll have to be more careful."

Sharing lunch with Adam was a mistake. It served no purpose to sit across the table and fall into his blue, blue eyes every time she looked up from her plate. She had no need to catch a whiff of sawdust and sweat over the aroma of lasagna. It certainly didn't calm her mind or her nerves.

"Have you been to Miz Henderson's shop yet?"

"Claudia's Attic? I was there this morning."

He drained his tea glass and reached for the pitcher to refill it. "What did you think?"

"I think I need to figure out what it's worth so I can decide what to ask for it."

"So you're going to sell it."

He sounded . . . disapproving, and it irritated her. "Of course I am." Who was he to disapprove of anything she did? "It's the only practical thing to do."

He shrugged. "You could always hang on to it—let a manager run it."

"Why would I want to do that, and be responsible for taxes, permits, all sorts of legal issues? No, I don't see the point in all that."

He shrugged again. "It was just a thought."

They fell silent and finished their lunch. Adam drained a third glass of tea, then went back to work, leaving Whitney feeling oddly adrift.

It wasn't as if she didn't have anything to do. She just wasn't ready to start.

There. She had admitted it. She didn't want to start going through her aunt's things yet.

She didn't want to call her boss yet, either, to tell him she wouldn't be back by the end of the week, as she'd originally thought.

Now that she knew what she didn't want to do, she needed to come up with something she did want to do, because she couldn't simply sit around and do nothing.

Her gaze lit on the empty lasagna dish.

* * *

Whitney stood on Betty Roberts's front porch and shifted her weight from one foot to the other, turning the lasagna dish around and over in her hands.

This was a stupid idea. Pathetic, really, returning a baking dish to avoid facing a tedious, painful task. But before she could do the smart thing and turn around and go home, the door before her opened.

"Whitney!" Betty cried. "What a wonderful surprise."

"I finished the lasagna. It was delicious, and saved me from having to cook." Whitney held out the dish. "Thank you."

Instead of taking the dish, Betty grabbed Whitney by the arm. "Oh, you're more than welcome. Come in, come in. I was just thinking of you."

The aroma hit Whitney before she realized what was happening. It weakened her knees, made her stomach rumble as if she hadn't eaten in a month, and tossed her back in time to a warm summer day in her childhood. All because of the aroma of freshly baked oatmeal cookies. She would bet her next month's salary that they were still hot from the oven.

". . . still hot from the oven," Betty was saying. "I've even got lemonade, made fresh not an hour ago. You'll have some, won't you?"

Whitney swallowed the saliva pooling in her mouth. "Oh, I—"

"Of course you will. Come on back to the kitchen. I'll even send some cookies home with you, with a couple of extra for Adam. I know he likes my cookies."

"I'm sure he does." Whitney followed Betty to her

kitchen, that heavenly aroma getting stronger the closer they got to the source.

"I'll just have to trust you to take pity on him and share a few."

"Now I'll feel guilty if I don't," Whitney complained.

Betty chuckled. "That's the idea, dear. Nothing works like a little dose of guilt."

"I'll have to remember that," Whitney murmured.

The cookies and lemonade were ambrosia to Whitney. The cookies melted in her mouth, the lemonade went down smooth, and despite Whitney's resistance, Betty made her feel, if not quite at home, then close to it.

When, after thirty minutes, Whitney insisted that she had to leave, Betty packaged up a full dozen cookies to send home with her.

"Oh, not so many," Whitney protested. "Won't your husband want some?"

"He'll get some, don't you worry. Tommy never misses out on my cookies. Besides, I figure maybe they'll help you get through the torture of all those thank-you notes you're having to write."

Whitney bent down quickly to brush away imaginary crumbs from her slacks so that Betty wouldn't see the shock and dread on her face. Good God, the thank-you cards. How could she have forgotten that little chore?

She remembered well enough from her parents' deaths that it had to be done, even though she would rather set her own hair on fire than tend to such a tedious chore.

Her lack of enthusiasm for the job in no way reflected any disrespect for the dearly departed nor disdain for those who had so thoughtfully sent flowers and cards. She had loved Aunt Claudia, just as she had loved her mother and father, and she respected, even appreciated, the thoughtfulness and caring of those who sent their sympathies, in whatever form. She simply found the finer points of etiquette to be the most tedious endeavors imaginable.

That was probably why her unconscious mind had allowed her to leave in her car the big box the funeral home gave her that contained all the cards that came with the plants and flowers. She had asked them to donate the potted plants to the local nursing home where Aunt Claudia used to volunteer. With those out of her mind, she had conveniently forgotten about sending thank-yous.

Betty patted her on the shoulder. "I'm sure if the funeral home supplied any thank-you cards it wasn't enough. You'll want to pay a visit to Randi's Cards and Gifts, about halfway down Main. She'll have what you need. And if you want some help with those cards, you just say the word, dear."

"Oh, thank you." The offer, so graciously offered, was more tempting than Betty could know. But Whitney resisted the temptation and said, "I really appreciate it, but I'm sure I can handle it. Especially since I have these cookies to see me through."

The rest of Whitney's afternoon was spent on a succession of chores and errands. When she left Betty's she dropped the cookies and lemonade off at Aunt Claudia's house. Or, rather, at home. She supposed it was her home for now.

She felt Adam's eyes on her the instant she stepped through the back door. From the living room he watched her walk to the refrigerator and store the lemonade.

"Not gonna share that?" he asked.

"Not on your life," she answered. "Until today, I haven't had lemonade like this since I was eleven years old. I'm going to savor every last drop of it myself."

Adam frowned at her and grumbled, "Stingy."

"But you can have a couple of cookies."

His face brightened like a little boy's would at the same prospect. "Oatmeal?"

"Of course." Feeling generous, she pulled three cookies from the package Betty had sent home with her and wrapped them in a paper napkin. "There you go." She placed them on the breakfast bar, then turned toward the back door.

"Leaving again?" he called as he bent down to examine a baseboard.

"I need something from my car."

Dammit, she thought, why was she answering to him? She was going to stop that.

She went to her car and carried the box from the funeral home into the house. At the kitchen table she went through the material and discovered that the funeral home had indeed included some thank-you cards for her use. A rough estimate told her she had enough to cover maybe a fourth of the cards she needed to send.

"I'm going to the store," she called over to Adam. Then she cursed herself. He wasn't her keeper. It wasn't his business where she went or what she did. She didn't owe him any explanations.

So why the hell did she keep offering them? Even when he didn't ask? Shaking her head, she grabbed her purse and headed out the door, then down Main to find Randi's Cards and Gifts.

She suddenly realized she should have called her boss before she left. She checked her watch and calculated the time difference. If she hurried she should be able to buy her cards, then get back to the house and call him before he left for the day. The sooner he knew she wasn't coming back at the end of the week, the better she would feel about it.

At least, that was what she'd thought, until she actually spoke with him an hour later, after she'd returned from buying three dozen thank-you cards—all they'd had—at Randi's Cards and Gifts. She had placed the call to New York the minute she had returned to the house.

Her boss was not happy with the news.

"Look," she said, getting exasperated. "It can't be helped, all right? And it's not as if I don't have the time coming."

"Is that supposed to make me happier?" he demanded.

"Since I'm not there to suffer the consequences, am I supposed to care whether you're happy or not?"

"Only if you want a job to come back to."

There was a little more bite to his words than she liked. He was definitely not pleased with her, and that made her less than thrilled with him. He had no right to be angry over her time off. "You're threatening me?"

"See?" he bellowed in her ear. "This is why I don't like people taking time off. They get all paranoid and defensive, lose their sense of humor. Just come back as soon as you can."

"I'll do that. And thank you for your condolences."

"I sent flowers."

"Now who's sounding defensive?"

"Take care of your business there, Sheridan, and get back to work."

She would have answered, but he hung up. She hated it when people did that. She slammed her receiver down. "Jerk."

"Trouble?"

She flinched as if slapped. Adam stood in the doorway looking at her.

"Mind your own business," she snapped.

"Sorry." He raised both hands, one of which held a paintbrush. "Just asking."

"Well, don't."

The kitchen table seemed the best place to sort through the cards to see how many of them contained addresses. There were so many cards, from the flowers and potted plants, plus regular sympathy cards from those who didn't send flowers. So many, many cards. Aunt Claudia had been well loved by a lot of people.

The very idea of how much Aunt Claudia had been loved made Whitney feel small. When she died, she figured maybe two or three people would show up. If she was lucky. The upside would be that she wouldn't be around to feel the humiliation and embarrassment.

And on that depressing thought, she opened the first box of thank-you cards and set to work.

* * *

Every time Adam looked over toward Whitney where she worked at the kitchen table, her face appeared a shade more ashen than before.

He didn't want to care.

He supposed he was mildly surprised. He had judged her cold and hard, yet every now and then, such as right now, she seemed neither. She seemed human, vulnerable. Sad and hurting.

She would surely be just as glad if he didn't notice. He didn't want to notice. He wanted to do exactly as she had ordered and mind his own business. The trouble was, he couldn't seem to do that.

He tucked his thumbs beneath his tool belt and ambled her way. "Got any more of that tea left?"

She looked up, her eyes glazed, and flexed her right hand. "What?"

"Tea."

She blinked.

"Never mind. I'll check for myself. What are you doing that takes so much concentration?"

She stretched her neck one way, then the other. "Thank-you cards. And, no, I don't think there's any more tea. I think you drank it all at lunch."

He looked in the fridge. No tea pitcher. He finally found it in the dishwasher, along with the plates and utensils they'd used at lunch. It didn't matter. Tea, he admitted to himself, had only been an excuse to talk to her. And that was a bad, bad sign.

Yet even knowing that, he still strolled back to her side at the table. "Thank-you cards, huh? From the funeral?"

"Yes."

"I don't envy you that. You'll probably get writer's cramp. There were enough flowers there to fill a greenhouse. But does it really take so much concentration? Just address the envelope, sign the card, and you're done."

She was shaking her head before he finished speaking. "That would never do. If you knew Aunt Claudia the way you say you do, then you know what a stickler she was for good manners and proper etiquette. If they just sent a card, then all I have to say is thanks for the card. But if they sent flowers, I need to tell them how pretty they were, how much Aunt Claudia would have appreciated them. If they sent a potted plant, they need to know what's become of it."

Adam gaped. "You're kidding."

"Aunt Claudia would have expected no less."

"You really think she would expect you to sit here until you go blind and your hand falls off?"

That got a chuckle out of her. But then her smile faded, her eyes turned sad. "It's what she taught me to do when my mother died, and she helped me do it again two years later when Daddy died."

Adam started to reach for her, to touch, to offer sympathy, comfort. Something. He had never lost anyone close to him. He even still had both sets of grandparents and most of his great-aunts and great-uncles, and there were a slew of them. He couldn't imagine what it must feel like to have no one left, no one at all. To bury your parents . . . the thought shook him.

Logically, he knew that, barring his own untimely death, he would one day have to bury his parents. But he didn't spend time thinking of it.

For Whitney it had already become a reality. Adam had a large, boisterous family, any one of whom would drop whatever they were doing and come running if he called. Whitney had no family left at all. He hoped, for her sake, that she had a close friend or two, someone to lean on now and then.

"Doesn't sound like much fun," he said.

Her only answer was a grunt.

"Hang in there." He gave her shoulder a quick massage. "You'll get through it. And if you need a break, you could always get up and make another pitcher of tea."

"Oh, ha, ha. Make it yourself."

"Hmm. Don't mind if I do." He meant to walk away, but his hand, of its own accord, lingered on her shoulder.

She looked up at him, and for a moment, their gazes connected. He didn't know what she saw in his, but in her rich brown depths he saw confusion, wariness. A look that said she didn't trust him, but with an underlying yearning that made him feel needed.

Too much, he thought, giving her shoulder a final, gentle squeeze and walking away. He was reading way too much into that brief look. Perhaps it was his own confusion and wariness he'd seen. His own distrust.

But if that was true, did it mean the yearning was his, too?

Chapter Five

The only reason Whitney finished so many thank-you cards that Monday afternoon was that she'd be damned if she would let Adam see her quit. It was a stupid reason, but good enough to keep her at it until he left for the day. Which was a good half hour after the point when her hand had started cramping, but she wasn't about to admit that, either.

Between the ache in her hand and the hot tingling along her shoulder where he had touched her, it had been more than difficult to keep her mind on the task at hand. For all she knew, she had thanked the wrong people for the wrong thing. If so, she hoped they would chalk her mistakes up to grief.

Tuesday morning, just as she was trying to talk herself into starting in on the next batch of cards, she got a call from Carla at the shop.

"You said you wanted to sell the shop?"

"Yes," Whitney answered.

"When do you think you'll have an asking price?" Carla asked.

"I don't know," Whitney said honestly. "I need to find a commercial appraiser. Is there any particular reason you're asking?"

"Well." There were nerves in Carla's voice. "If the

price isn't too high and if I can come up with the financing, I'd like to make you an offer."

Interesting, Whitney thought. "You want to own Claudia's Attic?"

"If I can, yes. I'd love it."

"Why don't I come down there? We'll talk about it."

Whitney spent most of the morning at Claudia's Attic. Not that there was much she and Carla could talk about, since neither had a dollar figure in mind. But as long as Whitney was at the shop, that meant she could postpone tackling the next batch of thank-you cards.

The morning was not a total loss, however. Three different customers, after extending their heartfelt sympathies for the loss of her aunt, gave her recommendations for appraisers. But the real coup came when the town's only real estate agent showed up.

"I'm Doreen Miller, Realtor, Miller Real Estate." Her handshake was firm and vigorous. "I'm so sorry for your loss. Claudia Henderson was one of the best-loved people in this community, and I mean that. She taught all three of my kids, and I'll tell you true, they're better people for it."

"Thank you," Whitney said. "She would be pleased to know you thought so."

"I admit I came in here with more than one purpose in mind."

"Oh?"

"Yes. First, to extend my condolences in person, and second, to see if you need the services of a Realtor. If you're not ready to talk about business yet, or if you have already made other arrangements for your aunt's property, just say so and I'll butt out. But if you need me, I'm here and willing."

"As a matter of fact," Whitney said, "I am ready to talk about business. I've got a business to sell, and a house that won't be ready for an appraisal until the remodeling is finished in a few weeks."

"Oh, don't worry about the remodeling. Any appraiser worth his salt can work around that and take it into account."

"Yes, but he'll be able to appraise it higher if he can see a finished, high-quality house."

The Realtor started to say more, but Whitney raised a hand to stop her. "No appraisal on the house, not even an informal one by you, until it's finished. That's final. But I would like to discuss the shop."

And so they did. Whitney made it clear that she wasn't promising to let Doreen handle the sale of the shop. In Whitney's mind, she might want to do an owner-financing deal, and if so, a Realtor's commission might complicate things unnecessarily. Still, even if Carla bought the shop, having a Realtor handle all the paperwork might be worth the commission.

In the end, Whitney did promise Doreen first crack if she decided to use an agent. Together they determined that Doreen, because she was a nice person and because she hoped to get Whitney's business, would contact the appraiser and have him call Carla to set up a time when he could come. Carla would call Whitney, because Whitney wanted to be there, even though she knew her presence wasn't necessary.

* * *

Whitney intended to tackle the next batch of thank-you cards that afternoon, but Adam was spraying texture onto the walls of the living room, and she didn't care to be anywhere in the house until the air had a chance to clear. Still, she knew if she put off those thank-you cards until tomorrow, it would be that much easier to think of an excuse to put them off again.

She walked back down Main to the Dairy Mart for lunch and brought home two large soft drinks, one of which was for Adam. He'd managed to make her feel guilty for not having any tea made for him today. When she returned home she settled on the front-porch swing with the thank-you cards and Aunt Claudia's lap desk with its padded underside.

Yesterday she'd thanked everyone who sent potted plants. Today it was cut flowers. Unfortunately, about five times as many people sent flowers as sent plants.

Shame, Whitney thought, for thinking that sending flowers was unfortunate. These people thought highly enough of Aunt Claudia to go to the trouble and expense of sending flowers, which weren't cheap these days, either. Whitney was glad, very glad, that so many peopled loved her aunt. If even a fraction of this number remembered her when she died, Whitney would feel honored.

"So stop griping about it, and thank them," she muttered. "This isn't supposed to be about me. I've got nothing to whine about."

"Did you say something?"

Whitney screamed and slapped a hand to her

chest to keep her heart from jumping out and landing at her feet. Dammit, she hated it when people snuck up on her. It made her feel stupid, which made her furious. "Jesus H. Christ," she snapped. "You scared the shit out of me."

"Oh-ho. I must have also scared the good humor out of you," Adam taunted. "If you ever had any."

"If I did, what makes you think I'd show it to some bozo who gets his kicks out of sneaking up on people?"

He rolled his eyes. "Lighten up and get over it. It's not like I came at you with a knife."

Whitney stuck her tongue in her cheek and looked down at the screwdriver in his hand. "No, not a knife."

"Oh, look! She does have a sense of humor."

"Get over it." She did enjoy tossing his own words back at him.

"It's kinda warm out here," he said. "I hung plastic to keep the spray out of the kitchen and dining room."

"And I appreciate it," she said. "I just prefer to be outdoors this afternoon." She also preferred not to tempt fate. She hadn't had a single headache—except her first morning in the house when Adam had woken her up after barely four hours of sleep—since leaving New York. She wasn't going to chance breathing in paint fumes. She had forgotten what it was like to get through a day without pain. Now that she remembered, she decided she liked it.

"Have it your way," Adam told her. "Just watch out for the wind. If it starts gusting, you could have a mess on your hands. I see you've got company coming." He motioned toward the driveway.

A small green car pulled in. The woman who climbed out was someone Whitney knew she had met at the church after the funeral, but she couldn't remember her name.

"Who is it?" she whispered to Adam, trying not to move her lips so the woman wouldn't realize she was asking.

"Hey, Avis," he called to the woman. "She's got a twin sister named Mavis," he added in an aside to Whitney. "They played cards with your aunt once a month."

Whitney remembered, vaguely, something about Bridge Tuesday or Bridge Thursday or something.

"Hello, Adam," Avis called as she swung her car door shut. "How's the house coming?"

"It's coming," he called back. "But I don't guess you came to see me, so I'll get back to work."

"Oh, but I thought you wanted a break," Whitney said, not wanting to be left alone to visit with a woman she didn't know.

"I did," he answered, "and now it's time to get back to work. I want to get that texture on so it'll be dry enough by tomorrow that I can paint."

How could she argue with that without looking like a desperate idiot?

"Adam, dear," Avis called. "Be a good boy, will you, and come carry in this baked ham I brought?"

"I don't know." He tucked his thumbs in his tool belt and sauntered to the edge of the porch like an Old West gunslinger about to elbow his way between the swinging doors of the saloon. "Do I get to eat any of it?"

"That will be up to Whitney, since I brought it for

her. But I would imagine you won't get a bite if you don't carry it in."

Adam grinned and winked. "Point taken." He jumped down the steps and took a large, foil-wrapped baking dish from the backseat of the car. With barely more than a cheeky grin at Whitney, he climbed the porch steps and carried the ham into the house.

The rat. The jerk. The asshole. Leaving her out here alone this way.

Whitney put her cards and notes in their box and set the box on the porch floor beside the swing. With a deep breath to fortify herself, she rose and prepared to . . . God help her, socialize.

"Good afternoon, my dear." Avis smiled as she climbed the steps to the porch. "I hope you don't mind my dropping by like this,"

"Of course not," Whitney lied.

"Mavis would have come with me, but this is her day at the beauty shop and I didn't want to wait any longer to make sure you were doing okay in this big old house." She looked toward the porch ceiling. "I never did understand why Claudia had to have such a big old house for one tiny person, but that's a nev-ermind. We wanted to see if there was anything you needed, and wondered if you have any idea yet how long you'll be in town."

How long Whitney intended to stay seemed to be the biggest question around town these days. It was the main thing everyone asked her.

"I'll be around for a few weeks," she offered. "Until the house is finished."

"Oh, Claudia would be pleased by that. That you're taking an interest in her home. She was so looking forward to the day all her remodeling was finished. Do you need anything while you're here?"

Whitney shrugged. "Not that I can think of."

"Well, all right then. But if the mess gets to be too much and you need a place to stay for a few nights—or longer—you just give a holler. I've got plenty of room, and so does Mavis, and Dorothy, and Betty, for that matter. There's just no lack of places you can stay in this town."

"Thank you." But if she needed a place, Whitney knew she would pick the local motel rather than impose on a stranger. "I'm sure I'll be fine right here."

Avis smiled. "I imagine you will be. That Adam will see to it. He's a fine young man, that Adam."

"So he seems to think," Whitney muttered.

"I beg your pardon, dear?" Avis leaned forward and cocked her head.

"Oh, sorry," Whitney said. "I was just talking to myself. Won't you have a seat? Can I get you something cool to drink? I still have some of Betty's lemonade, and there's iced tea."

"Oh, how sweet of you, but, no, thank you. I won't be staying. I see you've got your work cut out for you today." She nodded toward the box of thank-you cards. "I'm so glad to hear that you'll be in town for a little while. Next week is Bridge Thursday, when Mavis, Dorothy, Claudia, and I would have gotten together for our monthly card game at Dorothy's. Since you're going to be in town, we wondered, well, that is, we'd like you to come in your aunt's place. If you want to, that is."

"Bridge?" Whitney felt a case of claustrophobia coming on.

"Don't say no yet," Avis urged. "Just think about it,

and one of us will get back to you. Oh, and if you have time and want to get away from the house for a while, you could go to the nursing home to read. Claudia used to do that. She said it always lifted her spirits to bring joy to others. It's Shady Oaks, over by the Dairy Mart. Just ask for Edna Freeberger, the head nurse. She'll give you a book to read, or you can take one of your favorites. Believe me, they'll be happy to have you read anything at all, any time you want to drop by."

Whitney was speechless. Such a thing as her being rendered unable to speak rarely happened, but, then, it wasn't often that someone expected her to step into the footsteps of the dearly departed and live that person's life. Good God.

"I'll let you get back to your cards, dear."

Whitney finally had the presence of mind to thank the woman for the baked ham, but that was the best she could do.

"I don't believe it," she muttered a few minutes later as her tongue decided to work again when the little car backed out and Avis drove away. "I just don't flipping believe it."

"Are you talking to yourself again? Where'd Avis go?" Adam stepped out the front door carrying a tray with two pitchers—one of lemonade, one of tea—and two tall, ice-filled glasses. "I guess she didn't want anything to drink."

"No," Whitney said grimly. "She wanted me to step into my aunt's life and take up her activities. Have you ever heard of such a thing? It's outrageous." She felt steam build in her veins. "What's the matter with people around here? I am not my aunt and I don't want to be."

"Whoa, there." Adam eased his tray onto the small round table beside the wicker chair across from the swing. "What brought that on? Who wants you to be your aunt?"

"Everybody!" She waved her arms in the air. "I'm supposed to go to ball games because my aunt liked them. I'm supposed to read to the old people at the nursing home because she enjoyed it. I'm supposed to play bridge because she did. *Bridge,* for crying out loud. The only card came I even know how to play is poker. That'd knot their knickers, wouldn't it?"

Adam muttered something that sounded vaguely like, "You might be surprised," then shook his head. "You're reading them all wrong."

"Wrong? Oh, no," she fired back, wagging her finger in front of his face. "I don't think so. Everyone is making it very plain that I'm supposed to step in and take over for Aunt Claudia, to live her life. Well, I've got news for them."

"You've got rocks in your head is what you've got," Adam with disgust.

"What the hell's that supposed to mean?"

"Or, more accurately, one big chunk of granite where your heart's supposed to be."

"You leave my heart out of this."

"I'll have to, won't I? Since you don't seem to have one."

"That's mean. That's nasty. It's low. And it's not true."

He leaned down and got right in her face. "What are you going to do, tell my mommy on me?"

She leaned closer to him. "Bite me."

"Oh, come on, is that the best you can do?" he taunted. "Poor baby, so mistreated, so put upon."

"Kiss off."

"People offering you friendship."

"Go away."

"The nerve of them."

"Don't you have walls to texture?"

"Why don't you just tell them all to go to hell?"

"Why don't I start with you, Burkett?"

"Never mind that they're hurting nearly as much as you are over your aunt's death. She was their friend. A close, personal friend they loved. They've seen her and talked to her every day for more than thirty years. She was part of their lives. Never mind that now they've all got this huge hole in their lives, in their days, in their hearts."

"Oh, and I don't?"

"Never mind that having you here makes them feel like she's not completely gone. That having you here eases some of their pain and helps them start to accept her loss a little easier. Never mind that getting to know her friends, learning a little about the life she led here, might help you, too."

"Go remodel something besides other people's lives."

"So they want you to read at the nursing home, or go play a game of cards. Would it really hurt for you to do something useful with your time?"

"I'm plenty useful, I'll have you to know, in New York."

"Oh, yeah, sure," he said with a sneer. "Selfish, self-centered, big-city woman who can't wait to shake the dust of this little town off her Guccis. I know your type. Been there, done that, got the broken heart to prove it."

"So *that's* why you don't like me. Because of some other woman from your past."

"Career woman, too busy to be bothered with pesky things like friendliness, common courtesy, compassion. Family. Yeah, I know your type. You just go ahead and say no to all your aunt's friends. Why should you bother with other people's feelings when you don't have any of your own?"

"Go to hell, Burkett."

"You're repeating yourself."

When Avis left after delivering her baked ham and her invitation to Bridge Thursday to Whitney, she drove straight to Mavis's. She let herself in and waited for her to get home from the beauty shop. Thank heaven she didn't have long to wait. Mavis pulled in five minutes after Avis, the sun glinting off the blue tint of her newly coifed gray hair.

"Finally." Avis held open Mavis's door for her.

"How does my hair look?" Mavis had her priorities.

"You got a perm."

"Yes. I think she did exceptionally well this time. Now. Did you go see her?"

"I did."

"Did you ask her?"

"I did."

"Well?" Mavis demanded, getting impatient. "Do I have to drag it out of you?"

"She said she would think about it. That was the best I could get out of her. I think she's feeling a little lost, stuck here in this small town, surrounded by strangers."

"I'm sure I'd feel the same," Mavis said. "But, oh, I hope she decides to come. I just can't stand the thought of facing our first Bridge Thursday without Claudia."

"It would help, wouldn't it, to have her niece there. Let's call Dorothy and tell her where we stand."

"Yes, let's."

For the rest of the day, Whitney nursed her bruised feelings and swore she would never forgive Adam Burkett for once again sticking his nose into her life. That he could hurt her feelings at all was ridiculous, but the truth of it hovered over her as she finished the second batch of thank-you cards.

He thought she had no heart, no feelings.

Why should she care what he thought?

Damn him, he had no right to make her question herself. To accuse her of not caring about Aunt Claudia's friends.

Throughout the evening, the night, and into the next day Whitney seesawed back and forth between anger and guilt so many times that by the time she finished the final batch of thank-you cards, she didn't know how to feel any longer. She wanted to hang on to her anger. Anger was an emotion she understood, one she could use to her advantage.

She was equally familiar with guilt, but she had never learned to function well beneath its burden. The best she could do was push it aside and ignore it. But that was before she came to Washita. Here, practically everything added weight to the guilt. And dammit, she was tired of feeling guilty.

True, she had deliberately kept distance between herself and Aunt Claudia, particularly in the years since Whitney's parents had died. She could not allow herself to lean on Claudia, to rely on her for support, for happiness. To let her peace of mind depend on someone else was to court disaster, and she knew it.

So she had stayed away from her aunt. Each year it became easier to call less frequently, to send fewer cards and letters. To stop sending funny little gifts for no reason other than that they reminded her of her aunt.

Now she didn't need to worry about it. There was no one left in her life to concern herself with. No one.

Out of sheer desperation, to erase that depressing thought from her mind, she used the smell of Adam's spray paint as an excuse to leave the house. She started walking down Main and ended up at the Dairy Mart, when a trace of nostalgia struck her, and she stopped and ordered a root beer float. She sat at one of their covered picnic tables and indulged herself until she had slurped and sucked every last drop through the straw. Since she hadn't eaten lunch, she was probably going to be as sick as a dog, but just then she didn't care.

She wasn't ready to go back to the house yet. First, she wasn't ready to be alone with her thoughts, and second, Adam was painting the living room. She sure wasn't in the mood to deal with him. Why would she want to be around someone who so thoroughly disapproved of her?

She stood on the sidewalk in front of the Dairy Mart, but instead of continuing on down Main or going back to the house, she turned up the side street. Half a block later she stood before the Shady Oaks Nursing Home.

Not have a heart? She'd show him, the jerk. What did he know, anyway? Of course she had a heart.

With determination that bordered on the grim, she mentally pushed up her sleeves—they were too short to push up for real—and crossed the street.

Three shallow concrete steps led to the covered porch and a large glass door. The door was heavy when she pulled it open. The air that hit her in the face was cool and made her nose want to close itself off to keep from taking any of it in. It smelled heavily of antiseptic, air freshener, and old age, with a faint tinge of urine for good measure.

She couldn't remember the name of the head nurse she was supposed to ask for, but it didn't matter. The scowling woman at the front desk wore a name badge that said she was the head nurse, Edna Freeberger. That was good enough for Whitney.

"Hello," Whitney said. "My name is Whitney Sheridan. I'd like to volunteer to read to your residents."

The scowl on Nurse Freeberger's face melted away into a beaming smile. "Well, of course you would."

The woman had the face and hair of Aunt Bea from Mayberry, and a voice like ground glass. Like Burgess Meredith playing Mick, Rocky Balboa's trainer.

"Like aunt, like niece?" Freeberger teased.

Whitney gave her a wry smile. She should have known the woman would know who she was. Everyone else in town seemed to. "I don't know about that," she said. "I just heard you needed volunteers. Is now a good time, or should I come back?"

"As a matter of fact, right now is fine. Miss Ella is awake, and if I'm not mistaken, she and Miz Henderson were halfway through the latest Stephanie Plum story. Are you familiar with those books?"

"Yes, I am." She'd had to read them, because everyone at work talked about Janet Evanovich's books every time a new one came out. Actually, Whitney enjoyed the stories about modern-day bounty hunter and basic screwup Stephanie Plum. "But I don't have a copy to read from."

"Not to worry. Miss Ella has them all. She'll be able to tell you which book they were on and exactly where they left off. Just follow me. It's so good of you to do this. Miss Ella doesn't have any family at all. She'll be so glad to see you, especially because you're Miz Henderson's niece."

Good God, Whitney thought as she followed the portly nurse down the hall. What had she gotten herself into?

Miss Ella occupied the far bed in the fourth room facing the street. The near bed was empty, the mattress bare and somehow sad-looking.

There was nothing sad about Miss Ella's half of the room, however. Above her bed hung a giant paper sunflower with a happy face in its center. Photographs of all sizes hung around the flower and on the adjoining wall. Other photos stood in various sized frames on a nightstand, small dresser, and bookcase, all interspersed with more cheery flowers.

"Miss Ella," Nurse Freeberger called. "You have a visitor."

The small woman barely made a hump in the bed linens that covered her. Her left arm and leg shifted; the left side of her mouth curved up. "I do?" Her voice was only slightly slurred.

"This is Whitney Sheridan, Claudia's niece."

The one-sided smile widened as did the woman's faded gray eyes. "Well, praise be, so it is."

"Ms. Sheridan, this is Ella Fields."

Something stirred in the back of Whitney's mind. There was something about this woman. . . ."Fields?" Then her eyes widened. "Mrs. Fields who used to read me stories?"

"Oh." With one shaky, blue-veined hand, Ella Fields covered her mouth as tears filled her eyes. "You remember?"

A hard lump rose in Whitney's throat at the woman's reaction. "Of course I remember." She moved forward and slid onto the tall stool next to the bed. "How could I forget the woman who taught me to love reading?"

As she said the words, Whitney remembered how much fun it had been to read a book when she'd been a child. When and why had she lost that enjoyment? These days she read a book only to keep up with what the people at work were talking about. She read for self-defense rather than enjoyment. There was something so sad about that.

What was that old saying? People who can read and don't are no better off than those who can't. What, she wondered, did that make her?

"Well, what do you know about that," Nurse Freeberger said. "The two of you know each other?"

"Mrs. Fields was the librarian when I used to come spend summers with Aunt Claudia when I was a kid.

She introduced me to *Ramona the Pest, The Hobbit,* all the Judy Blume stories, all sorts of books. Every time I finished one book, she was ready with another one she'd picked out for me to read. She never steered me wrong."

Listen to me, Whitney thought. She was running off at the mouth like an excited teenager. Actually, seeing Mrs. Fields made her feel even younger than that. Sure, she remembered Janey, and Betty Roberts. But seeing Mrs. Fields again, having the woman remember her, somehow moved her more than seemed reasonable. All this nostalgia must finally be getting to her.

But that was okay, wasn't it? Hadn't Adam just chastised her for having no feelings? So, here she was, proving him wrong. If he wasn't there to witness the event, that was too bad.

"The nurse says Aunt Claudia was reading a book to you."

"Oh, she was, child. She hasn't been gone a week and I already miss her so much. What am I going to do without her?" A giant tear rolled down each of Mrs. Fields's wrinkled cheeks.

"I miss her, too." Whitney slid one hand over Mrs. Fields's. "Very much."

"There, now, you two." The nurse tugged at the bedcovers, straightening them. "You keep this up, you'll have me in tears, too, and you know, Miss Ella, how much I hate to cry. Why don't you tell Ms. Sheridan which book you want her to read from?"

Mrs. Fields sniffed as two more tears ran from her eyes.

"Maybe now isn't a good time," Whitney offered. "I can come back tomorrow, if you'd rather."

"No." Mrs. Fields squeezed Whitney's hand with surprising strength. "No, stay, please. If you can, that is."

"Of course I can." Whitney squeezed back gently. Her heart ached for this poor woman who had once been so vital but was now confined to this lonely bed in this place where people came to die. She thanked God that Aunt Claudia hadn't ended up in a place like this. "I can stay as long as you like, Mrs. Fields."

"Please." Mrs. Fields sniffed. "Call me Ella."

"I'll call you Miss Ella if you'll call me Whitney."

"Very well, dear."

Miss Ella told her which book she and Whitney's aunt had been reading the last time Claudia had come to read to her.

Whitney was surprised that with the few books she had read in recent years, this happened to be one of them. She turned to the place her aunt had marked, and started reading.

Miss Ella fell asleep an hour later with a smile on one side of her face.

Whitney left with a lump in her throat and an ache in her heart.

The lump was still in Whitney's throat, the ache still in her heart when she walked home and saw Adam's truck still in her driveway. Adam, the man who thought she didn't have a heart.

Facing him was the last thing in the world that interested her.

"Hello-o!"

It was Betty, calling and waving from her front porch.

Saved, Whitney thought. Not by the bell, but by the holler. She turned up Betty's sidewalk and joined her on the porch.

"Help me drink some lemonade?" Betty offered.

"Thank you. That sounds wonderful."

Betty poured Whitney a glass of lemonade. "Have you been out for a walk?"

Whitney told her where she'd been and why, and that she'd remembered Miss Ella from her child-hood trips to the library.

"She was always so active," Betty said. "It's hard to see her now, trapped in that bed, in that place. Not that Shady Oaks is a bad place, it's just . . ."

"A one-way trip?"

"Yes," Betty said soberly. "Claudia tried to bring her home with her, you know."

"No," Whitney said, stunned. "I had no idea."

"They grew so close over the years. With their age difference, they could have been mother and daughter, but they were the best of friends."

"So why didn't Miss Ella come to live with Aunt Claudia?"

"Because she refused to allow Claudia to take care of her that way, what with her being bedridden and all. Said it would be too much work, and she didn't want her friend to become her caretaker. Besides, she claimed that she'd been paying insurance pre-miums her whole life. As far as she was concerned, it was time to let them take care of her. But Claudia wouldn't allow her to simply lie up there in Shady

Oaks. She went sometimes every day, but at least a couple of times a week."

"Can't she use a wheelchair or something?"

"I honestly don't know, but I doubt she would be able to get herself in and out of one. What did you read to her?"

Whitney's lips twitched. "A story about a female bounty hunter in New Jersey. Aunt Claudia had started it last week."

Betty clapped her hands and grinned. "One of Janet Evanovich's Stephanie Plum books."

"Exactly."

"I imagine Miss Ella really enjoys the Grandma Maser character."

"Oh, she does, but her favorite is Lula. According to Miss Ella, that's who she wants to be when she grows up."

Betty slapped her knee and laughed uproariously. "Oh, my stars. She wants to be a fat black prostitute? Why, Miss Ella, I had no idea."

"Oh, no, no, no," Whitney protested. "That's more or less what I said, too, but Miss Ella corrected me. Lula was not a prostitute, she was a ho. But Miss Ella didn't care about that, what she wants is to be able to wear Day-Glo Spandex and use a stun gun on the bad guys."

"Oh, oh, oh." Betty laughed so hard she nearly fell out of her chair. "I just can't imagine our dignified town librarian saying such a thing. I guess when you're over eighty and bedridden you can say just about anything you please."

"That sounds like something we should all aspire to."

"What?" Betty asked. "Being over eighty and bedridden?"

"Feeling frisky enough to say whatever you want."

"Ain't that the truth."

The women's laughter drifted across the yard on the evening breeze, across the driveway next door, and in through the window Adam had opened to help dissipate the smell of paint. He had no trouble discerning the identities of the laughing ladies. It sounded to him as if Whitney and Betty were having a high ol' time over there.

All afternoon he'd been feeling guilty as hell for jumping down Whitney's throat the way he'd done when Avis had left. He should have kept his mouth shut. He didn't know what it was about this woman, other than the unforgivable way she had ignored her aunt these past years, that set off his temper. He was normally an easygoing guy, if he did say so himself. But with Whitney Sheridan, things were different. He was different.

He looked around the new living room and shook his head. The texture he had sprayed onto the walls yesterday had been perfectly dry this morning. The subsequent painting had gone off without a hitch. Afterward, to make the house as pleasant as possible—if such a thing was possible during the middle of renovations and remodeling—he had opened the living room windows and propped open the front and back doors to circulate some fresh air.

After the way he'd chewed on Whitney, he figured he owed her something more than a little airing out. He spent no small amount of time cleaning the room of his own debris. Then he mounted the mantle back over the fireplace, vacuumed the carpet, uncovered the furniture, and put the room back together again. He even unwrapped all of Miz Henderson's little knickknacks and set them around on the mantle and end tables. If he did say so himself, the room hadn't looked so nice in years. New furniture would make it even better, but since Whitney would be selling the house, there would be no new furniture.

But did she come home and let him offer the new room as an apology?

No-o. Not Whitney Big-City Sheridan, no sirree, Bob. She had more important things to do, like prance around town, then sit out along Main Street laughing like a loon.

The fresh flowers he'd cut from the backyard mocked him from their new location in a crystal vase on the coffee table. He sneered back, but he wasn't quite small enough to throw them out to deny Whitney the pleasure of them, no matter how pissed he was at her.

Then, suddenly, there she was, the bane of his existence, walking through the front door.

He should have left while she was still at Betty's.

"Wow." She blinked as she looked around the room. "You've been busy."

He snorted. "You could say that."

"It looks wonderful."

He tried not to let her compliment soothe his ruffled feathers, but he wasn't altogether successful.

"It looks so . . . new, so fresh. And you put everything back in order. You didn't have to do that."

"I didn't do it for you."

"And don't think I don't know that," she snapped back. "But that doesn't mean I can't still be grateful."

"Yeah, you sound real grateful."

She threw her hands in the air. "I can't win with you, can I?"

"I didn't know you wanted to win with me."

The sound that came from her throat was as close to a true growl as he'd ever heard come from a human.

"Go home," she said tightly. "Please tell me you're finished for the day and you're going home. Right now. Right this minute. Before I respond to that jackass comment and say something we'll both be sorry for."

If a jaunty whistle escaped from between his lips as he sauntered out the door with his hands in his pockets, well, hell, he couldn't help it, could he? He'd pissed her off, and that did his heart good. What better way to end a long day?

Chapter Six

It couldn't exactly be said that Whitney and Adam tiptoed around each other for the next couple of days. The truth was, they more or less clomped and stomped and kicked their way through the house as Adam set to work remodeling the downstairs bathroom from floor to ceiling.

Whitney was prepared to swear that her own body was betraying her. She couldn't remember ever having to go to the bathroom so frequently in her life as during those next few days. At least, it seemed frequent, but it could have simply been that while Adam worked on the downstairs bathroom, Whitney had to go upstairs.

She was also ready to swear that Adam was deliberately taking his own sweet time, getting some sort of perverse pleasure from her having to traipse up and down the stairs all day.

Two days into the bathroom remodeling, and they had yet to speak to each other. He, the jerk, obviously still had his nose out of joint over something. As near as she could tell, he'd wanted her to be grateful for the extra trouble he'd gone to in putting the living room back together.

She'd been grateful, dammit. She'd said so, hadn't she?

He'd told her before that she needed to be nicer to people. Well, she'd been nice, hadn't she? But had he given her a chance to tell him about it? To prove herself to him?

And why, by all that was holy, did she feel the need to prove herself to Adam Burkett or anyone else?

Oh, God, all she wanted to do was go home. In New York she knew who and what she was. In the WNN control room her confidence was never shaken. She always knew what to do, how to relate to the various people she came in contact with. She was in control, in charge, the big kahuna. No one came down on her for anything. At least, not and lived to tell about it.

In Washita, Texas, she was a fish out of water, and she didn't care for the feeling.

Adam felt like an alien in his own skin. How many bathrooms had he remodeled in his life? Too many to count. During the course of tearing through those bathrooms, he'd had occasion to smell just about everything, good and bad. Most of the time, he never even noticed.

This time, however, he kept smelling . . . Whitney. Her perfume, her shampoo, her hair spray. Whatever. There were several distinct fragrances lingering in that bathroom, and each of them whispered her name in his ear, so softly, so close, the hair on the back of his neck stood on end.

He didn't need this. Didn't need to think about her, wonder about her. Smell her. Didn't need it, didn't want it. It reeked of obsession, and that wasn't like him at all. *He* wasn't much like him these days.

A perfect example of how unlike himself he was lately came up the afternoon Whitney got the phone call from Carla at Claudia's Attic. He knew the call was from Carla because he heard Whitney say her name.

"Yes, Carla. What can I do for you?" Then, "Turned you down? The bank? I'm sorry to hear that . . . Other offers? Not yet, but I haven't listed the property yet, either . . . Work something out? What did you have in mind?" After a longish pause, Adam heard Whitney say, "I don't know. Let's both give it some thought, but I'll be honest . . . yes, exactly. I'm sorry, Carla, but maybe this is only a temporary setback. Maybe things will work out in the end. I'll see you in a day or two."

Adam hadn't meant to eavesdrop, but the bathroom where he was working was right off the kitchen and dining area. He couldn't avoid hearing her. Of course, he could have shut the door.

Nah. He wasn't *that* polite.

The news hadn't sounded good. Leaning slightly to the left he had a clear view of the breakfast bar, where the phone was. Where Whitney sat, holding her head in her hands.

Dammit, he shouldn't care, but something drew him out of the bathroom and across the floor.

"Bad news?" he asked quietly.

Whitney jumped at the sound of his voice. It was the first time either had spoken to the other in two days, and it took her by surprise. "What?"

"Sorry," he said. "It's none of my business. It just sounded like you'd had bad news."

"Why do you care?"

Adam sighed. "I guess I had that coming. Look, I'm sorry about the other day. I had no business saying those things to you."

"Damn right you didn't."

"I said I was sorry, didn't I?"

She held up a hand. "Okay, you're right. Now I'm sorry. I'm just not used to not being able to make things happen. I'm used to being in charge."

"What's happened that you couldn't control?"

She shook her head. "Carla wanted to buy the shop."

"That's great. That's perfect. She's been almost as devoted to it as Miz Henderson."

"Yes, but the bank won't lend her the money."

"Oh. That's too bad. Maybe she should try another bank, or one of those online loan companies."

"She said she was going to look elsewhere, but she didn't sound too hopeful."

"If you're bent on selling the place—"

"Why wouldn't I?"

"You should take your aunt's place at the monthly Chamber of Commerce luncheon coming up in a few days."

She frowned. "Why would I want to do that?"

"Because," he explained as if she were dim-witted, "all the local businesspeople will be there. Potential buyers? Potential lenders?"

Her lips quirked. "You want to be careful giving me legitimate advice like that."

"Why?"

"Because I might actually start to like you."

"Oh, no, not that," he protested.

"It could happen," she warned.

"I'll have to be more careful."

* * *

Whitney stood at the breakfast bar for a long time after Adam returned to work in the bathroom. She had to get over this inertia that had gripped her since coming to Texas. There was so much to do, and she had done none of it. Hadn't even started.

So, she would start.

She took the china tea set from its shelf and carefully wrapped it. Then, not wanting to be rude by simply disappearing without a word, she went to the bathroom door to let Adam know she was going to Betty's for a few minutes.

The bathroom had not been modernized since it was built back in the early 1900s. There was no vanity, no cabinet or countertop. Simply a porcelain sink mounted on the wall, with one worn faucet for hot, another for cold. Adam was on his knees and bent practically in two to reach the plumbing beneath the sink with his wrench. His jeans and T-shirt were stretched taut across his back and butt.

Whitney had the strongest urge to reach out and spread her hands, one across his back where muscles flexed and bulged, the other, lower, across the seat of his jeans.

Stunned by her own reaction, she gasped and stepped back.

He must have heard her, for he swiveled on his knees toward her and raised his head. But he raised his head too soon, and too far. He whacked it hard against the bottom side of the sink. A stream of swear words, vile and inventive, echoed in the small room.

"Pretty impressive," she said.

He rubbed hard at the top of his head. "I'm glad you liked it."

"Did you hurt yourself?"

"You don't have to sound so damned pleased about it."

"I'm not. But you should be more careful."

His eyes narrowed. He moved from beneath the sink and rose to his feet.

With a chuckle, she took a step back from the glint of retribution in his eyes. "I, uh, didn't mean to startle you."

"Didn't you?" He advanced another step.

This time she stood her ground. "Of course not."

"Then what did you come in here for? To check my progress?"

"Progress?" She glanced around at the walls stripped bare of their wallpaper, the bathtub filled with the torn remnants of that wallpaper; the baseboard standing upright in one corner; the dome gone from the light fixture, leaving nothing but a bare bulb glaring at her. She smiled. "You call this progress?"

He looked around the room. "Yeah, I call this progress."

"You would." She laughed at the look of outrage on his face. "I just came in here to tell you I'm going next door for a few minutes."

"You and Betty seem to be getting pretty tight," he noted.

"Actually," she told him, "I'm following up on something your mother suggested."

"The General? She'll be pleased. She loves to be obeyed."

Whitney laughed again. "She didn't issue me an

order. She simply said that my aunt would want Betty to have her china tea set. So I'm taking it to her."

He paused and tilted his head. "That's nice."

She smirked at his comment.

"No," he said. "I mean it. That's real nice of you."

"Golly." She batted her lashes at him. "Is that approval I hear in your voice?"

He pursed his lips. "For now. For this particular instance."

"Oh, well, I'm glad you qualified it."

Whitney stayed at Betty's only a few minutes, long enough for Betty to stop crying and for Whitney to stop being embarrassed. She hadn't realized just how deeply Betty would feel about the tea set.

On the way home she shook her head at herself. She needed to get back to New York, the sooner the better, before she changed so much she no longer recognized herself. Teasing and making nice with Adam Burkett. Bringing the next-door neighbor to tears. Reading to an old lady at the nursing home.

She could almost laugh at herself, except none of it was funny. Hour by hour, day by day, something pressed down on her heavier and heavier. She couldn't explain it. Maybe because she was unwilling to look too closely at herself, her life.

And, really, where was the need to look closer? All she had to do was take care of her aunt's belongings and get back to New York, where everything was familiar, where she could be herself again and not worry about how a neighbor would react to a gift, how three elderly ladies would feel when she declined to play bridge with them.

The disappointment a manager would feel in not being able to purchase the shop where she worked.

The sooner she finished her aunt's business, the sooner she could go home. It was past time to start going through the house in earnest.

She marched into the house, hollered at Adam that she was back, and took the stairs to the one room she'd been avoiding from the beginning— Aunt Claudia's bedroom.

She stopped for a moment in the doorway, her breath coming harder than the short climb up the stairs warranted, her hand on the light switch beside the door. It smelled of her aunt, the room did. That flowery, powdery fragrance that had always, always surrounded Aunt Claudia like a gentle aura. The smell meant love and safety, security and warmth. Similar to Whitney's mother's smell, but different enough that she had never confused the two.

Standing in the doorway wasn't getting the job done. She moved into the room. She looked around and breathed a sigh of relief. Aunt Claudia had changed nearly everything since Whitney had last been here. Gone was the heavy, dark oak furniture, the Chinese lamp with the fringed red silk lampshade, and the chenille bedspread.

The furniture was more modern in style, lighter in color. The lamp was Victorian, though, and a handmade quilt covered the bed with hundreds of tiny green and white squares. If she remembered what Carla had told her, it was the Irish chain pattern. It gave the entire room an open, airy feel.

Her breath came easier. Until she saw the framed picture on the wall over the bed. She brought a hand to her mouth to hold back a cry. She'd kept it.

All these years, and Aunt Claudia had not only kept it, but framed it and hung it over her bed. Whitney didn't know whether to laugh, or groan in horror. The childish finger painting was the most god-awful combination of colors, from mud brown to prison-jumpsuit orange, lime green to teal, and everything in between that clashed.

Whitney had done that in kindergarten. And Aunt Claudia had kept it all these years.

Suddenly Whitney lost any urge to laugh. Behind her eyes a hot pressure built. Quickly she blinked it away and sought something else to look at besides her own childish artwork, pitiful indeed, yet treasured by her aunt.

No, there was no urge to laugh.

On the bedside table rested a journal. Whitney wasn't ready to look at something that personal yet. Instead she reached for the photo album on the shelf beneath the table. Not exactly impersonal, but she couldn't keep putting everything off. Just the journal. That, she would work up to.

The photos in the album started with ones taken when Claudia and her sister, Whitney's mother, were children. Whitney had seen them many times during her life, but they still brought a smile to her face. So, too, did the organization of them into an album. Aunt Claudia had kept her photos—the ones that weren't framed and hanging on a wall—loose in a box. In several boxes. She had liked the surprise of not knowing which decade or subject matter she would find next.

It seemed she had finally changed her mind and organized everything, as this album seemed to lay the photos out in order, if the first few pages were anything to go by.

Whitney remembered, as a child, being unable to grasp the concept of her mother and aunt having once been children themselves, regardless of how many times she saw these old black-and-white pictures. It simply hadn't computed in her young mind. But the older she got, the easier it had become to envision the two sisters in their childhood, growing up side by side, Karen, the baby of the family, and big sister Claudia, some nine years older than Whitney's mom.

The advancement in photographic technologies was evident as the parade of photos continued. Claudia's high school graduation photo was in black-and-white, as had been the earlier snapshots. But her college graduation was in color, as were both of Karen's graduation pictures and her wedding pictures.

There were pictures of Whitney from her infancy. So many of them. Whitney'd had no idea Aunt Claudia had so many pictures of her. Some of them must have been sent to her by Whitney's mother, because they were obviously taken at home rather than here. Christmas, Easter. A succession of childhood Halloween costumes.

But there were things other than photographs included in the album. Aunt Claudia had apparently kept every card Whitney had sent her. Cards for holidays, special occasions, birthdays, and cards just to say hello.

Whitney's throat tightened.

All these things, kept all these years. How much love must have been there. Heat stung the backs of

Whitney's eyes. She blinked, and the card before her came into focus.

> *I love you Aunt Claudia.*
> *Be my Valentine*
> > *Hugs and kisses,*
> > *Whitney*

The card blurred. She'd been nine years old when she sent that card. Aunt Claudia had kept it all these years.

"And I hadn't even called her in months," she whispered, her voice shaking through her tight throat.

Then a lump rose and closed her throat completely, and the hot stinging moved to the front of her eyes, and the blurry vision began to swim. And suddenly her cheeks were wet and her chest was heaving. For the first time since her mother's death ten years earlier, Whitney Sheridan was crying. Great, gut-wrenching sobs that shook her and drove the breath from her lungs.

Downstairs, Adam stepped out of the bathroom to get himself a drink. With a tall glass of iced water in his hand, he leaned back against the breakfast bar and mentally outlined the ongoing work in the bathroom. He was, he decided, right on schedule. Maybe even a little ahead.

She would like that, Whitney would, if he finished early. That way she could return to New York that much sooner, which would make her that much happier. It wouldn't displease him any, either, to see the last of her. Then maybe his emotions wouldn't keep seesawing from anger to anticipation to humor, and back to anger and mistrust.

He hadn't felt so many different things for one woman since Monica. And that had been an unmitigated disaster.

The sooner he got back to work, the sooner he would finish and Whitney Sheridan would be on her way out of his life.

He pushed away from the breakfast bar, and could have sworn he heard a small animal cry out in pain. Thing was, there were no small animals in the house. At least, there weren't supposed to be.

Then he heard what could only have been a sob, and realized the sounds were coming from upstairs. From Whitney?

He didn't remember crossing the dining area or taking the stairs, but suddenly he was inside Miz Henderson's bedroom, sitting on the side of her bed and reaching for Whitney. God, he'd never seen a woman cry so hard. This was no dainty sniff and tear-up. This was gasping, bone-wracking sobs, with great streams of tears. This was heart-wrenching. This was a heart and soul tearing themselves to shreds.

"Whitney?" Tentatively he placed a hand on her arm. "Whit, honey, what's wrong?"

"I am."

"What do you mean?"

All she could do was shake her head and sob even harder.

He found a box of tissues on the dresser and carried it to the bed. There he put a tissue in her hand. She didn't seem to know what to do with it, so he used another one to mop at her cheeks. Then he slipped an arm around her shoulders and pulled until she leaned on him.

"Go ahead," he told her. "Cry all you want. It's about time you let go. You'll feel better once you get it all out of your system."

She continued to cry, so he continued to talk quietly. "You never really get it all out, but you can ease the pressure so it doesn't hurt quite so bad. For a while. But you gotta let it out or it'll choke you. That's it, hon, just let it out."

Whitney heard the deep murmur of his voice and pressed herself into his chest to get closer to the comfort of the sound. God help her, she couldn't quit crying. The tears wouldn't stop, her breath wouldn't be controlled. Her face was wet, her eyes burned, and she couldn't breathe in or out through her nose at all. She hated this.

But she couldn't stop. The pain inside, the guilt, the regret, were all too great. The deep, crippling ache would not subside. It was closing over her head and she was drowning in it. All she could do was hang on to the warm voice, the strong arms, and try to survive the storm.

The human spirit is able to maintain a peak emotion for only a certain amount of time before it exhausts itself. The storm gradually subsided. Her sobs turned to sniffs, her gulps to swallows and breaths.

"Better?"

The deep voice roused her from a stupor. In the next second she became aware that she was curled up in Adam Burkett's arms as if it was the most natural place for her to be, a bird snuggling in its nest.

"Oh, God." With one hand she covered her face; with the other, she pushed herself away from Adam. "I am so sorry you had to see me like this. I don't know what came over me."

"Don't you?" He used his index finger to smooth a strand of hair away from her damp cheek.

Why did she want so desperately to lean into that finger, to feel it stroke her face?

"It's only natural," he said. "You've lost your aunt. Grief is not only justified, it's essential."

Whitney straightened her back and gave a sniff, striving for some semblance of dignity. "That doesn't mean it's all right for me to fall apart and blubber all over you. I'm sorry I lost control that way. Thank you for your help. I'm fine now."

"That's bull."

Whitney stood and arched her neck to look down at him. "I beg your pardon?"

"Ooh, there's that queen-to-peasant tone again, but it's not going to get me off the subject."

"We don't have a subject, because this discussion is over." She turned to walk away.

He snagged her wrist and held her there. "Why do you do that?"

"I'm not even going to ask what you're talking about. Let go of me."

"Why do you get so defensive every time we strike up a conversation?"

"Maybe because your idea of a conversation is you telling me what's wrong with me and how I should act. Now, let go of me."

"Okay, sure." He let go. "Go ahead and run away again. Don't face your own emotions. Bottle it all up until you explode. I can't imagine why I even care what happens to you. Just be sure, when you're pushing away those feelings that keep trying to get the best of you, that you know what those feelings are and what it is, exactly, that you're hiding from."

Whitney gave a toss of her head. "I don't hide from anything. And I don't run."

"Of course you do," he accused. "You're doing it right now."

Whitney propped a hand on her hip. "You know, I'm a pretty smart person. But I'll admit, I don't have the slightest idea what you're talking about. And, what's more, I don't care to know."

"What I'm talking about is that you've got bigger issues going on that just grief over your aunt."

"You're crazy."

"Certifiable. But I'll get the truth out of you before you leave town."

"Why?" Whitney demanded. "Why bother? You like poking at people, exposing their pain?"

"Don't be any more dense than you have to be," he said. "Of course not. I just don't like to see people tear themselves apart when maybe talking about it might help."

"There's nothing to talk about," she stated flatly.

"I can see why you wouldn't want to talk to me, but it looks to me like you damn sure need to talk to somebody."

Whitney felt her stomach tighten and her temper soar. "You're so damn full of yourself. I don't need you; I don't need anybody."

"Like you didn't need your aunt," Adam taunted. "Which is why you just spent thirty minutes crying so hard you damn near made yourself sick."

"Which just proves my point," she snapped.

"Point? You have a point?" he asked, incredulous.

"My point is," she said distinctly, "that the crying jag I just had is a perfect reason to keep my distance, to never get too close to people, since I'll just lose them, anyway."

"Lose them? You mean they'll die?"

"Aunt Claudia did."

"She had a heart attack," he said tersely.

"Yes, and my mother had a brain aneurysm, and my father got himself killed by a drunk driver. When I was eight, my best friend moved away and I never saw her again. When I was sixteen my boyfriend dumped me for a girl with bigger boobs. Who happened to have been my best friend since I was nine."

"Okay," Adam said. "You've had it rough. That's too bad. You have my sympathies. But cutting yourself off from caring about anybody is no way to live. Isn't the pleasure of having had your aunt in your life worth the pain of losing her?"

His words make her heart clench tight.

"Besides," he went on. "Your aunt will always be in your heart, so she'll never really be gone."

"That's cold comfort, don't you think?"

"Is it? I always thought it was the best comfort of all, to carry somebody in your heart, to know you're in theirs. To me, the heart is a house filled with an infinite number of rooms—more than enough rooms to hold every person, place, or thing you could possibly care about or love in your whole life."

Whitney gave him a sarcastic laugh. "Yeah, well, all the rooms in my heart have collapsed in on themselves. They're destroyed and useless and empty, and you should mind your own damn business."

"Yeah, you're right." He stood and nodded his

head. "You're right about that. I should mind my own business and let you wallow in your misery."

She smirked. "I hear a *but* in there."

"But," he said, raising his arms out to his sides, "what can I say? Repairing destroyed or damaged rooms is what I do."

Whitney shook her head and rolled her eyes. "Why do you even care what I feel, what happens to me? You don't even like me, because I remind of you some other woman."

Adam had the good grace to blush. "I was wrong about that. You're nothing like her, and even if you were, it's still not fair of me to treat you badly because of it."

She sniffed. "How do you know I'm not like her? What did you call her? Career woman, too busy to be bothered with pesky things like friendliness, common courtesy, compassion? Family? That sounds pretty much like me, don't you think?"

He shook his head. "No, but even if it did, it doesn't matter. You see, the problem with Monica was, I thought I was in love with her." He smiled. "I don't have that problem with you, now, do I?"

"Good God, I hope not."

That evening, after Adam left for the day, Whitney squared her shoulders and marched back to her aunt's bedroom. She would face the memories and put them behind her. And she would do it this time without a witness.

She set the photo album aside. She would keep it, of course. But she wouldn't look at it anymore for now. Later, when she was home again and her emotions were steady, she would take it out and enjoy going through the pages.

For now she turned to Aunt Claudia's closet.

Clothes, shoes, handbags. None were Whitney's style or size. Perhaps the church could sell them in their next rummage sale. She would leave them where they were for the time being.

On the top shelf, in the back, she found a large box, the size that would hold a case of paper. It was filled with more books like the one on the nightstand. Journals.

Whitney carried the box from the closet and set it on the bed. There was no writing on the spines. She took one from the top and leafed through it. The entries were dated last year.

Wondering how far back the journals went, Whitney took them all out and checked the date of the first entry in each. The oldest was from before Whitney was born.

What was she to do with the journals? Most people assumed and expected that the things they wrote in their journals would remain private. Aunt Claudia certainly never intended for anyone to read her entries, surely.

But to simply throw them away? The idea was unthinkable. It would be like dismissing Aunt Claudia. Throwing her away. She couldn't bear to throw them away.

But to read them? Should she? What would Aunt Claudia want?

Whitney ran her hand over the fake leather jacket of the oldest journal. Something inside her urged her to read the journals, to use them to get to know her aunt, get close to her, keep her memory alive.

At first the thought startled her. But when she thought about it, she realized that she was gripping the book tightly. She was going to read them. She would take her time. There was no hurry.

But she would start now.

She opened the first journal.

> *June 23*
>
> *My baby sister got married today. Imagine that. I don't know why I was surprised when she and Steven announced their intentions last winter. The two of them have been in love for ages. I guess I was surprised that Daddy gave his permission, as determined as he has always been to keep both of us by his side.*
>
> *And, all right, I'm envious. Karen's only twenty-five, after all, while I'm whithering on the vine, as it were, at thirty-four.*
>
> *Envious, yes, but not jealous. Karen is so dear to me, and I'm so glad she's happy. Maybe someday there will be a man for me. And if not, well, I am not unfulfilled. I have my students, and they are always a joy. And I have Daddy to take care of, as always. Seeing Karen wed makes me feel like the mother of the bride. She has been my charge, my responsibility since Mama died when Karen was only five. She's been mine ever since. Karen and Daddy both have been mine to care for and tend to.*
>
> *Yes, I am fulfilled. And envious.*
>
> *For now I will be happy for Karen and her Steven, and dream of a love of my own. After all, no one ever died of loneliness, did they?*

Whitney sniffed and blinked to clear her vision. No, she thought, no one ever died of loneliness. But her aunt's loneliness fairly leaped from the pages of her journal.

"Oh, Aunt Claudia, I wish things could have been different for you."

With a new ache in her heart, Whitney set that first journal aside and repacked the others, placing them in reverse order, newest on bottom, so she could get to the next book in sequence. She would read a little each night.

But no more tonight. Tonight she was too sad.

Chapter Seven

Late that night, thunderstorms boiled across the Texas Panhandle, wreaking havoc along the way. No tornados, praise God, Whitney thought. She'd never seen a tornado, never been in the vicinity when one touched down. As far as she knew, they didn't have them in New York. She wasn't in any particular hurry to meet one up close and personal, either.

The town, not just Whitney, was lucky. No tornados struck that night. But straight winds blew strong enough in places to tear off roofs and blow down barns and power lines.

In Washita, damage was light. A couple of sheds and outbuildings suffered damage, and several roofs would need repair. All of it was on the opposite side of town from Whitney, for which she was grateful.

She knew all of this because Betty came over to check on her bright and early, and while she was filling Whitney in, Adam called.

"Are you all right?" he asked.

"I'm fine."

"I'll swing by and check the place over for damage later this morning, but I'm not going to be able to finish the bathroom today."

"You're not?"

"A couple of my regular clients have roof damage, and if it rains agin before it's fixed . . ."

"I get the picture," she said, visions of rain dripping down through the ceiling making her vow to go outside and check her own roof.

"You're sure you're all right?"

"I'm sure. You do what you have to do."

"All right, then," he said. "I appreciate your being so understanding about this."

Whitney understood the need for Adam to work on other houses. She had no quarrel with waiting a few days, although, naturally, she would like to get the work done on Aunt Claudia's house sooner rather than later. In this case, the delay couldn't be helped.

"Just hurry, will you? I really need this work finished as soon as possible," she said.

"I know. I'll drive by and look at your roof and trees, then get to work on these other houses. If you need me before I get back to you, you've got my cell number there on the breakfast bar."

Whitney started to make a crack about needing him when hell froze over, but the next couple of days, or however long it took him to finish the other work, loomed large and empty before her. That she should actually miss him appalled her. She nearly swallowed her tongue.

Whitney spent the next two days going through Aunt Claudia's belongings room by room, closet by closet. She got suggestions from Betty as to what Aunt Claudia's bridge partners and Miss Ella might like to have as a keepsake, and set those items aside.

And every once in a while she picked up the journal and read another few pages. Actually, more than a few, she realized when she finished the first volume and picked up the second. She had read more than two years' worth of entries since that first one, about her parents' marriage, when the tone of the entries changed from dutiful and steady to delirious.

> *August 17*
>
> *My life changed today, I just know it did. The world is a brighter place, sunnier, more exciting. I met a man! And oh, what a man! His name is Harry. How dashing and handsome he looks in his army uniform.*
>
> *He's young. At twenty-seven (Karen's age) too young for me, people will say, and they'll be right. But when I pointed out our nine-year age difference, he laughed. "So what?" he said.*
>
> *So what. Imagine a twenty-seven-year-old man saying such a thing to a thirty-six-year-old spinster.*
>
> *I don't know if people still use the word spinster, but that's how I have seen myself, particularly these past two years that Karen has been married.*
>
> *But I digress. I know I've known Harry only one day, but I honestly believe he is the one.*
>
> *I understand how pathetic that sounds, but I don't care. One look at him, and I knew, in my heart, that I would love him and no other man.*
>
> *And joy of joys, I think he feels the same. There is love in his eyes when he looks at me. Or maybe that is my love for him being reflected there.*
>
> *Harry is stationed at Fort Benning, right here at Columbus. He has just finished basic training. I try*

*not to think about the fact that he will probably be
sent to Viet Nam.*

*I wondered how he had managed to avoid the draft
since turning eighteen. He said the avoidance had
not been his idea. He had wanted to join, to serve his
country. But the Army kept rejecting him for high
blood pressure.*

*Every year he tried again to enlist, and every year
they rejected him, until finally, this time, his blood
pressure was normal and they signed him up. He
said he was glad, and he has always been eager to go
wherever they send him. But, he said, now that he's
met me, he is not so eager to leave.*

How can I not love a man such as him?

*Tomorrow he's taking me to a movie. I don't care
what we see. It will be enough to sit close to him in the
intimate darkness and hold his hand.*

Whitney couldn't read any more. It seemed too
personal, as if she were peeking through the window
shades into someone's bedroom.

Tomorrow, she thought wryly, she would read
some more. She went back to work sorting her
aunt's belongings.

By the time Janey called and invited her to her
youngest son's T-ball game, Whitney was so ready to
get out of the house that she accepted the invitation
almost eagerly.

The Robert Simms Memorial Park, named for the
late father of the local banker, occupied fifteen acres
a short distance behind Claudia's Attic and across
from Shady Oaks Nursing Home. It was home to the

town swimming pool, a playground, three ballparks, a soccer field, and lots of grass and trees for those who liked to run and play, or spread a quilt and laze away a warm afternoon.

Janey had said the game started at five-thirty, so Whitney had timed herself to arrive a few minutes early. Apparently that meant she was late. At least, later than a whole bunch of other people. Small children ran every which way on the field while parents, siblings, and other fans stood in line at the VFW Sno-Kone machine or the Rotary Club concession stand before making their way up into the bleachers.

The players down on the field were adorable. All of them, according to Janey, were around six years old. Janey's youngest, Bobby, and his teammates made up one group, but Whitney didn't know if they were the ones in the blue shorts and blue and white T-shirts, or the red shorts and gray T-shirts.

Whitney approached the bleachers from the side, trying to locate Janey, but it was hard to see faces from that angle.

Maybe this wasn't such a good idea. That soft spot in the head that all babies were born with must never have grown over on her own head, Whitney thought. She couldn't come up with any other reason for finding herself attending a game of T-ball. She barely knew what T-ball was, and what little she did know, she'd had to glean from Janey when she'd called. And, okay, so she was a tad on the anal side— she had looked it up on the Internet.

As near as she could tell, the game was like softball, except there was no pitcher, at least not for these little kids, although for older ones a coach or someone might pitch. Otherwise the ball stood on an adjustable tee so it could sit at the right height for each batter, and the batter swung at it.

The game was played this way, she'd read, because the players were little bitty kids, too little to be able to pitch any distance with any accuracy.

So here she was, approaching the bleachers in search of Janey and her family in order to watch Janey's youngest, six-year-old Bobby, and his teammates play ball. Because Aunt Claudia used to come to all the games. Because Janey was so proud of her kids that she wanted to show them off to her childhood friend. Because Whitney was tired of her own company, tired of fighting Adam's arguments about the need for people to care about. Tired of being lonely.

"Oh, look, Adam, there's your Whitney."

At the sound of her name—being linked with Adam's, no less—Whitney jerked to a halt. A good thing, too, else she might have run right over Adam's mother.

"Mrs. Burkett," she said, not daring to let her gaze wander to Adam, at his mother's side.

"It's Mary, dear. You must call me Mary. Did you come to watch my son play softball? Or," she added with a wink, "my grandson play T-ball?"

Whitney nearly gulped, but managed to keep her wits. "I didn't know your boys were playing." She added a hint of surprise in her voice for credibility. In truth, she hadn't known, though in a town this size, perhaps she should have thought to ask. But it never would have occurred to her that the big boys would have a game following the little kids.

"I'm meeting Janey."

"Janey Woods?" Mary asked.

Whitney frowned. "She used to be King. I don't know her married name."

Mary nodded. "That would be Janey Woods, married Frank Woods a number of years ago. Her little Bobby plays on the same team as our Kenny. Isn't it nice that Whitney came to the game, Adam?" She pulled her youngest son around by the arm so that he and Whitney were forced to acknowledge each other.

"Sure is," Adam said, fighting back a smirk. He hadn't counted on running into her here at the park, but if he had, he would have hoped for a friendlier greeting than the slight scowl she offered him now. Especially considering they hadn't seen each other in two days. He could have hoped, if he'd let himself, that she might have missed him just a little.

But not Whitney Sheridan, no sirree, Bob. She was too damned independent and self-sufficient to miss someone. To care enough to miss someone. To need enough to miss someone.

"You're going to play ball?" She looked him up and down, eyeing his WASHITA BUILDING SUPPLY softball team uniform.

"Yeah. You gonna stay and cheer me on?"

"Maybe I'll root for the other side," she said.

"Yoo-hoo!" came a call from up in the stands. "Whitney, up here!"

Saved, Whitney thought, by the yell.

If Whitney had been lonely at home, there was no chance of the loneliness following her here. There had to be from eighty to one hundred people in and around the stands, and that didn't count the two teams of youngsters out on the benches that substituted for dugouts.

One team—the red and gray—started shouting and ran out into the ball field.

"Okay!" Janey placed two fingers between her lips and let out a sharp whistle. "Let's go, Cubs! Come on, Bobby, make your mama proud!"

"Mo-om," her eight-year-old, Steven, whined. "Guys need cheerleaders when they're playing ball, not mamas."

"Oh. Okay," Janey said. "I'm sorry. I forgot."

Steven rolled his eyes in disgust. "Mothers."

"Yeah." From the row behind them, Steven's father, Frank, wearing a team uniform that didn't match Adam's, ruffled his oldest son's hair. "But what would we do without them, huh?"

Steven looked up at his mother and grinned. "Yeah, I guess."

While Whitney watched the family byplay and laughed, several people clomped up behind her in the bleachers.

"Coming through. Make a hole."

Whitney stiffened. The voice was unmistakable. Dammit, she'd thought she was done with Adam Burkett for the day, but no-o, there he was, with his parents, both brothers and their wives and the two youngest Burkett grandkids.

Four-year-old Barry stood on the seat between his parents and pointed toward the field. "Kenny."

"Yes," his mother, Debbie, said. "Kenny's going to hit the ball now." Barry's brother Kenny, a red and gray Cub like Janey's Bobby, was coming up to bat.

It was like no ball game Whitney had ever witnessed. Not that she had witnessed that many, but she'd been stuck watching a few on television in the past. She wasn't a sports fan, but she understood the game and knew the major rules.

Unlike adult or even Little League games, this one was first and foremost, democratic. It didn't matter how many outs there were, an inning was over when everyone on the team had batted. The young boys in their shorts and tees ran the shortened baselines, bumped into their opponents, and sometimes their own teammates. Some performed spectacular slides while others hopped and skipped along, waving to a parent or sibling in the stands.

After four innings of laughs and tears, shouts and cheers, the game was declared over. No losers, all winners.

Whitney was surprised at how much she enjoyed herself. And not all of her enjoyment was centered on the ball field. She got a hell of a kick out of watching Janey angst over her son's performance, cheer him on, laugh at his antics.

What did it feel like, she wondered, to watch a part of yourself learn to run and play and meet life on his own, away from you, separate from you, relying on his peers instead of his parents?

The joy, the pride, the pain of it all would cripple her, Whitney feared.

But since she wasn't in Janey's shoes, she was free to enjoy herself, or not. And seemed she had chosen to enjoy.

So, too, had everyone in the stands. Whitney glanced casually around and realized that she knew a number of people present. Janey and her family, and the Burketts, of course. But also Betty and her husband were there. So were Avis and Mavis, and their friend Dorothy, with a man who was probably Dorothy's husband.

Then there was the older woman from the café, Ada. She sat with a man about her own age, plus the young waitress, Franki, who had a toddler on her lap and a gorgeous guy at her side.

Carla from the shop was there, and other people Whitney recognized but whose names she couldn't recall.

It felt odd to recognize so many people at a public event. Back home, if she went to an industry function there would be hundreds of people she could call by name. But out in public? She doubted she would run into anyone she knew, no matter where she went.

She wondered what that said about her and the life she led. Wondered, but not enough to think too hard on it, lest she not like the answer.

After T-ball with the little kids came adult softball. The men's game, Washita Building Supply against the Dairy Mart, had nothing to do with democracy and everything to do with testosterone, complete with butt-slapping, crotch-scratching, and all the other things guys do to prove they're real guys.

Before the first inning was over Whitney silently determined herself to be a lifelong fan of butt-slapping. Who would have thought?

Oh, she'd looked at male backsides before and even appreciated a few of the finer specimens. She'd known Adam had a fine butt. However, seeing him in his white, form-hugging uniform gave her a new appreciation for the male tush, and his was a fine one, indeed. She wouldn't mind slapping it a time or two herself. Or maybe bite it.

"Did you say something?"

Whitney jerked and turned to Janey. "What?"

Janey laughed loudly. "The look on your face! God, it's priceless. You looked like you were picturing the entire team buck naked."

"I did no such thing," Whitney cried.

Janey laughed so hard she rocked against Whitney's shoulder. "Methinks thou doth protest too much, or however the saying goes."

Whitney scrunched up her face and studied her childhood friend. "Just why was it I liked you when we were kids?"

"Because I let you use my little brother's skateboard."

"Oh, yeah. That's right," Whitney said. "Of course, you only did it so you wouldn't be the only girl around with skinned knees."

"Worked, didn't it?"

Whitney chuckled. "Like a charm."

"What are you two talking about?" Eight-year-old Steven leaned in from his mother's other side.

Janey ruffled his hair. "The olden days."

"Your mother's skinned knees," Whitney corrected.

"Huh?"

"Never mind," Janey told him.

From the row behind them, one of Adam's sisters-in-law, Cindy, stood and urged her husband to steal third. "Go-go-go, Brian! Run, baby, run!"

"Daddy run?" Little Crissy jumped up and down beside her mother. "Whee! Run, Daddy, run!"

Brian ran. The ball flew a little wide. The third baseman had to step off the bag to catch it. Brian hooted and jeered as he hit the base and the call came: safe.

Half the people in the stands cheered. The other half shouted insults, most of which were good-natured.

Janey's Frank came up to bat and, ignoring the chatter from the stands, hit a single. The runner who had been on first made it to second, but Frank's hit was a line drive, barely inside the third-base line. Brian never had a chance to make home.

Now the bases were loaded. Whitney fought the urge to squirm in her seat as Adam came up to bat. It was ridiculous to get excited. He was barely an acquaintance, and this was only a silly softball game. But when he popped a foul high and to the left she barely restrained a moan.

She did not restrain a yell. "Come on, Burkett, you can do better than that."

Beside her Janey snickered.

Out at home plate, Adam turned and arched his brow. His gaze narrowed and zeroed in on her. He grinned and winked.

Whitney wanted to shrink down into the wooden bench beneath her. What had possessed her to speak out that way? She had never done such a thing before. She never attended ball games at all, let alone yelled at the players, for heaven's sake.

"Oh, ho," his mother said from behind her. "Tell me I don't know what's what. I knew there was something between those two."

Whitney felt heat sting her cheeks. The very fact that she was blushing both amazed and appalled her. She didn't suppose a hole was going to open in the bleachers and conveniently swallow her, so she squared her shoulders and pretended everything was normal.

On the field, Adam turned back to the business at hand. He tapped the end of his bat against one shoe and then the other, leaned forward, wiggled his hips in a way that made Whitney smile, and raised his bat.

The pitch was right on. The crack of bat against ball echoed through the park. The crowd cheered. Adam ran. He ran all the way to home plate.

It was silly, really, to feel such a thrill, Whitney admonished herself. After all, she didn't particularly like the man. Right?

Right.

Sneaking home early was, by all measures, a cowardly thing to do, but that didn't stop Whitney from doing it, although she didn't like to think of it as sneaking. Slipped. That was it. She had slipped away, not sneaked. Slipped away to avoid making Janey or Mrs. Burkett feel as if they should invite her over, or out for coffee or a beer or whatever, after the game.

Okay, okay, she thought. To avoid Adam. He was bound to gloat after that home run that brought in three other runners. If she opened her mouth, something snide was bound to come out and spoil things. She really didn't want to ruin the evening for Janey or the rest of the Burketts. Better to simply be gone by the end of the game.

She had stayed for most of it. Long enough to know that it would take a miracle for Dairy Mart to come from behind and overtake Washita Building Supply. Adam's position as hero of the game would be safe.

The sun was just setting as she left the park for the short walk home. From the bleachers behind her came a loud roar. Someone had done something very good, or very bad. She fought the urge to turn around and see if she could tell which. She didn't need to get any more involved in the lives of the people in Washita than she already was. And it wasn't like her to feel a tug of regret at that realization, but there it was. A sharp little tug around the region of her heart at the thought of not knowing if Adam scored any more points. Or if Janey's husband did, or Adam's brothers. Had Adam's mother been disappointed in the speed with which Whitney had left the game? There was no fooling that woman. She had seen right through Whitney's flimsy excuse of wanting to get home before dark.

Janey hadn't been as discreet as Mary. "Why?" she had asked. "I mean, it's not like you can get lost, is it?"

Whitney rolled her eyes at the memory of her own attempt at humor when she'd said anything was possible, since she wasn't used to small towns. "If there's not a mugger around every corner or a subway station on every block, I have trouble finding my way."

Everyone had dutifully laughed, and had stopped hassling her about leaving. She thought she had probably gotten off easy. She had mixed feelings about that. But, then, she didn't really want people to invite her to stay, to convince her she should. She wanted her independence, didn't she? She prized and treasured and guarded it zealously, didn't she?

Which did not explain the emptiness she felt as she walked up the driveway toward her own porch. The house seemed to welcome her, but the warmth it generated within her felt . . . undecided. As if the house knew it was supposed to make her feel at home but couldn't decide, as she stepped inside, if it really wanted her there or not.

Well, that made two of them, she thought.

No, no, no. This was stupid. Houses couldn't think, and she had nothing to decide. Finish the work on the house, put it and the shop and the Cadillac up for sale, and get the hell out of Dodge.

The Cadillac. She hadn't given it a thought since her first day in town. She hadn't even been out to the garage to look at it or see what else might be out there.

She crossed through to the back door and stepped out onto the back porch, barely half the size of the front porch. She started toward the steps that led to the sidewalk to the detached garage, but halted at the top step. It was nearly dark. The Cadillac would still be there tomorrow in the bright light of day.

She turned to go back into the house, but a movement at the corner of the garage caught her eye and she paused. City girl that she was, she knew that whatever had moved was too small to be a person, so she wasn't about to be mugged or shot or raped. But if it was too small to be a person, that meant it was an animal. She glanced around and realized that she was at the edge of town. The very edge. The last house. Beyond her was nothing but open country.

Farmland, pastures, wild animals. City girl that she was, she knew next to nothing about wild animals.

Discretion being the better part of valor, she reached for the handle of the screen door, then saw the movement again.

It was a cat. A scrawny, scraggly gray cat that looked to be about half grown and mostly starved. From clear across the yard she felt his yellow eyes assessing her. He wasn't sure, she thought, whether he should come forward or just stand his ground. Either way, he wouldn't run. Not without a direct, imminent threat. Too much of the scrapper in this one. Whitney knew just how he felt.

"Hey, fellow."

His tail flicked.

Surely if Aunt Claudia had a pet, someone would have mentioned it.

If this was a neighbor's cat, it looked as if it had been sorely neglected. Surely it was a stray. It looked like a stray. Tough. Alone. Homeless. Hungry.

He probably liked being alone, and he had the whole outdoors for a home—and there were surely plenty of mice around for dinner. He didn't need some stranger putting scraps of food out for him. This fellow looked more than capable of fending for himself.

None of this reasoning, however, stopped Whitney from going inside and digging around in the fridge until she came up with scraps of ham and roast beef. She put them on a saucer, added a bowl of water, and set them both on the back porch while the cat eyed her from beneath the tree. He had moved closer.

She waited, but he came no closer. Probably

wouldn't as long as she was there, so she went inside and peered out the window.

He sat beneath the tree and peered back at her.

After several minutes Whitney gave up and went to catch up on the national news on her aunt's cable TV.

It had, apparently, been a slow news day. Maybe the network should have sent a crew to cover a neighborhood T-ball game. At least then there would have been something fun and exciting in the newscast.

The next morning she found a can of tuna in the kitchen pantry. It took less than a minute to open it and dump the contents into a small bowl. She stepped out onto the back porch and looked around.

The saucer from the night before was empty. A large brown June bug swam on its back in the water bowl.

The cat stood warily beneath the tree.

"Hey, fellow. Here's some tuna for you." She set the bowl down and picked up the empty saucer. "There's a little extra protein in your water, too."

The cat blinked at her.

"No, huh? Okay, I guess I can dump it and get you some clean."

How pathetic was it, she wondered as she tossed the water and the bug into the grass, that after two days without Adam underfoot and in her way every minute, she was reduced to talking to a stray cat.

She went inside and got fresh water, then brought

it back out and set it down next to the tuna. The cat hadn't moved.

"Come on, boy. It's for you."

"You know if you feed him, he belongs to you. You're responsible for him from then on."

Whitney glanced over her shoulder to find Adam standing at the corner of the house.

"Not me," she protested. "I don't have pets. I'll have him included in the appraisal. He'll go to the new owners with the house."

Adam shook his head and looked out at the cat. "Forget it, pal. You won't get anywhere with this one. She says she doesn't have a heart."

It wasn't true, Whitney realized. She did have a heart. She knew, because just then, with the slight sneer in Adam's voice, it hurt like hell.

Damn man.

Damn cat.

To hell with both of them.

Chapter Eight

Later that morning Whitney was boxing up her aunt's rather sizable collection of sweaters, to be given to the needy, when Adam clomped up the stairs and stuck his head in the door.

"Today's that Chamber of Commerce luncheon, if you're still interested in going."

She frowned. "I don't know that I was ever interested."

Adam shrugged. "Whatever. I just thought you wanted to meet more people who might be in a position to either buy the shop or lend money for someone else to buy it." He shrugged again. "If you'd rather not, it's no skin off my nose."

Whitney took a slow breath. "You're angry with me."

"What makes you think so?" he asked.

"You haven't been nagging me all morning about anything."

"I've been busy," he said. "The downstairs bath's finished except for the wallpaper."

"You have been busy. Are you doing the wallpaper today?"

"Yes. Are you going to the luncheon?"

"Why does it matter to you?"

Adam threw his hands up in the air and turned to go. "I give up. Never mind. Go, don't go, I don't care."

"Adam, wait." She didn't know why she called him back, but it seemed important.

Adam didn't know why he stopped, but it seemed he couldn't help it. "What is it?"

She took a half-step toward him and raised one hand. "I . . . thanks for reminding me about the lunch."

"You're welcome." He turned away again and made his way back down the stairs, cursing himself with every step. He wanted . . . hell, he didn't know what he wanted. To be friends with her. For her to like him. But what was the point, when she'd be gone in a few weeks?

Does there have to be a point? A voice in his head asked.

He considered the question, and wondered. Why couldn't they like each other simply because they were—or could be—likable people? They didn't have to want a lasting relationship, for crying out loud. Two ships passing, and all that.

But she didn't seem interested in being friends. She had barely spoken to him at the game last night, and had slipped away before the end of his game. She hadn't been interested in passing any of her free time with him at all.

If he was more disappointed by that than was reasonable, it would have to be his little secret. He didn't know why he'd thought things would be any different. But dammit, he wanted them to be. He'd wanted her to . . . to what? Flirt with him?

Yeah. Yeah, he'd wanted her to flirt with him.

Short of that, he'd at least wanted her to appear glad to see him this morning. Instead, he'd blown it with his crack about her not having a heart, and she had wasted no time in sticking her nose back into the air.

So make it up to her.

That voice in his head was busy today. Make it up to her? How? And perhaps more important, why?

But in the end it didn't matter why, only that he try. He didn't want to spend the next two or three weeks with the two of them at odds.

So the question remained: how to make it up to her?

He wasn't worried. Something would come to mind. But it had to be perfect. And then he thought he knew just what to do.

In the end Whitney decided to attend the regular monthly luncheon meeting of the Washita Chamber of Commerce. It was held in the private side room at Good Eats Café. When Whitney entered the café, Ada Puckett herself, the owner who had been seated at the cash register mouthing off to her waitress the last time Whitney had been in, led her to the meeting room and introduced her around. She met Eugene Dowd, who owned the feed store; William Frazier of the Dairy Mart; Bob Haskell, the owner of the building supply company that sponsored Adam's softball team. She met the grocer, the drugstore owner, and several other local business owners, including the banker, Bobby "not Robert, just Bobby" Simms.

No one had a problem with her attending in her aunt's place. They all made her feel welcome and expressed their sorrow over Claudia's passing. No one used the words "death" or "dead" or "died." Miz Henderson had passed, or passed away, or passed over, or passed on, or "we lost her."

"Did I hear," Bobby Simms, the banker, said, "that you're planning on selling Claudia's Attic?"

He had heard well enough, Whitney thought, when Carla had applied for a loan to buy it. "I'm exploring my options," she answered.

He checked his watch. "We don't have time right now. I've got to introduce our speaker. I'm the Chamber president, you know."

No, she thought. She hadn't known. Nor cared.

"Perhaps we can talk after lunch about those options you speak of," he suggested with a toothy smile.

This was exactly why she had come to this meeting, to find people interested in buying, or at least financing the shop. Simms hadn't made an offer yet, but he had something in mind or he wouldn't have brought it up. But she wouldn't make him any promises, because she didn't care for that good-ole-boy charm he was laying on a little too thick, while the look in his eyes was sharp enough to draw blood.

"Perhaps," was all she said to his suggestion.

The guest speaker for the month was a financial planner from a brokerage firm with a branch office in Amarillo. After his talk on planning for one's financial future, lunch was served.

Out in the main dining room Adam tucked himself into a booth and ordered a cheeseburger and fries. Never mind the meatloaf sandwich his mother had sent with him. He had needed to come here, to follow Whitney.

To make a fool out of himself? Only if she realized what he'd done and why, and he would deny it with his dying breath, so he figured he was safe enough.

He just wanted to make sure nobody gave her a hard time.

And wasn't that asinine? Nobody in the Chamber meeting was going to give Whitney a hard time. They were probably in there doting on her at that very moment, treating her like a long-lost relative.

When Karen Jean brought his cheeseburger, he wolfed it down and got the hell out of the café before the meeting broke up and Whitney came out of that room and spotted him. That was all he needed, to look like he was following her around town, checking up on her.

Wouldn't she just love that?

As he walked back down Main, he tried not to think of how much he wanted to get on her good side. Was he falling for her? How stupid would that be, to get caught in that trap again. With another city woman, no less.

But what the hell. He told her to take a chance on friends. Shouldn't he do the same with her? Shouldn't he be brave enough to risk his heart, after urging her to risk hers?

Besides, he didn't figure he had any better chance with her than a snowball did at a summer barbeque. But, what the hell. Nothing ventured, nothing gained. No pain, no gain. And all those other sayings.

* * *

When the meeting broke up Bobby Simms caught Whitney at the door. "May I give you a lift home?" Charm fairly oozed out of him.

"Thank you," she said. "But it's so close, I'll just walk."

He held the door open for her. "If you don't mind the company, I'd like to walk a ways with you."

"It's a public sidewalk." She smiled to take the sting out of her words.

He chuckled. "That it is." Out on the wide sidewalk, they started walking east, side by side. "I might like to make you an offer on Claudia's Attic, if you've a mind to sell it."

His words were not unexpected, but they left her with mixed feelings because she knew Carla wanted the shop. "What kind of offer?"

He named a price that, to Whitney, seemed low. She knew prices were drastically lower in this part of the country compared to New York, and she hadn't studied the books enough, nor had an appraisal done, so she couldn't be sure, but it seemed low.

"You know I haven't had the property appraised yet."

"I know, but I'm in a position to know what property is worth in this county. I think when all is said and done, you'll find my offer a fair one, especially considering you don't have a lot of time."

"So you're willing to, what, take it off my hands, out of the goodness of your heart?" She kept a smile on her face. There was no need to offend the man. Not yet, anyway.

From the corner of her eye she thought she saw Adam entering the grocery store across the street. She wondered what he needed in the middle of the day, when he'd brought his lunch, as he did every day.

Simms laughed. "Out of the goodness of my heart? I'm not that altruistic."

"Of course not," she said. "At that price I imagine you could turn a nice profit when you sold it."

"What?" He splayed a hand across his chest in mock innocence. His Texas twang got twangier. "You don't think I look like the needlepoint type? Why, I'm crushed, ma'am, simply crushed."

"I'm sure you are, but I'll keep your offer in mind."

"I hope you will," he said, his laughter fading. "You probably won't get a better one around here."

"I'll let you know," she told him. "There's the bank." She nodded across the street, where the bank and its parking lot took up the entire albeit short block, except for the corner occupied by Claudia's Attic. "Thanks for the company. I'll see you around."

She didn't wait for him to say anything. She took off at a quick clip toward the house, leaving Bobby Simms and his offer behind.

If she had any brains at all she would turn around and leap at his offer, low or not, and be done with the shop. Surely he would keep Carla on as manager, so Whitney wouldn't worry about that. As long as she got enough to pay off any debts. . . .

The attorney hadn't mentioned any debts, but perhaps Whitney would be wise to make sure on her own.

Wisdom, however, had nothing to do with this new reluctance to leave town that stirred in her. If she stayed much longer she was going to lose her edge. That sharp, nervy feeling that kept her going day in and day out.

The idea that she might not mind losing that edge, living at a slower pace, shocked her to her core. Such a thing was simply not in her nature.

Neither was it in her nature to acquire a pet, but that didn't stop her from rushing through the house and out onto the back porch looking for a certain scruffy cat.

"Hey, Scruffy," she called softly, staring intently into the flickering shadows beneath the tree and the rustling bushes beside the garage. He had cleaned up the food she'd left that morning, but now seemed to be nowhere in sight. "You out there, fellow?"

"You've already named him?"

With a gasp Whitney spun toward the side of the house. Adam stood there with a grocery bag in one arm.

"That was you," she said.

"It was?"

"On my way home I thought I saw you going into the grocery store."

He shrugged and offered the bag to her. "I picked up a few things I thought might come in handy."

"What?" She took the bag and looked inside. He had bought two cat dishes, a small bag of dried cat food, cans and pouches of moist cat food, a little bag of kitty treats, a yellow ball, a red mouse, and a brown fuzzy creature of some sort, all three stuffed with catnip.

"Adam," she said. "I don't know what to say."

"No need," he told her casually. "It's just my contribution to the cause."

She gave him a rueful look. "It may be too late. He's nowhere to be found."

He grinned. "You mean Scruffy?"

"I had to call him something," she said defensively. "But now he's gone."

"I wouldn't worry," Adam told her. "He'll be back."

"How can you be so sure?"

"Are you kidding? You offered him a can of tuna. To a cat, that's heaven. If you offered me heaven, I'd come back."

After a startling spike in her pulse rate, Whitney ignored that last part, waved it away with her hand. "But he's afraid of me."

"Big deal." He stepped onto the porch and moved close to her. "So am I."

"You are?" He was suddenly so close that Whitney had to arch her neck to look him in the eye. Breathing became difficult. Unimportant. "Afraid of me?"

"Terrified." He leaned closer, bent down. "But that wouldn't stop me."

His face was so close that she could see herself reflected in the blue of his eyes. "It wouldn't?"

"It wouldn't."

He leaned forward another two inches and their lips met.

How long had it been, Whitney wondered, since a man's lips had touched hers? Weeks? Months? It didn't matter, because they hadn't been these lips. They hadn't tasted of Adam or of sunshine or . . . mustard. She smiled and parted her lips, all the better to taste him with.

Oh, she did like this. She liked the way his full lips felt against hers, the heat of them, the soft firmness.

She liked the heat emanating from his body, the weight of his hands on her shoulders, the circling of his thumbs against her collarbone.

She quickly lost track of all the reasons she liked kissing him and simply enjoyed.

Then his chest was pressing against her breasts, his thighs against hers. He slipped his arms around her and pulled her close, and she returned the favor.

She welcomed the physical pleasure that washed through her. The sharp tug of emotion, however, surprised her. She didn't know what to do with it. She could fight it, but there didn't seem to be enough time, as it flooded over and through her in intense waves and left her shaken. If they hadn't had such a tight grip on each other, she might have slid to the porch floor and melted into a puddle at Adam's feet.

After several long minutes, the intensity eased, as did his hold on her. Their lips separated slowly, one fraction of an inch at a time. Whitney blinked her eyes open and looked into his.

"Wow," he said with feeling.

"Yeah," she admitted. "Wow."

"That was . . ."

"Yeah." She swallowed and stepped back out of his arms, stunned by what had just happened between them. Without his arms around her, the eighty-plus-degree day felt cool. "It was."

Adam brushed the backs of his fingers across her cheek. "I better get back to work on that wallpaper."

"Oh. Sure. I'll just . . ."

"Feed your cat."

"Cat. Right."

* * *

Bobby Simms sat behind his big oak desk and drummed his fingers on the glossy top. He wasn't used to being told no.

Of course, she hadn't said no, precisely, but it had been in her voice. Miz Henderson's niece didn't want to sell the damn shop to him. And that wouldn't do.

He was president, CEO, chairman of the board, and co-owner, along with his mama, of First Washita Bank and Trust. It was the only bank in town. He was used to getting what he wanted, and Claudia Henderson's building would be no exception.

There was no reason for the niece to hold on to the shop. A big-time WNN news producer from New York City wouldn't want to own a craft-and-consignment shop in Nowhere, Texas.

But it was too soon to go after her again. She said she would keep his offer in mind, would let him know. He could wait.

Bobby Simms waited two days. When he hadn't heard from Whitney by then, he got tired of waiting. He picked up his phone and drummed his fingers on the desk.

"Brenda," she said when his secretary picked up her extension. "Get Claudia Henderson's niece, that Whitney Sheridan, on the line."

"Sure thing, Mr. Simms."

Brenda Rowlett was twice Bobby's age and had known him all his life, but from the day he took over the bank, after his daddy's death, he insisted that she call him Mr. Simms.

She went along with it, he knew, to humor him, and because he signed her paycheck. And because she had promised his mother she would.

He didn't give a damn what her reasons were, as long as she did as he asked. He hung up his phone and waited for her to buzz him back.

Whitney was on her way out the door when the phone rang. For that past couple of days, if she'd been in the house, it had been only for a few minutes. Since that kiss they'd shared on the back porch over plastic dishes and catnip, she and Adam had given each other a wide berth.

The choices for Whitney were two: stay away from him, or jump his bones.

She decided to keep her distance, as much as possible. She had been reading at the nursing home a great deal. She and Miss Ella had a fine time with their books, and sometimes they put the books down and just talked.

Today Whitney looked forward to finishing the current book they were reading, but when the phone rang she turned back into the house. She had never developed the ability to ignore a ringing phone when she knew it was for her.

If it was a telemarketer, she would fry the poor soul's ears for delaying her departure. Prepared to give somebody hell, she grabbed up the receiver. "Hello."

"Ms. Sheridan?" a woman said.

"Yes."

"Please hold one moment for Mr. Simms."

"I don't think—" But the woman had already put her on hold before Whitney could tell her what she thought of some joker named Simms who was too hoity-toity to make his own frigging phone call.

Simms. Bobby Simms? Surely that Texas good ole' boy wouldn't pull a stunt like having his secretary place his calls for him. That cute little power play some men liked to use, making the person they called have to wait for them to come to the phone. Personally, Whitney had always thought it meant that the caller was too stupid to learn to push numbered buttons on a phone.

"Whitney," came Bobby Simms's booming voice over the phone.

"What can I do for you, Mr. Simms?" Whitney purposefully let the smirk on her face enter her voice.

"Well, darlin', first you can call me Bobby."

"And second?"

He was silent for a minute. Possibly because there had been a bite to her tone. "I'll bet I've caught you at a bad time," he said.

"I was on my way out the door," she admitted, "but I've got a couple of minutes."

"And here I was hoping you could spare me enough time to come on down here to my office at the bank and talk about that little shop of your aunt's."

Whitney frowned. Was he deliberately trying to be condescending, or did it come naturally? If he had been standing before her, she would have sneered in his face and walked away at such an insulting tone.

"I'm not from Texas," she said carefully.

"Of course you're not."

"In New York, when someone wants something from another person, they don't call them on the phone and ask them to come to their office."

"Ah. I guess that didn't come off quite the way I meant it to," he said.

"And they don't call them darlin', darlin'."

"Is my apology any good?" he asked quietly.

"It might be, if it was a little more sincere."

"Ouch."

"You asked."

"Okay, look. I'm sorry. I'm too used to being in charge, to ordering people around. I wanted to talk to you about buying your aunt's shop, and I thought you would rather come here than have me come to the house."

"You're right that I don't want you to come to the house, but don't take it personally," she said. "I'm in the middle of remodeling, as I'm sure you know."

"I had heard," he allowed.

"So the house isn't fit for company."

"Well, actually," Bobby told her, "the house was one of the things I wanted to talk to you about."

"The house?"

"Yes. I'd be willing to make you an offer on it, too. A package deal, if you like. Both properties for one price. That way you wouldn't have to wait until the remodeling is done. You could get back to your life and your job in New York and stop worrying about things here."

"You want to buy the shop and the house?" Whitney asked carefully.

"Yes, ma'am."

From what Whitney had overheard at the Chamber luncheon, Bobby and his wife lived with his mother in the big white house on the hill overlooking half the town. He had no need for a house. He would either turn around and sell it, or rent it out.

Renters? In Aunt Claudia's house?

Aunt Claudia would turn over in her grave.

Besides, Whitney did not care for Bobby's pushy, smarmy attitude.

Of course, whoever bought the house could end up reselling it or renting it out. That would be beyond Whitney's control. But she didn't have to sell it to someone she knew had those plans from the beginning.

Nevertheless, she said, "That's an interesting idea."

"Is it?" he asked and named a figure that, like the one he'd named the other day for just the shop, sounded too low to Whitney. It was past time to get those appraisals done.

"I'll have to give it some thought. When I've made up my mind, I'll get back with you. Thanks for calling."

She hung up so fast that Bobby pulled the receiver away from his ear and stared at it blankly. No one hung up on him. No one. Not ever.

And no one put him off. No one told him no.

She would think about it? He didn't want her to think about it, he wanted her to sell, damn her hide.

He hung up the receiver, then picked it up again. This call he would make himself. If Ms. Sheridan needed a little incentive to sell that worthless excuse for a shop sooner rather than later, he would give it to her.

Claudia's Attic was about to plagued with problems. The first of those problems would come in the form of a plumbing leak an hour after dark that night, long after the shop was closed and everyone had gone home.

When Carla opened the front door the next morning she was met with an inch of water flooding the shop.

"Whitney, it's a mess," Carla told her when Whitney arrived. "I hated to call you with this, but I knew you'd want to know."

"No, I'm glad you called." Whitney could see the standing water on the kitchen floor from the front doorway. "How's the plumber doing?"

"He's about got the problem repaired, but he says the fix is temporary. He says we need a serious plumbing overhaul."

"Don't they always say that?" Whitney said. "How do we get rid of all that water?"

"And that's only half of it," Carla said. "The back room is flooded, too."

"We should call the insurance agency and see if the damage from the leak is covered," Whitney said.

Carla called the insurance agent while Whitney ran home to meet Adam, who was due there any moment. He would know what to do about all that water.

He was just pulling into her driveway when she got there.

"You're out early this morning," he noted.

"I've got a problem over at the shop, and I was wondering if you would mind looking at it and seeing what you think we need to do."

Adam draped his wrist over his steering wheel and left the engine running. She was asking his advice on something? Hot damn. That was a definite turn of events. For the better, as far as he was concerned.

"Get in," he said. "You can tell me about it on the way."

As he backed out of her driveway and drove the few blocks to the shop, Whitney told him about the leak that had flooded the back room and the kitchen.

"Must have been one hell of a leak," he said.

"I guess. The plumber's still there. I haven't spoken with him. But how do we get all the water out? The floor must slope, because it looks like it's about an inch deep in places."

Interesting, Adam thought. Her reaction to the current crisis was strictly typical. She was concerned, but not upset. She wanted to get busy cleaning up the mess and repairing the damage. The kicker was, she cared. She genuinely cared about Claudia's Attic, the floor, the baseboards, the furnishings, the plumbing. It was the caring that surprised him.

Then again, it shouldn't surprise him at all. She had cared enough about Janey to attend her kid's T-ball game. She cared enough about Miss Ella to go to Shady Oaks every day or so and read to her. She visited Betty often. She had cared enough to not offend his mother when she'd invited her to the cookout.

She couldn't be Miz Henderson's only living relative and not be a caring, responsible person.

She couldn't have kissed him the way she had a couple of days ago if she didn't have the ability to care about something. He hoped.

"A lot of water, you say?" He pulled into the parking lot next to the plumber's truck.

"Yes. I'm worried about the floor. Will it be ruined?"

Something sharp and primitive stirred inside Adam that made him want to throw back his head and laugh. She was looking to him for help, for reassurance. How ridiculous that such a thing could make him feel more of a man than he'd felt in ages.

God, when had he gotten so pathetic?

He killed the engine and opened his door. "Let's have a look and see how bad it is."

It wasn't too bad. Adam called his dad and had him bring over an industrial sized wet vac to suck up all the water and a large fan to speed the drying process. They spent the rest of the morning mopping up, cleaning up, assessing the damage.

One strip of baseboard would have to be replaced, but the linoleum, already old and worn, was none the worse for the soaking.

To thank everyone for their help, Whitney took Carla, Adam, and Joe, the plumber, to lunch.

Whitney had never been out in public when she was so unkempt, but she was apparently the only person who cared. Her companions were equally damp and dirty, if not more so. But since they were eating at a picnic table outside the Dairy Mart, she figured their appearance made no difference.

"What caused the leak?" Whitney asked Joe while they waited for their orders.

"Well, now," Joe said, scratching the side of his face. "Funny thing, that."

"Funny?" Whitney asked.

"What do you mean?" Adam asked.

"I mean, I worked on that faucet not more'n two months ago—"

"Two months?" Whitney asked.

"That's right, two months. Now, for no good reason, the cold-water connection comes loose enough to leak a mighty stream. Hmph. Wasn't loose two months ago, and I doubt Carla here's been under there with a pipe wrench workin' it over."

"Of course I haven't," Carla protested. "I wouldn't even know what to do."

"My point exactly," Joe said. "No reason I can think of for that line to come loose that way."

Whitney stiffened. "Are you saying it was tampered with?"

"I never said that," Joe told her quickly. "Just saying it's a little peculiar. But, then, plumbing can be peculiar sometimes."

Personally, Adam thought Joe was making more out of a simple leak than necessary. Pipes leaked. It happened all the time. If it didn't there wouldn't be any plumbers, and if it didn't sometimes happen in a big way, a way that caused damage, guys like Adam wouldn't have as many jobs. It was the way of the world.

This little problem was mostly behind them. He would do another walk-through after lunch to see if anything else needed to be done, but otherwise it was back to business as usual at Claudia's Attic.

The girl at the order window called out their order number, and within a matter of minutes the foursome was chowing down on burgers and fries at their picnic table.

"Since there's not much left for you to do," Adam said to Whitney, "you won't have to worry about missing your card game with the ladies."

Whitney paused with her burger halfway to her mouth. "My what?"

"You know. Bridge Thursday. Avis, Mavis, and Dorothy?" Adam grinned over his root beer float. "Don't tell me you forgot."

"No," she said slowly. "I didn't forget. I never said I was going."

"You never said you weren't. Oh, look." He nodded and waved at the car pulling in behind Whitney's back. "There's Dorothy now. Hey, Dorothy. Getting a little lunch before the girls come over this evening?"

"Looks like I'm not the only one getting a little lunch." Dorothy Gonzales climbed from her car and strode toward their table. "Good afternoon, everyone."

The others at the table returned her greeting.

"We were just talking about today being Bridge Thursday," Adam said. "Isn't that right, Whitney?"

The look she shot him might have felled a lesser man, but she managed a tight smile. "Yes, we were."

"Oh, good," Dorothy said, placing a hand on Whitney's shoulder. "Does this mean you're coming?"

"Well," Whitney began.

"Of course she is," Adam said.

Beneath the table, Whitney's aim was dead on. She kicked him in the shin, exactly halfway between his knee and ankle. Hard. And she smiled.

"Wonderful!" Dorothy clapped her hands. "The

girls will be so excited. Did Mavis tell you the time and place?"

"Yes," Whitney admitted. "She did."

A short time later, as Dorothy drove away with her to-go order and the four of them returned to the shop, Whitney marched past Adam and snarled. "I'll get you for that."

Adam chuckled. "If you don't thank me for it afterwards, I'll give you a formal apology. But Miz Henderson always had a ball at those things."

"How many times," she managed between clenched teeth, "do I have to say it? I am not my aunt."

"That doesn't mean you can't enjoy yourself," he told her.

"I know, I know. And it doesn't mean I can't be nice to her friends. But bridge? Really. The only card game I know how to play is poker."

Adam smiled and patted her shoulder. "You'll do just fine. I just recommend that you walk instead of drive."

Whitney frowned at him. "It's only three blocks. Of course I'll walk."

He gave her another pat, which, he could tell, irritated the hell out of her. He wondered what she'd do if he kissed her. But since they had an audience, and Carla was staring unabashedly, he decided not to find out just then.

Later. He would kiss her again later.

Chapter Nine

They called it Bridge Thursday because, well, it took place on a Thursday. And because there was a deck of cards involved, and there was a bridge. It was made of teak and spanned the small fishpond in Dorothy Gonzales's backyard.

That was as close to Whitney's vision of four elderly ladies sitting around sipping sherry while playing a respectable hand or two of bridge as things got.

In reality, it was potent Mexican beer, corn chips and salsa, fat stinky cigars, and five-card stud outside on Dorothy's covered patio in her very private backyard.

Once she was over the shock, Whitney settled in for one of the most outrageously enjoyable evenings of her life—at least, of those spent with women, she thought with a laugh. Girls' Night Out had never been so much fun back home.

One by one each woman told her at least twice how glad she was that Whittney had come. They missed her aunt terribly, and having Whitney there helped ease their loss, as they hoped being with her aunt's friends helped ease Whitney's.

It was sweet of them, she thought. They must have

truly loved her aunt for them to care so much about a long-absent niece.

"Oh, but you were so important to her," Avis proclaimed. "She talked about you all the time."

Whitney felt her throat swell with emotion while her stomach churned with guilt.

"Now, look, sister," Mavis chastised. "You've made our Whitney all sad. Let's not talk about sad things tonight. Let's just play cards and have a good time."

Mavis went on to win the first hand. They didn't use money, but Dorothy's supply of poker chips instead. Whitney took the next two hands, raking in a goodly pile of chips.

By the end of the evening a thick layer of smoke hung over Dorothy's backyard. The quantities of beer and corn chips and salsa had been seriously lowered. Each lady had won at least one poker hand.

"Ladies," Whitney said, the quantity of Corona she'd drunk lending a grand tone to her voice, "I have never had a more enjoyable time."

Avis gave her a look of pity. "Oh, how sad for you, my dear."

Whitney and the others burst out laughing.

"Let me rephrase that," Whitney offered. "I've never had a better time with women."

"Much better." Avis beamed.

"Does anybody need a ride home?" Dorothy asked.

"Not from you," Mavis said tartly. "You drank more than the rest of us."

"That may be," Dorothy admitted, "but Ben will be home soon."

"Oh, and they don't drink down at the Elks Club?" Avis asked.

Dorothy frowned. "Good point. Never mind."
Then she smiled slyly. "But I bet we could get that
hunky Adam Burkett to give our Whitney a ride
home."

"Or anywhere else, for that matter," Mavis added.

Avis patted her twin sister's hand. "Don't snicker,
dear, it's unseemly in someone our age."

That, of course, merely set Mavis to snickering all
the harder. Which set off the rest of them. It was several long moments before anyone was steady
enough to leave.

Streetlights provided ample light for Whitney's
walk home. The night was warm, the air heavy with
humidity despite the southerly breeze. She hoped,
in case anyone looked out a window and saw her,
that she wasn't staggering.

The thought made her giggle. She slapped a hand
over her mouth. Good God, she hadn't giggled
since . . . since . . . hell, she couldn't remember the
last time she had giggled, but it had to have been a
good twenty years ago, and wasn't that sad. Not sad
enough to keep her from giggling about it, but sad
nonetheless.

Every time she swallowed a giggle, she thought
of the evening she'd just spent, pictured Aunt Claudia there with her friends, and broke out in giggles
again.

Adam heard her muffled laughter when she was
still three houses from home.

He'd never been told, but he had a good idea that
a lot of drinking went on at those Bridge Thursday
events. He had come back to her house to sit on her

front porch and wait to make sure she made it home in one piece. She had left a light on in the living room, so he sat beyond the window, in the shadows.

From the sound of things, it appeared Whitney was going to make it home just fine, and damned happy about it she was, too. Funny, but he would never have pegged her as a happy drunk, much less a giggler.

He could see her now, approaching the front of Betty's house next door. Betty's front door opened.

"Whitney?" Betty called. "Is that you?"

"Hi, there, Betty!" came Whitney's cheerful reply.

"Are you all right, dear?"

"Fine and dandy." Whitney gave her a cockeyed salute. "Just fine and dandy."

"Are you sure?" Betty called, coming out onto her porch. "You sound a little funny."

Whitney giggled. "You mean I sound a little snockered?"

"I never—"

"I never, either, until tonight." Whitney laughed loudly, then clapped a hand over her mouth. "Oops. I better get on home before I get arrested for public trunk—drunkenness."

Adam stepped back deeper into the shadows of her porch and stifled the urge to laugh in delight. He'd known it. By God, he'd known that if she would only let herself, she would have a great time with those three ladies. He wasn't sure exactly what went on at the Gonzales house on the second Thursday of each month, but it was obviously something pretty damned special to turn straight-laced, uptight Whitney Sheridan into a happy drunk.

"G'night, Betty!" Whitney called as she came up her own driveway.

"Good night, dear." Betty chuckled and went back into her house.

Adam stepped forward, intending to announce his presence so as not to scare the living daylights out of her, when she started up the steps and tripped.

"Son of a bitch!" Her cry was loud and sharp, and followed by a stream of swear words that Adam was surprised to find she even knew.

He let out a low whistle. "Pretty impressive."

She shrieked.

"Sorry, didn't mean to scare you."

"Scare me?" Doubled over to hold one hand against her bruised shin, she hobbled up the steps. Even in the semidarkness there was no mistaking the glare she shot him. "You scared the living shit out of me. What are you doing lurking around my porch this time of night in the dark? What are you doing here this time of night at all?"

He took her by one arm and led her toward the swing. "I just wanted to make sure you got home okay."

She sneered. "I'm used to navigating New York City after dark. I think I can manage three blocks in Washita, Texas."

He stepped back and raised both hands. "My mistake. Sorry. Didn't mean to offend."

"Oh, bite me, Burkett."

He couldn't help it. He grinned. "Do I get to pick the spot?"

Under other circumstances, he was sure, she would have thrown something at him, or given him a cold stare, or somehow gotten even for his suggestive remark. But after whatever went on at Bridge Thursday, he had to conclude that she wasn't exactly herself. She snickered.

He leaned forward. "What was that?" he asked.

"I didn't say anything."

"I know. You snickered. Or at least, that's what it sounded like."

She snickered again. "I was just trying to picture the look on your face if I actually told you where I wanted you to bite me first."

For a moment, words backed up in Adam's throat. "First?" A hard, hot shiver racked him from head to toe. He gulped, not knowing whether to laugh like a loon, beat his head against the front of the house, or throw back his head and howl at the moon. "God, what I wouldn't give to have you say that to me when you're sober."

She pushed herself to her feet and swayed slightly. "What do you mean, sober? I'm not drunk."

He caught her by both arms and steadied her. "Of course you're not."

"I'm just a little . . . tipsy."

"If you say so."

"I do. Now, if you'll excuse me . . ." She mustered what dignity she could and stuck her nose in the air. "I'd like to go inside."

"Certainly, your highness."

Whitney blinked at him, then laughed uproariously. "Highness! Drunk. High. Highness. That's a good one, Burkett." She patted him on the cheek as she passed him on her way to the door.

It was pure reflex, along with a few latent desires, that made him turn his head and plant his open mouth in her palm, where he caressed her skin with lips and tongue.

Whitney sucked in a sharp breath. Fire shot from her palm, up her arm and down her spine. Hot, shocking fire. Her knees weakened, and way down deep inside, moisture gathered.

"Oh," she whispered.

"Yeah." Adam took her hand in both of his and held it to his mouth. "Oh."

He did things to her palm with his tongue that she didn't know could be done with such a supposedly simple act. Explosions of electric current burst through her, wringing a moan from deep in her throat.

"Damn, damn, damn." Adam freed one hand and slid it around her neck to pull her close. "I wish you were sober."

"I told you—" She placed a kiss against his jaw. "I'm just a little tipsy. Maybe," she said, trailing another kiss after the first one. His skin was on the rough side, with a day's worth of beard rasping against her lips. "Maybe just tipsy enough."

Damn, damn, damn, he thought. *Don't ask, don't ask. Dammit, don't ask.* "Tipsy enough for what?"

Those clear, dark eyes of hers, eyes the color of rich coffee, stared up at him, and he would have sworn she was stone-cold sober. If he didn't know better.

"For this." She cupped his face in her hands and pulled his head down toward hers.

She may not have been stone-cold sober, but he was. In addition, his mama didn't raise no fool. No way in hell he was passing up this invitation. Just because Whitney might not know what she was doing didn't mean he shouldn't let her have what she wanted. He met her mouth with his own and dove in.

The buildup to searing heat came slowly. It started with a tiny gasp—hers. Then came a low moan, from him. Lips molded, tongues danced. She tasted of . . . Good God.

He tore his mouth free. "Cigars and beer?"

She looked puzzled. "You've got something against cigars and beer?"

"Not on principle, no, although I am anti-smoking. I'm just surprised, that's all." He chuckled. "I knew those ladies were doing something naughty over there every month."

She chuckled back, but her laugh was sultry. Deliberately so, he thought. "And do you like naughty ladies?" she asked.

He nudged his nose against hers. "More than I should."

"Why do you say that?"

"Because you've had too much to drink, and if this goes where I want it to go, tomorrow morning you'll accuse me of taking advantage of you."

"I'll accuse—?"

"And you'd be right."

"I can't believe we're going to argue about this."

"I can't either." His nose nudged hers again.

She nipped his bottom lip with her teeth. "Let's see if I've got this straight." She took a step back and bumped up against the front door. "I drink a few beers—three, to be exact—"

Adam put his arms around her and linked his fingers together at the base of her spine. He laughed.

"Three beers makes you walk down the street giggling?"

"It was Mexican beer," she said in self-defense. "It was pretty strong stuff."

"How do I know it wasn't some three-two, light beer? Maybe you're just a wuss. Maybe you just can't hold your liquor."

She snorted with disgust. "It was Corona, the strong stuff, but let's stick to one argument at a time, please."

"Why do we have to argue at all?"

"We don't." She peered up at him from beneath her lashes. "You could just shut up and kiss me."

"Been there." He nudged closer. "Done that." His belt buckle nudged her abdomen. "More than eager to do it again." He swooped.

She met him halfway. Her mouth demanded more than merely a simple kiss. She asked for heat, but not without offering it in return.

She scorched him, and he reveled in it. He set his hands free, and they filled themselves with the trim, supple back, her narrow waist, the gentle flair of her hips. Pulling those hips firmly against his seemed the most natural of movements.

They were made to fit against his. All of her was made to fit him, he was sure of it. He wasn't sure he was comfortable with it, but there it was, undeniably true.

Then there was the taste of her, once he got past the beer and the cigar. Beneath those flavors he found the sweet, dark taste of woman, mysterious, addictive.

A car drove by and honked. It was an abrupt reminder that they were standing on Whitney's front porch, and that both his hands were in the process of cupping her backside.

Whitney groaned into his mouth.

He flexed his hands, hidden from anyone on the street by the bulk of both their bodies. "What's that?" He traced one finger around a shape in her hip pocket.

"Front-door key," she managed while kissing his throat.

He dipped his fingers into the pocket. "Do you mind?"

"Not at all." If a woman could purr, she did.

He slipped the key from her pocket and worked it into the lock. Whitney's shoulders had been pressed against the door. If he hadn't had his arms around her when it opened she would have fallen into the house.

"I saved you," he pointed out.

"Oh." For a New Yorker, she gave a more than credible Southern Belle sigh. "My hero."

Who would have thought, he thought as he kissed her again, that fooling around with Whitney Sheridan could be so much fun? Humorous even.

When she deepened the kiss, he forgot about fun, forgot about humor. In truth, he nearly forgot his own name. All he knew was that at any moment he might disappear inside her and never find his way out again. Never even try. And that was fine with him.

Without breaking the kiss, Adam managed to move them far enough into the room so that he could close the front door. With a flick of his fingers, the dead bolt clicked into place.

"You've locked yourself in," Whitney murmured

against his mouth. She pulled back slightly and met his gaze. "How handy."

"How's that?"

"Because you've locked us in together, and locked everyone else out. I think I like that."

"You really have had too much to drink, haven't you?" It was pitiful how much he regretted that fact.

"I can't want to be alone with you unless I've had too much to drink?"

They were swaying now, back and forth, to some tune only they could hear.

"You're alone with me every day. You don't usually want to kiss me."

"How do you know?"

Adam grinned. "Oh, yeah? Do tell."

Slowly she shook her head from side to side, while their lips still touched. The friction was exquisite.

"I'm really not in the mood to talk," she whispered.

"Oh." He flicked his tongue across her upper lip. "Well, then." She was right. Kissing beat the hell out of talking any day of the week. Especially on Thursday.

His hands, shame on them, started roaming again. This time they found her firm, full breasts, just made to fit his palms. Through blouse and bra he felt her nipples peak and harden. Felt her move against him, all the better to fill his hands.

The pressure of his hands on her breasts sent warm honey flowing through Whitney's veins. She wanted more from Adam than she had realized. Much, much more. She wanted it all. Everything. That hot, intimate joining of a man and woman who wanted each other.

Maybe it was the drink. Maybe the cigar, she thought wryly, although she'd had only one puff, and that merely to satisfy the ladies. Maybe it had been the walk home in the moonlight. Or his having waited on her porch for her to come home.

But, secretly, she figured it was more likely the cat food he'd bought that had made her want him. Now that she had him in her arms, she couldn't get enough of kissing him, of touching him. She'd known he was leanly muscled, but to feel the hardness of those muscles beneath her hands, against her thighs, was nothing short of heaven.

It had been a long time since she had let a man get close to her, since she had wanted one to. Now she found herself drawn to a man all wrong for her, too young for her, and she didn't care. He was here, and so was she, and what would it hurt to share the night with him?

"You feel good," he told her, his fingers flexing against her breasts.

"I do when you do that," she answered.

Adam smiled. "Glad you like it."

She closed her eyes and moaned. "Glad you're doing it." She ran her own splayed hands over his chest in a mimicking movement.

With a slight groan, he took her mouth again with his. "This," Adam said against her lips, "could get out of hand fast."

"Promises, promises."

Adam kissed her again, then pulled back slightly. "Are you sure?"

She smoothed her fingertips across his cheek and smiled. "I promise not to blame you tomorrow if you won't blame me."

He gripped her hips and pulled them flush against his again. "Sounds like a plan."

"I thought so." She took the lead then, by pulling his shirttail free and sliding her hands up the bare skin of his back.

Adam shuddered at this new, flesh-to-flesh contact. Pulses pounded all through his body, then gathered low, below his belt, and hardened there.

Oh, yeah, he thought, this could get out of hand real fast. He didn't know whether to be alarmed or grateful. A new urgency built in him and he deepened the kiss. Whatever cautions or worries he'd had out on the porch jumbled together in the fog of lust in his mind and became meaningless. He wanted her. She, God knew why, seemed to want him in return.

And want him, she did. She told him with her hands, her lips and tongue. With every movement of her body against his. Every way a woman could tell a man, without words, that she wanted to feel his hands on her, his mouth. Wanted to feel him inside her.

In the end, they took each other, right there on the living room carpet amid scattered clothing and rasping breaths. She pushed him onto his back and rose over him, lamplight gleaming across her bare breasts.

"God, you're good to look at," he told her with feeling.

She ran her gaze down his body, slowly. So slowly, so deliberately, that he swore he could feel it as if it were her hands instead.

"So are you." She lowered herself until her breasts were crushed against his chest. Her hair fell forward and brushed his cheeks. Her bare legs entwined with his bare legs. "And you feel good, too."

With a neat twist of his hips and torso, he rolled until their positions were reversed. He was on top, nestled cozily between her legs.

Now he could taste her wherever he wanted. He started at her forehead and worked his way down, pausing for several heart-stopping minutes at that generous mouth before moving on down to her soft, soft neck.

"You taste good, too." He could have nibbled on her neck forever, but even tastier flesh awaited him farther down. He kissed his way along her collarbone to her shoulder, then back again, and down. Down the valley between her breasts. Up one soft rise to the nipple, peaked with arousal against his tongue. He drew it into his mouth and suckled.

Whitney gasped and arched her back. Had he not been lying on her she might have risen clear off the floor. Mindless pleasure danced from her breast, down her middle, straight to that place between her thighs that throbbed with wanting.

What she wanted, was for him to never stop.

When he left her nipple she cried out in protest. Then he drove her wild by suckling on her other nipple.

Oh, yes. Don't stop. Don't ever stop.

Then he slid his hand down her side, her hip, over her abdomen and back again before slipping down to the folds that hid the very core of her.

His fingers were skilled, soothing and arousing at the same time. With a moan, she clenched her thighs together to keep his hand there, just there.

Adam groaned. She was honey beneath his lips,

wet heat at his fingertips. She was as ready for him as he was for her. He was so ready, in fact, that when she took his erection in her hand he nearly lost control.

And then he was inside her, and she was wrapping those long, elegant legs around him. His world narrowed to her, to the two of them joined the way a man wanted to be joined to his woman. He refused to consider that she didn't belong to him beyond this moment. There would be time to worry about that later. For now, they had each other and the heat that exploded between them

They moved together, faster and hotter and harder, breath rasping, hands grasping, sweat slicking skin that burned.

Whitney came first, throwing back her head and crying out as the world erupted around her in bright, swirling colors. She held on to Adam with all her strength and rode the wave until she felt him follow her off the edge of the earth.

They didn't speak, not even when their breath returned. Silently, as if by prior arrangement, they gathered their clothes and stumbled up the stairs, Whitney leading the way, Adam trailing kisses down her back as they went.

She led him to her room, to the narrow bed there, where they made love again. Twice.

And finally, in the wee hours of the morning, they slept.

* * *

As was his habit, Adam woke at dawn. The window was a pale rectangle in the dark room. Not his room.

There was no moment of disorientation. Even in his sleep he'd known where he was. He'd known the woman in his arms was Whitney, that he was in her bed. That she had turned him every which way but loose, more than once, before sleep—or more accurately, at least on his part, exhaustion—had overtaken them.

He smiled before he even opened his eyes, because he could feel her gaze on him. He opened his eyes and saw that he'd been right. She was awake and watching him.

"Well," he said, rolling until they lay on their sides facing each other. "Now that we got that out of our system . . ."

She placed a hand on his chest to stop him from kissing her. "Meaning?"

"Meaning . . ." He threaded his fingers through hers and lifted her hand from his chest to his lips. "Now we can take our time."

Her smile was slow, her voice sultry. "You'll get no argument out of me."

The bed was narrow, which meant they had to stay really close to each other.

There was no argument there, either.

They took their time in the early morning light, with lazy touches, slow kisses. But lazy and slow were not enough for long, for soon the sizzle and heat rose up and singed them.

Whitney pushed him onto his back and straddled his hips. When she rose above him, he smiled and cupped her breasts in both hands. Whitney sighed.

With her head flung back, she closed her eyes, took him in her hand and guided him inside.

Adam gripped her hips and pulled her down tight against him, even as he thrust upward. She was so hot, so slick. So tight. She began to move, and he helped her, faster, faster, harder.

Whitney grasped his shoulders and held on as the pleasure and the pressure built.

The explosive climax hit them both at once. She cried out sharply. He growled.

She fell forward onto his chest, and he held her there until their racing hearts slowed down.

"If the house caught on fire," he said lazily, his eyes closed, his arms still around her, "I'm afraid the fire department would find me right here in this bed."

"Now there's a cheery thought."

"I don't think I can move."

"Well . . ." Whitney stretched, still on top of him. "If it's fire you're worried about, we could get in the shower."

Intrigued, Adam tugged gently on her hair until she raised her head and looked at him. "Can't catch fire in the shower," he said.

"Not when you're all wet." Her voice was husky. From sleep. From sex. "When water is streaming down every inch of you." She trailed her fingers down his sides. "Soaking you, drenching you, making your flesh slick."

Life stirred again in a part of him he'd thought was finished for the morning. "Damn, woman."

They barely made it out of the shower before the hot water turned cold.

* * *

What an odd night, Adam thought as he walked the back streets home. He'd left his truck at home last night, and a good thing, too, unless he wanted everyone in town to know he'd spent the night with Whitney.

Not that he cared what anyone thought, but broadcasting their night together wouldn't be fair to her.

Why was it people always looked down on the woman, but not the man?

He shook his head and stuffed his hands deeper into his front pockets. All of this was off the point, something else to think about other than what had actually happened between him and Whitney last night. Because the truth was, he wasn't sure what had actually happened between them.

Sex, sure. Great sex. Terrific sex. The hottest sex he'd had in years. Maybe ever.

For a man who wasn't looking for commitment, last night had been perfect. Hot sex with a beautiful woman who was in town for only a few weeks. No promises, no emotional blackmail, no "will you still respect me in the morning." In fact, there had been no talking at all until dawn, and then it had been of no consequence.

The perfect sexual encounter.

So why wasn't he jumping for joy? Why did he feel as if he should have handled things differently, made the night more special for the two of them. They should have talked to each other. They should have at least talked before he left this morning, but she'd practically booted him out the door. Smiling, but with her hand practically shoving at his back. She had to go to the shop to meet the appraiser. He had to go home, then come back and start work on the new linen closet. No time to talk. See you later, alligator.

He didn't know whether he felt used, or was he the user? Sap or jerk? Both? Neither?

He turned the corner onto his street. For now he had to shake off the questions in his mind and instead brace himself for the questions his mother was about to hurl at him as soon as she realized he hadn't spent the night at home.

She surely already knew. She wouldn't have seen the lights in his apartment over their garage come on. He was late to breakfast.

It certainly wasn't the first time. He was, after all, a grown man.

A grown man whose mama still cooked his breakfast every day.

What could he say? He loved his mama, and her cooking, and she set a place for him. What was he supposed to do, tell her no and eat his own cooking, then walk right past her kitchen as he left for the day?

A man could take adulthood and independence too damn far, that's what he thought.

Chapter Ten

Whitney set a new record for keeping herself busy, her mind occupied, from the instant Adam left that morning just past dawn. She dressed quickly but carefully, then walked to the other end of town for breakfast at Good Eats. She walked slowly, taking note of every building she passed, the type of business it held, thinking about how each business related to the others in town. Concentrating on the community. The cracks in the sidewalk. The planters with flowers, and a few without. The single traffic light in town.

There was a lot to see and think about. There was no need to think about the night just past. No need to relive the hottest, sexiest, most exciting night of her life. No need to think about Adam's body, the taste of him, the smell of his hair, his skin. The feel of his bare flesh against her bare flesh.

No, no need to think about any of that.

She must have been out of her mind.

And thank God for it, she thought. Otherwise, in a saner moment, she might not have had the nerve to instigate a night of wild sex with a man she barely knew. And instigate she had, there was no denying that. Yahoo, Mexican beer.

But she didn't feel as if she barely knew Adam. She felt as if she knew him well. He certainly seemed to know her. Last night he'd known instinctively where to touch, exactly how to pleasure her. But even before last night he'd had her pegged, with his comments about her holding in, denying her emotions, keeping to herself to avoid messy feelings.

They had crossed a line last night that, intellectually, she knew they should never have crossed. However, there was no going back, for either of them.

How was she supposed to look him in the eye? What was she supposed to say to him?

Conversation hadn't been a problem last night. That, too, had been at her instigation. She had deliberately discouraged talking. She hadn't wanted false promises or fake compliments from him, hadn't wanted to offer any.

So why did she feel as if she had made a mistake?

She shook her head and put it aside. The whole point of this morning to was to avoid thinking about last night. At least until she had a little distance between her and all that hot, unbridled sex.

A shiver of electricity raced up her spine at the mere memory.

With grim determination, she entered the café.

"Hey, there, Miss Whitney." Ada May, the owner, sat perched on her usual stool at the cash register and gave her a wave. "You sure look pretty this morning. Got a glow about you. Must be getting some good lovin' from somewhere, huh?"

Whitney nearly choked.

"Out for an early breakfast?"

"Yes, ma'am."

"Ma'am." Ada slapped her knee and hooted. "I like that, yes I do. Franki! Gotta a real polite customer out here who'd like to eat."

"This is the place for it." Franki Malone sailed through the swinging kitchen doors and into the dining room. "Oh, hi. We must not be too bad, since you came back."

"Not too bad at all," Whitney acknowledged. She took a seat at a side booth and looked forward to the show Ada and Franki were sure to put on.

After breakfast she met Carla at the shop, and they waited for the appraiser, who was due at Claudia's Attic any moment.

"Wow." Carla gave Whitney the once-over. "You look like you got a great night's sleep." She grinned. "Or something."

"I don't know what you're talking about." Hell, did it really show on her face that she'd spent the night having one orgasm after another? Sheesh.

She was saved from whatever response Carla might have made by the arrival of the appraiser.

Whitney followed him around as he took his pictures and measurements and made copious notes—partly to keep Carla from making any more comments about how Whitney had spent her night, partly because she wanted to see what the man did.

"Really, Ms. Sheridan, it's not necessary for you to accompany me. I assure you I'm used to finding my own way."

"Oh, that's all right." She gave him a pleasant smile. "I promise not to get in your way."

The look on his face announced plainly that he would rather she find some out-of-the-way place to sit, and stay there. But she had never watched an appraiser work and found it interesting that from a few notes and measurements, and a comparison to similar properties that had sold recently in the area, he could arrive at a value for the building.

He took his time, poking into every room, checking doors, inspecting windows. He spent about an hour at it.

"I'll have to look up the comparables at the office. The appraisal should be ready in about a week."

"All right." Whitney shook the man's hand. "You'll call me when it's ready?"

"Certainly. I understand you also have a home in the area that you'll be selling? I do residential appraisals, too."

"That's good to know. But the house isn't ready. I'm having quite a bit of work done on it. When that's finished, then I'll see about an appraisal."

Whitney had to leave the shop soon after the appraisal. She was more in Carla's way than of any real help. Still not ready to go home and face Adam, who would be hard at work by now, Whitney decided to pay Miss Ella a visit, see if she wanted to start a new book today.

It was a short, five-minute walk from Claudia's Attic to Shady Oaks, but the day was so humid, and already warm despite the morning hour, that she was hot and sticky by the time she arrived. The air conditioning was more than welcome.

Edna Freeberger, the head nurse, greeted her when she entered. "Miss Ella will be glad to see you."

"How is she today?"

"Feisty as ever. She had a good night last night. Have you done something different with your hair?"

Whitney frowned. "My hair? No." She had barely taken the time to comb it after it had dried.

Freeberger shook her head. "I can't put my finger on it, but something about you looks different. You're positively radiant today."

Whitney swallowed. "Uh, thanks. I'll just, um, go on back to Miss Ella's room."

"Sure thing."

When Whitney entered Miss Ella's room, the woman was propped up on two pillows, staring out the window beside her bed.

"Whitney," she cried, her face lighting up with a huge smile.

The woman was so glad to see her that Whitney was humbled. And so very glad she had decided to come.

"Good morning," she said.

"Aren't you a pretty picture today."

It was all Whitney could do to keep from rolling her eyes.

"You have Claudia's smile."

Whitney paused. "I do?" No one had ever told her that, and she had never noticed it herself. "Are you sure?"

"I'm positive. When you go home, look at a picture of her, then look in the mirror. The very same sweet smile. And you have a bloom about you. Like a woman in love."

Whitney gulped. "Oh, no. It must be the humidity, that's all."

Miss Ella laughed.

They started a new book, a Western historical romance this time, because Miss Ella loved cowboys and Indians. Whitney read until Miss Ella started to nod off. She closed the book and set it on the bedside table, then leaned down and kissed the elderly woman's cheek.

"I'll see you tomorrow, Miss Ella."

"You're so sweet to come see an old woman this way."

"Nonsense. I'm not sweet at all. I just do what pleases me. This is the least I can do after you taught me to love reading."

With no more reasons, legitimate ones at least, to stay away from the house after leaving Shady Oaks, Whitney walked the short distance home. She thought she might possibly have set a new record for slow walking.

It was too much to hope that, it being near noon, Adam would have taken off somewhere for lunch. She wasn't that lucky. His truck sat there, big and bold in her driveway. When she reached the front porch she could hear the country music blasting from his boom box. He never turned it up that loud when she was home. He was clearly taking advantage of her absence.

Her reluctance to confront him—no, that wasn't right. Why did there need to be a confrontation? Why was she getting all defensive? They had spent a wonderful night together. She'd heard of awkward mornings after, but this was shaping up to be beyond ridiculous if she couldn't even face him.

She was about to turn the knob to let herself in through the front door when she heard the whine of Adam's saw from the backyard. She almost had herself talked into changing direction and going back there to talk to him when the saw fell silent.

"Be brave," she told herself. She had faced worse situations. Egotistical reporters, maniacal bosses, and in her younger days out in the field, even an irate foreign head of state or two. She hadn't batted an eye at the prosepct of facing any of those. So why was she so reluctant to see Adam?

Oh, God, she was repeating her own questions, and had yet to come up with an answer. Angry with herself, she shoved open the front door and stepped into the house—at the exact same instant that Adam stepped into the kitchen from the back porch. They ended up facing each other, an expanse of carpet and tile flooring separating them.

"Hello," he said.

Whitney stood where she was, suddenly unable to move. His jeans were dusty, with a rip across one knee. His T-shirt was sweat-dampened and dirty. A faint sheen of sweat and sawdust covered him from head to toe.

Never had a man looked so damned appealing.

"Hello," she finally managed.

He was carrying a stack of boards. He set them down on the breakfast bar. He shuffled his feet, looked down, then back up, stuck one hand into his back pocket. "So," he said. "Is everything all right?"

"Sure. Everything's fine. The appraiser finally came. For the shop. Miss Ella and I started a new book. Everything's fine."

He gnawed on the inside of his jaw, then said, "I mean us. You and me. Are we all right. With each other."

"You mean because of last night?"

"No, I mean because it's Friday. Yes, I mean because of last night. Maybe you're used to spending an entire night doing what we did and not saying a single word to each other the entire time, but I'm not."

Whitney gave a toss of her head and admitted that her defenses were on alert. "It takes two to have a conversation. I don't recall hearing you say anything."

He grinned and shrugged. "I was busy."

She returned his shrug. "And I was supposed to talk your ear off? I was a little busy myself."

He cocked his head. "I guess you're feeling as awkward about this as I am, huh?"

Whitney swallowed. "Yeah. I guess awkward's a good word for it."

He stepped closer, pulled his hand from his pocket and dropped his arms to his sides. "Are you sorry?"

"About last night? Of course not."

"You're sure?"

"Adam, if you'll recall, I'm the one who initiated things last night."

A slight smile curved his lips. "Oh, yeah, I recall that well enough. I also recall the beer you had earlier."

"You still think I was too drunk to know what I was doing?"

"God," he said with feeling. "I hope not."

For the first time that day Whitney felt a knot of tension in her stomach ease. She laughed.

"It sure seemed like you knew exactly what you were doing."

"Is that a compliment?"

"You better believe it." He sidled closer to her and cupped the balls of her shoulders with his hands. "Are we really all right?"

Whitney placed her hands on his chest and smiled up at him. "I'd say so, yes."

"Good." He pulled her close and kissed her, slowly at first, then deeper, harder before breaking off and smiling. "Does that mean you'll come watch me hit a few homers tonight?"

"He-man wants to show off, does he?"

He stepped back and flexed his biceps. "You bet. Gotta impress the little woman, don't I?"

"Oh, and what little woman would that be?"

"Uh, gotta impress the woman from out of town?"

"That'll do."

"Then you'll come?"

"Since you asked so nicely."

"And can I come home with you afterward?"

The question took her by surprise. It also made her pulse leap in anticipation.

"If you're not comfortable with that, Whit, just say so."

"Whit?"

"Ms. Sheridan?"

"No, no," she protested when his voice turned cold. "I didn't mean it like that. It's just that no one's ever called me that."

"You're kidding. Not ever?"

"Not to my face, anyway."

"You don't like it?"

"I didn't say that."

"No, you didn't. We don't seem to communicate very well, do we?"

"We seem to do better when we don't talk."

"There is that."

"Maybe you could come over tonight, after your game, and we could . . . not talk some more."

With a smile, he swooped down and kissed her again. "Now you're talking."

Oh, Whitney thought, how good it felt to laugh again.

The Washita Building Supply softball team did not do as well against Washita Feed and Seed as they had the week before against Dairy Mart. It was a low-scoring game, and Adam swore he did his share by knocking one runner in and making it home himself. Then there was that fly he caught out in left field, putting out Lorne Dowd, whose father owned the Feed and Seed.

Still, when the third out in the bottom half of the ninth inning came and went, the Builders lost to the Farmers three to five.

"Damn Farmers," Mr. Burkett grumbled.

"Watch out, there, Teddy." Eugene Dowd, owner of the Washita Feed and Seed and sponsor of the winning team, nudged him in the shoulder on his way out of the bleachers. "Them damn Farmers whupped your boy's Builders, and did a handy job of it."

"Yeah, yeah." Teddy waved Eugene on.

"That means you buy the next round of coffee at the café," Eugene reminded his old friend.

"Yeah, yeah. When do you want it?"

"How about lunch tomorrow?"

"That's fine, but I'm not buying your lunch, just your coffee."

Eugene laughed and slapped Teddy's shoulder. "It was worth a try."

"Get on with you. I'll see you tomorrow. Come on, Mother." Teddy took his wife by the arm and helped her down the steps of the bleachers.

Behind them Whitney smiled. The two men had been pestering each other from the minute they'd entered the stands. It was easy to see that they had been the best of friends for years.

For a brief instant, Whitney envied them that friendship, that closeness and companionship. Then she closed out the thought. She'd had friends, and lost them, one by one, and the losing hurt too much.

Was their friendship not worth the pain? Adam's question still haunted her. She wondered if she would ever be brave enough, or rash enough, to try again, to open herself to another person again.

And then she was down out of the stands and Adam was striding toward her and she forgot everything but that she would soon have him all to herself again behind closed doors.

"Well," he said with disgust, "that was a pisser."

"Poor baby," she told him.

"Good game, son." Adam's father came over and clapped a hand to his son's back. "Good game."

"We lost, in case you didn't notice." Adam tugged off his cleats and put on his Nikes.

"It was still a good game," Mr. Burkett insisted. "But it's gonna cost me a round of coffee tomorrow at lunch. How 'bout I buy you a beer? You, too, Whitney."

"Thanks, but she promised me a root beer float. Will you take my shoes home?" Adam snatched Whitney with one hand and held out his shoes with the other.

His dad took the shoes in his work-worn hands.

"Thanks," Adam told him. "See you later. G'night, Mom," he called.

"Good night, son," she called back. "That was a nice catch on that fly."

"Thanks, Mom."

"Oh, Whitney." Mary Burkett drew her husband to a halt. "I hear you've got a new cat over at your place."

Whitney shot Adam a look from the corner of her eye. "Now and then," she admitted. "When he decides to stop by for a meal."

Mary laughed. "You feed him, he's yours." With a big grin, she wagged a finger at Whitney. "Same goes for men, too."

"It does?"

"It does," Mary confirmed.

"Thanks for the warning. I'll be careful."

"Good night, you two," Mary called. "Come on, Dad, let's go home."

"Hmph. I'm not your dad."

"I'm not your mother, either. That never stopped you from calling me that."

"Now, Mother . . ."

It sounded like an old and familiar argument to Whitney. One the Burketts were comfortable with, since there didn't seem to be any heat in their words as they headed out of the ballpark.

Whitney and Adam ended up in the middle of a group of eight that made their way down Main to the Dairy Mart, whose team did not play that night.

Adam was so cute, Whitney thought, maneuvering everyone else to leave a few people at a time until the two of them were the only customers left. They wouldn't remain that way for long, as the night was still young and teenagers by the dozen would pull in, probably several times each, before closing time.

But this way no one would notice that Adam walked home with Whitney.

"Whose reputation are you taking care of?" she asked after they left Dairy Mart and crossed the street on the way to her house. "Yours? Or mine?"

"How about both?" he suggested.

"No, no, no. You're supposed to say that your reputation is of no consequence, that you don't care what people say about you, but that you'll do whatever you must to protect my good name."

"Yeah, that's what I meant."

"You sweet-talker, you."

"On the other hand," he said, pulling her to a stop beneath a streetlight about a block away from her house, "maybe I should make a public statement, stake my claim right out here where anybody and everybody can see." He pulled her close and wrapped his arms around her.

"And spoil all your hard work of making sure none of your buddies realized you were coming home with me?"

"Oh, well, there is that." He planted a quick kiss on her nose, then another, not quite so quick, on her mouth.

When they reached her house and were inside,

Whitney turned to him. "I hope you won't take this the wrong way, but you're welcome to use my shower."

Adam broke out laughing. "A little ripe for you?"

"No, actually. I just thought you might be more comfortable, what with the way you slid at third base the way you did. And you ended up in the dirt when you caught that fly."

"So you're just looking out for my comfort. Is that right?"

"Of course."

"You stick to that story. It works pretty well. I'll use the downstairs shower. But I don't have any clean clothes to put on."

"Ah, well, we have this new invention. It's called a washing machine."

"You'd do my laundry for me?" he asked.

She grinned and pinched his chin. "No, but I'd let you do it."

Adam was so enthralled and delighted with this playful side of Whitney that he could only laugh at her refusal to perform a domestic chore for him.

"I'll do my own laundry if you'll scrub my back in the shower."

Her brows raised. Her lips curved. "Well, now, aren't you the lucky one. A hot, soapy back scrub in the shower happens to be my personal consolation prize to the left fielder of the losing team of tonight's second game of the evening."

"Sounds like you're right." He put an arm around her and led her toward the newly refurbished downstairs bathroom. "I am the lucky one."

* * *

The water was hot, the soap and Whitney's hands were slick. Adam could have sworn he'd died and gone to heaven.

"I'll give you an hour to quit that," he said.

Her laugh was low and seductive. "We stay in here an hour, we'll both be screaming. The hot water will run out long before that."

Still, she took her time running her soapy hands over his back, his arms, after she washed his hair.

"My turn." He turned around and faced her. He picked up the soap, lathered his hands, then touched her. Her shoulders first, her neck.

Whitney felt his touch all through her. She closed her eyes and tilted her head back, giving him easy access to her neck.

But he didn't linger on her neck. His hands, wet and slick and hot, slid down and cupped her breasts. With his thumbs, he flicked the tips again and again.

Whitney cried out at the sharp pleasure.

"You like that."

"Yes. Oh, yes."

He slid one hand down her stomach, between her legs, and slipped his fingers between her folds. "And that?"

Her knees nearly buckled. "Adam." She grabbed onto his shoulders to keep from falling.

"Easy," he crooned. "I've got you." He kept his hand between her legs and held her close against him with his other arm.

"Adam," she cried again. It was too much. She felt too much too fast. She couldn't hold it in. A sharp wave of pleasure struck hard and fast and spread out from his hand to every inch of her body. "Adam."

Her orgasm nearly brought on Adam's, but he

gritted his teeth and fought it back. He wasn't ready. Didn't want to let go yet.

But when Whitney regained her breath, she slicked her hands again with soap and, with her gaze locked with his, took his erection in hand and began to stroke him from base to tip.

The way his eyes widened and his nostrils flared made her pulse leap.

Adam took the exquisite torture as long as he could, then pushed her against the wall. "Put your legs around my waist."

She didn't question or delay. The feel of her silky legs sliding up his hips, one at a time, to his waist, made him groan. He held her by her hips and buried himself in her depths in one long stroke.

Whitney's breath left her in a harsh gasp, but not from pain. From the shock of incredible pleasure.

Again and again he plunged into her, and she clung to him, her arms around his neck, her legs around his waist. And when he came, she flew with him.

"I have a favor to ask."

Whitney finished wrapping the towel around herself and finger-combed her wet hair away from her face. The bathroom door was open, but the air was still steamy. "What's that?"

"Can we find a bigger bed tonight?"

Whitney gave him a mock frown. "You don't like being so close to me?"

"On the contrary." He wrapped his arms around her and pulled her close, burying his lips against the

side of her neck. "I want more room to roll around
with you."

She took him to the guest room, that room she
had avoided, as it had been hers years ago, and
found that there were no ghosts there, only a man
and woman engaged in the act of making love.

Chapter Eleven

Saturday was the strangest day for Whitney. Much as the previous morning, Adam left for home near dawn, on foot because, also as the previous morning, his truck was at home.

She, however, stayed home. She felt no need to keep her mind busy to avoid thinking about the night before. In truth, she wanted to relive it over and over in her mind, to wallow in the remembered passion.

Never had she had such an attentive lover as Adam. She could remember clearly every touch, every stroke and kiss from the past two nights. The difference between yesterday and today was . . . in truth, she wasn't sure what the difference was. Except, maybe she was more at ease with taking Adam as her lover now because they had talked. She didn't feel as if she had used him, or been used by him. What they shared had been mutual.

And, if she had anything to say about it, it wasn't over.

She would have fixed breakfast for him—she could cook when the mood hit her—but his mother would be cooking for him. No sense in alarming her two days in a row, as Whitney pointed out to Adam.

"She wouldn't be alarmed," Adam had told her. "Just curious. I figure you'd rather not have her poking her nose in any more than necessary."

"You figure right," Whitney had told him. The thought of having to answer to a man's mother . . . no, that held no appeal for her at all. Only terror.

In the end she might as well have fixed Adam's breakfast, because Mary Burkett followed him when he came back to Whitney's house to work.

"Mrs. Burkett." Whitney smiled. She wiped her suddenly damp palms on the thighs of her jeans and hoped her smile didn't look as tight as it felt. "This is a surprise." And that was putting it mildly. She didn't think she'd ever been confronted by a man's mother the morning after spending the night with him.

"It's Mary, now," Mrs. Burkett reminded. "You promised."

"Mary, then. Please, come in."

"Thank you, but I can't stay. I just wanted to bring this extra pie over here for you. It's blackberry. They ripened early along the river this year. And I need to talk to Adam for a minute."

"He's upstairs painting the new linen closet. Come in and have a seat while I go get him."

"Thank you, dear. I won't keep him but a minute, I promise."

Whitney set the pie on the breakfast bar, then rushed upstairs to get Adam.

"Hey, Sweetcakes."

"I'd make you take that back," she told him, "but your mother is downstairs, says she needs to see you."

Worry filled his eyes. "My mother? I just saw her an hour ago. Did she say what she wanted?"

"Just you. And she brought me a blackberry pie. Go see what she wants. She didn't look like anything terrible had happened."

Adam propped his paintbrush across the top of the can of paint and pulled a rag from his hip pocket to clean the white splotches from his fingers on his way down the stairs.

"Mom? What's wrong?"

"Oh, Adam, I'm sorry to bother you, but I was bringing the pie to Whitney, and I wanted to tell you in person that your Uncle Gary's gallbladder is acting up again, and he's going into the hospital today for surgery tomorrow. Your father and I are going to head for Amarillo right after lunch. Your Aunt Connie's at her wit's end and needs the moral support."

"I'll be home by one. Give me time to clean up and I'll drive you."

"Are you sure, son?"

"Of course I'm sure." He smiled and kissed her cheek. "That's what you wanted me to say, isn't it?"

Mary smiled and patted his cheek. "You're a good son, Adam."

"I'm the best. I've been telling you that for years. Now scoot so I can finish up here."

"All right. I'll see you later. I'll make sure your father has the car gassed up by the time you get home."

Whitney looked at her image in the mirror and swore. It was Saturday evening, Adam had been gone for only a few hours, and she felt lost. She missed him.

"Idiot," she hissed at herself. Since when did her mood, her happiness, depend on a damn man?

Since Adam Burkett.

Okay. There was that.

It was humbling and more than a little frightening if she thought about it too much, to realize that in just a few short days she had come to care for him a great deal more than was wise. A hell of a lot more than she had cared for any other man in recent memory.

She spent another hour moping around the house, then decided to cheer herself up by reading a few more entries in Aunt Claudia's journal. She started with the one written one week after Claudia met Harry.

> *August 24*
> *I can't count the number of sins I've committed during the past weekend, and I don't care. I was right about Harry. I am absolutely, positively in love. And wonder of wonders, he loves me, too.*
>
> *He got a weekend pass and called me. I told Daddy I was going to see a sick friend in Atlanta for the weekend. It is the first major lie I've ever told. Isn't that sad? At my age, I've never lied to my daddy. Never had reason to.*
>
> *Harry and I spent the weekend at a little motel on the south side of town. It could have been on the moon, for all we saw of the outside world. We might have starved were it not for pizza delivery.*
>
> *He is the most thrilling lover I've ever known.*
>
> *All right, here in these pages I can admit he's the*

only lover I've ever known. He is everything I ever dreamed of. We made love all weekend. It was the happiest time of my life.

And the saddest. He is shipping out next week. He didn't say, said they hadn't told him yet, but they'll send him to Viet Nam. Where else would the army send a new private in this day and age? I fear for him. I ache for my own loneliness to come. I love him so much!

Smiling softly, Whitney closed the journal and set it next to her bed. She'd had no idea Aunt Claudia had loved a man. She'd never thought about it, and that was her shame. Claudia Henderson had been a lovely woman, kind and smart and generous and fun. Any man would have been lucky to have her look at him, much less love him.

But something terrible must have happened to take Harry away from her, to have her never mention him, keep no pictures of him. Whitney was in no hurry to read those particular journal pages.

Sunday evening Whitney was putting away the vacuum cleaner when the phone rang. She had never vacuumed and mopped and dusted so much in her life as in the past week, but Adam's work generated a lot of dust, not to mention what he tracked in on his shoes going to and from the workbench he'd set up out back.

She closed the closet door on the vacuum, swearing she wouldn't touch it for at least three days, and went to answer the phone.

"Hi."

"Adam. Where are you? How's your uncle? Did the surgery go all right? Are your parents and your aunt holding up okay?"

In the visitor's lounge on his uncle's floor at the hospital in Amarillo, Adam smiled with delight. For a woman who claimed she didn't want connections with other people, she certainly seemed to care a lot about his family. He let out a small laugh.

"Let's see. In Amarillo, at the hospital. My uncle's out of recovery and in his own room now. The surgery went fine. My parents and my aunt are much relieved. Does that take care of it?"

"I guess so. Except you didn't tell me how you are."

"You didn't ask about me."

"Pretend I did."

"I'm fine. But I miss you."

There was a long silence on the Washita end of the connection. Adam wondered if missing her wasn't allowed in her book.

"Whit? You still there?"

"Wha— Oh. Sorry. I, uh, I miss you, too. It's been quiet around here."

"You mean no hammering or sawing?"

"No one to talk to," she said softly.

Adam's pulse took a leap. "That's the nicest thing you've ever said to me."

"If that's the nicest, I'll have to try harder."

"That might be interesting, but since I hear my mother coming up the hall, I believe I'll change the subject. How's the cat?"

Whitney loosened her grip on the phone cord as tension eased out of her. She could talk about the cat much easier than about missing Adam. She didn't know what had possessed her to admit to such a thing. Even if it was true.

"I haven't seen him today," she answered. "But it's just past dark. He didn't come yesterday until about this time."

"Does he like his dish I bought him?"

"Of course he does," she said with a laugh. "I get the feeling it's his first real possession. I think he's proud of it."

"Has he let you near him yet?"

"Are you kidding? He's a typical male. All he wants me for is to keep food in his dish."

"Hey, that was a chauvinist remark."

"It was a feminist remark, and it was true. When are you coming home?" She wanted the words back the instant they were out. They made her sound too eager to see him.

"You do miss me, don't you?"

"Don't let it go to your head. It was just a question."

"Still, you miss me. I can tell. We're going to stay here tonight. If Uncle Gary's doing all right in the morning, we'll head home. I'll give you a call."

Later that night Whitney wandered out onto the back porch. The air was warm and heavy with humidity. The frogs along the creek a quarter mile away screamed so loudly they made Times Square at high noon seem quiet by comparison.

How, she wondered, had she gone from a tightly self-contained, self-assured woman to someone who yearned for a glimpse of a stray cat and nearly ached for the return of a certain man? How could she come to care so much so fast?

She didn't trust these emotions. Didn't trust the people—or rather, the man and the cat—for whom she felt them. Adam said to let them into her heart, there was plenty of room. She wasn't sure she could do that, or even wanted to. She really wasn't interested in having her heart ripped to shreds again. It would be a long time healing from the loss of Aunt Claudia. She didn't need to lose any more loved ones.

Therefore, she would not love.

A simple, logical decision. She could like and enjoy and care about, but there was no reason to fall in love with anyone. That way lay disaster.

She took a deep breath of the heavy night air and smiled. With that decision made, she felt immensely better.

"Good night, Scruffy," she called softly, in case the cat was nearby, listening. "There's fresh food and water on the porch."

Monday morning brought another week and, along with it, another problem at Claudia's Attic. Not plumbing this time but electrical. When Carla opened up the shop, the first thing she did was reach over and flip the light switch, just as she did every single day.

But this day, instead of light, she got a loud *pop* and a sharp sizzling sound. A puff of smoke wafted from the switch.

Carla squeaked and jumped back. Then she held

her breath and tried another switch. No fireworks this time but no light, either.

As a grown woman, Carla was not helpless. She knew enough to check the circuit breaker. Flipping those switches didn't help any. Because of the pop and sizzle when she had flipped the first switch, she had no hope that the problem was with the power company. She didn't bother calling them. She called the electrician instead.

She did not want to call Whitney. That poor young woman did not need more trouble dropped on her doorstep. But, Carla realized, she would have called Claudia. It was only right that she afford Whitney the same respect and authority. So with a heavy sigh, she picked up the phone and called the shop owner.

The shop owner took the news in stride, but after she hung up the phone, she groaned. First the plumbing, now the wiring. What was next? Sewage?

Don't even think it.

As if that made a difference. She hadn't thought wiring, but that hadn't prevented this newest problem.

With a heavy sigh that, unbeknownst to her, matched Carla's, Whitney grabbed her purse and started for the front door. Only to realize she was barefoot.

How odd, she thought. At home she rarely went from bedroom to bathroom without something covering her feet. Socks, house slippers, sandals, something. She glanced around now and realized she hadn't had shoes on all morning. She trudged upstairs, fished out a pair of sandals, then headed for the shop.

* * *

Adam arrived that afternoon at the last house on Main, where Miz Henderson had lived for more than twenty-five years, to find Whitney pacing the floor, muttering under her breath. Something about wiring and strangling.

"I take it you've had an interesting day," he said.

She narrowed her eyes. "Interesting is not the word I would choose. How did you know?"

"You mean aside from the scowl on your face and the four-letter words bouncing off the walls?"

"Yeah." She managed a slight smile. "Aside from that."

"Keith, the electrician, was at the gas station when we stopped there on our way home."

"Ah, yes, good ol' Keith."

"You didn't like Keith?"

"Oh, Keith's fine. Nice guy. Pillar of the community. It's Martin Eads I'd like to string up by his thumbs."

"Our friendly city inspector."

"I guess I missed his friendly side. 'The wiring in this building is not up to code' doesn't sound very damn friendly to me, especially when Carla says he never mentioned a problem the last time he inspected the wiring."

"Really?"

"Really. And writing me a damn citation didn't seem very friendly, either. Nor was telling me I had thirty days to bring the wiring up to code my idea of friendship."

Adam rubbed his hands up and down her arms. "What can I do to make it better?"

She poked out her lower lip in a beaut of a pout. "You could go beat him up for me."

"Pound on him with one of my hammers?"

Her face brightened. "What a wonderful idea. Would you?"

"That depends. Will you pay my bail?"

"Oh. There is that."

"Yeah."

She heaved a sigh. "I guess I'll just have to bring the wiring up to code. But I'm not putting Eads on my Christmas-card list."

With his arms around her, Adam locked his hands together at the small of her spine, then leaned back and peered down at her. "You don't strike me as the Christmas-card-list type."

"What's that mean?"

"It means I bet you don't have a Christmas-card list at all."

"And your point is?"

"My point is . . ." He leaned down and nipped her chin, her lips. "I missed you."

"I missed you, too."

Her admission caused an ache somewhere in the region of his heart, but it was a good ache. "Then kiss me," he whispered.

Her lips were soft and warm. They welcomed his the way a man wanted to be welcomed, eagerly and with feeling.

It was those feelings that startled Whitney, the depth of them. She started to pull away, but Adam's hands rubbed her back and soothed her. She gave in to the need to hold him and wrapped her arms around his waist.

What could it hurt, after all, to stand in her living room and kiss a man? It was, after all, only a kiss.

An hour later, when Whitney's heart stopped pounding and she could catch her breath, she smiled.

Adam pushed himself up on his forearms to relieve her of some of his weight and saw her smile. As a welcome home, this topped them all.

"You look," he said, placing a kiss on the tip of her nose, "like the cat who just swallowed the canary."

"Really? Missing a few feathers, are you?"

"Are you saying I'm a canary?"

"Are you saying I'm a cat?"

"Tweet tweet."

Whitney laughed. "Meow."

"Want me to make you purr?"

"You already did. But I haven't heard you sing yet."

"No, and if you're lucky, you never will. Let me up, woman. I have to get at least some work done before the day's over."

"I'm not holding you," she told him.

"You're looking at me. Might as well be a set of chains."

Whitney opened her mouth for a smart reply, but none came. What could she say to a comment such as that? Her gaze held him as if he were chained?

Adam did manage to get some work done, and afterward the two of them grabbed a hamburger at the Dairy Mart on the way to the ballpark. Tonight Adam's team was playing the Electric Co-op.

While they were eating their burgers at one of the Dairy Mart's picnic tables beneath the awning, a big black Lincoln pulled in and Bobby Simms climbed out.

"Hey, there, Miz Sheridan, Adam."

"Mr. Simms."

"Bobby. How're things?" Adam asked.

"Can't complain," Bobby said. Then he looked over at Whitney. "Have you given any thought to my offer? From what I've been hearing lately, that building is getting to be more trouble than it's worth. You really ought to let me take it off your hands."

Whitney was appalled, and perhaps she shouldn't have been, that he would use the recent troubles at the shop to further his own ends.

"I'm surprised," she said, looking at him curiously. "A busy man like you having the time to listen to gossip about leaky pipes and faulty wiring. I would have thought a bank president would be way too busy to pay attention to such nonsense. But, you know," she added conversationally, "if anything else goes wrong at the shop, I'm going to start feeling downright unwelcome around here."

"Oh, come on," Bobby protested, a splayed hand to his chest and a grin on his face. "You can't think anyone would sabotage your plumbing and light switches."

"All I know," she said with a shrug, "is that they tell me things like this never happened to Aunt Claudia. What's a girl to think?"

"Don't let 'em fool you, Miz Sheridan." Bobby winked and started for the order window. "Leaky pipes and faulty wiring happen to everybody. Yes sirree, every single body."

"Bobby, honey." A woman opened the passenger door on the Lincoln and glided out of the car. She didn't climb or step out, she glided. "What's taking so long, sugar?"

"Just visiting, baby doll. Come on over here and meet Miz Henderson's niece. Debbie, we'll have us two root beer floats when you get a sec. Sue Ellen, this is Miss Whitney Sheridan of New York City. Whitney, my lovely bride, the former Sue Ellen Hawthorne, now, I'm proud to say, Simms."

"How do you do, Ms. Sheridan." Sue Ellen Hawthorne Simms was blond and petite, still young enough, mid-twenties, to bear the glow of youth. The kind of girl Whitney would have hated in high school. She'd bet her bottom dollar Sue Ellen had been not only the head cheerleader, but prom queen as well. Had undoubtedly never gone through a gawky stage, never had acne or bad-hair days, and never started her period in the middle of class.

Whitney hated her.

But she shook her hand and smiled. "Fine, thank you."

"I can't tell you," Sue Ellen said in a Southern accent thicker than molasses, "how sorry we all are at losing Miz Henderson. She was my favorite teacher of all time."

"Thank you," Whitney said. "She would be pleased to know that. She loved teaching."

"Adam," Sue Ellen said. "How you doin'?"

"Doin' pretty good. You?"

"The same."

"Since your husband has the bank to tend to all day, I assume you're the one," Whitney said to the woman, "who's interested in crafts?"

Sue Ellen blinked and frowned. "Krafts? Like, macaroni and cheese?"

Whitney started to laugh, but realized at the last instant that the blank look on Sue Ellen's face meant she was not joking.

Whitney mashed her lips together and managed to hold back all but a small squeak.

Beside her Adam coughed.

Over at the order window, Bobby picked up their floats and returned to his wife's side. "Ready to go, baby doll? Mama's waiting on us."

"Sure thing, honey-bunch. Bye, y'all. It was nice meeting you, Miz Sheridan."

Whitney held her tongue until the Lincoln had backed out and driven away. Then she let her head fall to the table and laughter shook her shoulders. "Oh, God. Macaroni and cheese? Tell me she didn't say that."

Adam snorted and laughed, which set Whitney off again until tears of laughter streamed down her face.

"That's our Sue Ellen," Adam said. "Pretty as a picture, but not the brightest bulb on the string. You get points for not laughing in her face."

"It was a close call," Whitney admitted, wiping the tears from her cheeks.

Bobby Simms steered the Lincoln up the hill toward the big white house that looked down upon the town of Washita. Not as in looking down one's nose. His mother saw it that way and approved. So did Sue Ellen, now that it was her home. But not Bobby. He saw it more as watching over the town from on high, to protect it.

"I didn't like her." Next to him Sue Ellen dipped the plastic spoon up and down in her root beer float and pouted.

"Whitney?"

She cut him a look. "You're on a first-name basis with her?"

"I'm trying to buy that building of her aunt's from her. It's just business, pumpkin, that's all."

"She thought I was stupid, but I get it now. Crafts. Like knitting or whatever. And I thought she meant Kraft Foods."

Bobby reached across the dark leather seat and patted his wife's silk-covered knee. "I'm sure she didn't think you were stupid."

"What do you want that shop for, anyway?"

"Because it's prime real estate. Which reminds me. Excuse me a minute, baby doll. I gotta make a quick call."

"You know they say it's not safe to use the cell phone while driving."

"There." He pulled into their driveway before the big white house and put the car in Park. "Now I'm not driving."

Sue Ellen squeezed her husband's hand and smiled. "Good. I wouldn't want anything to happen to you, sugar."

Or my money. But he thought it with affection, because he knew Sue Ellen really did love him, as much as Sue Ellen could love anyone other than herself.

She let herself out of the car and left Bobby alone to make his call in private.

He held the phone in his palm and used the thumb on that hand to punch in the number he wanted.

"It's me. Let's have a little vandalism. Nothing serious. But something obvious. Visible. And do it tonight."

Chapter Twelve

The crowd in the stands was, as always, lively during the game. Whitney sat between Janey and Franki, the morning waitress from Good Eats who liked to bicker with the owner, Ada.

"Hey, Franki." Janey leaned across her youngest son and Whitney to say hi. "Where's that adorable baby of yours?"

"Grandpa and Ada wanted her to themselves for the night."

Janey laughed. "You and Duncan finally get a night to yourselves, and you spend it here? Girl, you haven't been married *that* long."

"At least I didn't come all the way here from New York to spend my nights watching local softball."

"Hey, I'm getting hooked," Whitney said defensively.

"Word's out you're snakebit," Franki said.

"I'm what?"

"Snakebit. Unlucky."

"I don't—"

"Claudia's Attic? Plumbing? Flooding? Wiring?"

"Oh, that. Word sure gets around."

"You can say that again."

"Word sure—"

"Never mind," Franki said with a laugh. Then she pointed toward the field and jumped up. "Come on, Duncan! Knock a homer!"

"I didn't know your husband played on Adam's team," Whitney said.

"He doesn't, usually."

The first pitch was low and inside. Duncan Malone let it go.

"That's it, Duncan, wait for the right one!"

The second pitch must have been the right one, because he knocked a solid hit that put him on first before the other team could tag him.

"Way to go, Duncan! He's subbing," Franki said when she finished cheering, whistling, and clapping for her husband. "Half the damn team is off on vacation all over the damn country. He plays for the Farmers, but they're idle tonight, so he's filling in. Heaven forbid we should go one night without him getting to ground dirt into his jeans."

"Yeah, but I bet you make him do the laundry," Janey teased.

"You better believe I do, when it comes to his play clothes."

Janey and Whitney both snickered.

"Play clothes?" Janey managed. "Oh, I like that."

"Feel free to borrow the term, m'dear."

"By the way," Janey said to Whitney. "Speaking of Claudia's Attic, there's a rumor going around—"

"You mean besides the ones about the plumbing and the wiring?"

"Yeah, this one is about Bobby Simms wanting to buy the place from you."

On Whitney's other side Franki hooted.

"What's that mean?" Whitney wanted to know.

"Bobby Simms," Franki said calmly, "is a rat. I wouldn't trust him as far as I could pick him up and throw him."

"I think I figured that part out for myself."

"Good for you. A person's gotta wonder what a banker wants with a shop like that. You know he's not going to run it himself, or even keep it. Either he wants the building for something else, or he already knows of another buyer he can make a profit from when he resells it."

"I imagine you're probably right," Whitney admitted. "It's good to have my suspicions confirmed."

"So what are you going to do?" Janey asked.

"I don't know." Whitney shrugged. "Carla wants to buy the place, but the bank wouldn't loan her the money."

"Of course they wouldn't, if Bobby wants it for himself."

"Don't bankers have federal regulations they have to meet? Is that sort of lending practice—or rather, refusal—legal?"

"Who knows?" Janey said.

"Besides," Franki added. "When you're the only bank in town, and you're privately owned, I think you can do pretty much anything you think you're big enough to get away with. Some of us keep a real close eye on our money, I'll tell you."

Whitney stared. "You keep your money with a man you don't trust?"

Franki rolled her eyes. "I don't think he'll steal my money. But he'll lie and cheat and trick you to get what he wants. He's been known to try bullying and intimidation, too," she added. "But as for out and out stealing, naw, he doesn't have the balls for it."

Whitney squinted toward home plate in thought. "How about sabotage? Has he got the balls for that?"

"Oh, certainly. He'd do anything short of killing somebody. I don't think he'd kill anybody."

Out on the field a new batter hit a double, making it to second base. Duncan, having been on second, took third at a dead run and kept on going.

Franki jumped to her feet. "Run, baby, run! Go go go! Safe! Safe! All *right!*"

The next batter struck out, ending the inning. The two teams traded places.

"You're not thinking Bobby had anything to do with—" Janey shook her head. "No, that's too far-fetched."

Whitney arched her brow. "Is it?"

"But what would he want with Miz Henderson's shop in the first place?"

"That," Whitney said, "is the question of the hour."

"Did he give you a reason when he made his offer?" Franki asked.

"He didn't want me to have to worry my little head about it, or some such nonsense. He just wanted to help me out, take the shop—and the house, in his last offer—off my hands."

"Isn't that generous of him?" Franki batted her eyes.

"I thought so. I told him I'd think about it and let him know."

"And did you?"

"Not really. At the time I hadn't even had an appraisal done yet on the commercial property, and I won't get one done on the house until we're finished remodeling."

"You told him you'd think about it, and when you didn't accept his offer right away, you started having trouble. Is that about it?"

"It is, but that doesn't mean he had anything to do with the leaking pipe or the faulty wiring."

"No, but did you ever wonder why the city inspector showed up just when you had wiring problems?"

"You heard that, too?"

"I'm a waitress. I hear everything."

"Remind me to watch what I say in restaurants from now on."

"And beauty shops, and grocery stores, and dry cleaners, and—"

"All right." Whitney laughed at Franki's list. "I get the idea. Gossip comes from everywhere."

They let the subject of Bobby Simms die a natural death as the game on the field heated up. Adam caught another fly in left field, putting his team back in the dugout. Or rather, on the bench, since there was no actual dugout.

The Builders won this time, beating the Co-op eight to five.

"No contest," to hear the Builders tell it.

"We gave it away," according to the Co-op.

The teams poured off the field and made a run on the concession stand for beer. Whitney, Franki, and Janey and her two boys made their way out of the stands to meet and congratulate their conquering heros.

Janey kissed Frank while their sons talked a mile a minute about every play their dad had made.

Franki wrapped her arms around Duncan's neck and planted a big kiss on his lips.

Adam looked expectantly, hopefully, at Whitney. "Where's mine?"

Whitney laughed and gave him a peck on the mouth.

"Duncan, you'll love this," Franki said. "Bobby's trying to buy Miz Henderson's shop from Whitney. What do you think the sneaky bastard's up to?"

"Are you kidding? He's been after that property since I was a kid. My mother used to work for Bobby's father. I remember her talking about it."

"What for?" Whitney asked. "Surely it wasn't a craft shop back then."

"No, it was Mr. and Mrs. Beckerman's house until your aunt bought it. Bobby never cared what it was used for. He just wants to level the building and expand his parking lot."

Whitney stared blankly. "Level the building? After all my aunt's hard work building her business from the ground up? For what, three or four more parking spaces?"

"And an unobstructed view of his bank from that end of town."

"Oh, well, pardon me for owning an obstruction."

"Excuse me, Ms. Sheridan?"

Surprised by the tap on her shoulder, Whitney turned to find that same freckle-faced young officer who had stopped her and Adam as they had walked home from his mother's cookout when Whitney had just come to town.

"Hey, Jimmy," Adam said. "What's up?"

"I'm afraid there's been some trouble over at Claudia's Attic, Ms. Sheridan."

Whitney clenched her fists at her sides. "What kind of trouble?"

"Somebody broke out the front window. It doesn't look like they got in, but it'd be a good idea if you went over and checked."

"Yes. Certainly."

"Simms," Franki said darkly.

"Pardon?" Officer Jimmy said.

"Never mind." Whitney shook her head at Franki. "It's just speculation. No facts to go on. Let's go."

Because they had walked to the game, Adam and Whitney rode to the shop with Jimmy. It took fewer than five minutes to get there. Another policeman was there keeping an eye on the place until they arrived.

The big plate-glass window in the front of the shop had been smashed. The policemen's flashlights revealed broken glass all over the floor and the merchandise near the window.

Whitney used her key and opened the door. The lights still worked; after what they'd paid the electrician that day, it was a damn good thing, Whitney thought.

"Here's your culprits." Jimmy motioned toward two red bricks lying amid shards of glass on the floor.

"Does this sort of vandalism happen often around here?" Whitney asked after she managed to unclench her jaw.

"No, ma'am," Jimmy said. "This sort of thing just about never happens."

Jimmy went out to his patrol car and brought back a camera. He took a few pictures, made a few notes on his notepad, then suggested that Adam help her secure the window for the night.

Before he could make it back to his car to leave,

Carla sped up in her car. She jumped out and ran up the sidewalk.

"What—Oh, Good God." It didn't take but a moment for her to realize what had happened. "Somebody broke out our window? But why?"

"Can you tell if they took anything?" Whitney asked.

Looking bewildered, Carla peered around the room. "At first glance I'd say no, but I'll know more once I get this mess cleaned up."

They had plenty of help with the cleanup. Duncan and Franki arrived right after Carla, and Janey and Frank showed up a few minutes later, without their children.

While Adam and the men left to get plywood to cover the broken window, the women manned brooms and dustpans and took care of as much of the broken glass as they could. More pieces would likely come to light during daylight hours.

With every sweep of the broom, Whitney's resolve hardened. She had no proof that Bobby Simms was behind this incident or the shop's other recent troubles. But she now knew that he wanted to level the building. To expand his parking lot?

That may have been what he told others years ago, but she didn't buy it. She had passed the bank more than a dozen times since coming to town, and not once had she noticed a need for more parking space. With the front and back lots combined there was more than enough room for customers.

No, there was no need for more parking space. But leveling Claudia's Attic would give the bank exclusive use of the entire block. With nothing to obstruct the view from the east, the bank would be showcased the best it could be, short of leveling the rest of the buildings on Main Street.

Bobby Simms's quest to own this property had little or nothing to do with business, and everything to do with ego. Namely, his.

"We'll just see about that," she muttered.

"Did you say something?" Carla asked.

Whitney stilled her broom and studied Carla. "How much of the work in operating this shop did my aunt do?"

"It's like I said when we first met. She didn't want to be tied down to having to come in every day. In the beginning, when she first opened the shop, she did it all, and she did it alone. But for the past couple of years she left it all up to me."

"Everything?"

"Well, let's see. At tax time she took everything over to the accountant who does our returns. But the records themselves were done by us here at the shop. If you don't mind my asking, why are you asking?"

Whitney pursed her lips and made her decision. "If I keep the store instead of selling it, is there anything you couldn't, or wouldn't want to do? Would you be willing to stay on and run the place?"

"Of course."

"You didn't take much time to think about it."

"What's to think about? I love my job. Frankly, since I realized I can't buy the shop myself I've been worried about having to find other work. You're not going to sell? Really?"

"I'm thinking about it." But, in truth, she figured she had already decided. She would not see all her aunt's hard work bulldozed for extra parking spaces, or to feed Bobby Simms's ego. "But I'm not sure, so let's keep it between us for now." She didn't want word to get back to Bobby until she could deliver it personally.

"Okay," Carla said, eyeing Janey and Franki.

"Ladies," Whitney said. "Your discretion would be appreciated."

Janey crossed her heart and held up three fingers. "Scout's honor."

Franki mimicked turning a key on her lips. "Mum's the word. They'll have to torture me to get it out."

"Uh oh, man work." Janey pointed out the glass-less window.

The men were back. They'd left in Frank's SUV and returned in that and Adam's truck, which had two sheets of plywood in the back, along with various tools.

"Stand back, ladies," Frank announced. "The men have work to do."

Whitney rolled her eyes at Janey. "You live with that?"

"I think it's cute the way she lets him pretend he's in charge." Franki grinned.

Janey grinned right back. "Learned it at my mama's knee."

Whitney laughed. "I'm sure she's proud."

It took an hour to get the plywood up and the shop secure. From what Whitney observed, Adam could easily have finished in half that time if he hadn't had quite so much help. But he probably wouldn't have had as much fun. He plainly enjoyed Frank and Duncan.

They deliberately waited until everyone else was gone before loading the last of his tools and checking the locks one last time. Then they drove to Whitney's house in his truck.

He pulled up in her driveway and killed the engine.

"Are you coming in?" Whitney asked when he merely sat there.

He looked over at her in his dirty softball jersey. "I'd like to. If you want me to."

"Do I sense a problem?"

"Not from me," he said.

"But you think I've got one?"

"I think you've got a problem with Bobby Simms, but I can't prove it."

"Then we're thinking alike," she told him.

"You seem . . . I don't know. Like you're gearing up for battle or something."

"There's nothing I like better than a good battle," she admitted. "But I'm not going to give him a chance to fight back."

"What are you going to do?"

"I'm going to sleep on it."

"With all this on your mind, would you rather sleep alone?"

She reached over and traced a finger along the back of his hand. "I'd rather sleep with you, if you're interested."

"Oh, I'm interested," he said with feeling.

"Then why are we sitting out here?"

They went inside. Together.

They got very little sleep.

And not once did either of them think about Bobby Simms.

It was the next morning at dawn and Adam was getting ready to go home and change clothes before either of them thought about Simms or the shop again.

"What are you going to do this morning?" Adam asked her.

"I'm going to shower, get dressed, eat breakfast,"

"I'll see you in a couple of—"

"Go to the bank."

"—hours."

"Talk to Simms."

"What?"

"I'm going to see Simms this morning. I'm going to turn down his offer for the shop and the house."

Adam caught a militant gleam in her eye. "Are you going to give him a reason?"

"I'm taking them off the market. For now. If and when they go back on the market, I'll be asking more than he offered."

Adam pursed his lips. "He's not going to like that."

"I'm not obliged to do what he likes."

"Are you going to say anything about what happened last night?"

"I would if I could prove he had anything to do with it. But until I do, nothing happened last night at all."

A slow smile spread across Adam's face. "Can I come to the bank with you and watch?"

"Well," she said slowly. "I wouldn't mind, but I'm

afraid he'll think I brought you for backup. He needs to learn that I mean business, and I don't need anybody's help to make my point."

Adam nodded. "You're absolutely right."

"I'm glad you agree."

"But I still wanna watch."

And watch, he did. It didn't take much arranging to get to the bank about the same time as Whitney. All Adam had to do was take a seat in the waiting area outside the glassed-in offices in the back of the bank. Then he only had to sit back and watch the fireworks.

He didn't have long to wait.

Whitney saw him there when she followed the receptionist's directions to the secretary just outside the bank president's office. She pursed her lips and gave him a slight nod.

"Do you have an appointment?" The secretary sat at a dark wood desk neatly appointed with brass and greenery. She was in her late fifties, her hair and dress suit of the latest style.

"No. I need about two minutes of his time." She could see Bobby beyond the glass wall behind the secretary's desk. He was on the phone, facing the other way, leaning back, looking out the window at a maple tree planted next to the building.

"Just tell him Whitney Sheridan is here to talk about the offers he's made recently on some real estate."

"Oh, yes, certainly, Ms. Sheridan."

The secretary went into Bobby's office. He put his hand over the mouthpiece. She spoke to him, gesturing toward Whitney.

Bobby glanced her way, and the look that came

across his face could only be called smug. He was certain that he had her. He motioned for her to enter his office.

She and the secretary passed each other at the doorway.

"I'll just close this to give the two of you some privacy."

"There's no need on my account."

The secretary paused, then, with a nod, left the door open.

Bobby held up a finger as he wrapped up his phone call. "That's right. I said so, didn't I? Come on in tomorrow, and we'll have the papers ready for you. Yeah, good talking to you, too, Marv. See you tomorrow."

He hung up and rose to face her fully. "Good morning, Whitney." He smiled. "To what do I owe the honor? Wait, don't tell me. Let me guess. You've come to talk about selling your aunt's shop. Please, have a seat."

"That's okay," she said, declining. "I won't be here long enough. I just wanted to let you know that I've changed my mind about selling the shop."

His face with comically blank. "Changed your mind? What do you mean?"

"I mean I'm not selling it. I wanted to let you know right away so you wouldn't count on getting your hands on that particular corner of the block any time soon."

"Not . . . not selling? I don't understand. I would have thought that after all the trouble you've had lately—I even heard you had vandals last night. Most people would want to get rid of property that was so much trouble."

"I'm not most people, Mr. Simms."

"Come on, it's Bobby, Whitney."

"Mr. Simms and Ms. Sheridan will do until I stop thinking you might have had something to do with all these troubles the shop has had recently."

"Me?" He placed a hand on his chest in innocence. "You think I had something to do with it?"

"It doesn't really matter what I think. It's what I can prove. And even that's irrelevant. I simply don't want to sell the property. But Bobby?"

"Yes?" He looked confused, dazed.

"If anything else happens to that shop, you and I are going to have a serious problem."

He looked thunderstruck. "Is that a threat?"

"No, Bobby, that's a promise. Claudia's Attic isn't going away, and neither am I."

Whitney spun on one heel and marched out his door. She didn't even look over at Adam, who stood leaning against the wall, a cat-ate-the-canary grin on his face.

"I'm a business owner."

Whitney stood in her living room and stared at Adam in shock. When she'd left the bank, he had been right behind her. They hadn't spoken during the five-minute walk home. At least not about the subject at hand.

"You make it sound like the end of the world," Adam said, a little worried about the dazed look on her face.

"It's just . . . so . . . bizarre," she said. "I turned down the only viable offer I'm likely to get for Claudia's Attic and announced to the local Chamber of

Commerce president that I intend to retain ownership."

She looked around the room without really seeing anything and shook her head.

"You can always sell it later to someone else."

"No," she said faintly. "Today I made a commitment to the community. I'm a business owner. I employ three local citizens, do business with a local accountant, plumber, electrician. My sales generate tax revenue for the city and county. The shop brings business in from out of town, out of state, which means I help generate tourism dollars. Good God, what have I done?"

Adam couldn't have been more delighted. If it was true. If she meant to make a go of it.

He grabbed her by the shoulders and raised her to her tiptoes. "I don't know, but I sure like it." He kissed her with all the enthusiasm he was feeling. "I love you," he murmured against her lips. And wasn't even surprised to realize he meant it.

But he didn't want her to feel as if she had to repeat the words, or worse, explain why she couldn't return them. So he stepped away, brushed a light kiss on her cheek.

"I've got to get to work. The lady who lives here won't like me getting behind on my work."

"Yeah." Whitney felt a sudden need for air, and for something to lean against before her knees gave out. "I've heard that about her."

He loved her?

He couldn't have meant it.

Chapter Thirteen

Thursday afternoon, while Whitney was gone to the grocery store, Adam got his dad to come over and help him move the furniture out of the guest room so he could repaint it.

"How about I give you a hand with these boxes in the closet?" his dad asked.

"Thanks, but I'll get those. I'm already in enough trouble with Mom for getting you to do this much lifting."

"Your mother worries too much."

"Because she loves you," Adam said.

"Seems to me maybe there's somebody loving you these days." His dad wiggled his eyebrows. "Am I right?"

"Now, Dad, a gentleman never kisses and tells."

"That's true, son. I guess I taught you that myself, so I can't blame you for sticking to it. Here. Let me get this box." He stepped into the closet and stooped to get a white cardboard file box.

"That's exactly the kind of lifting Mom didn't want you doing," Adam protested.

"What? I can lift a bed and a dresser, and not a dinky little box? What does she think's gonna happen to—*argh!*" With the box barely six inches off the floor, he dropped it.

"Dad! Are you all right?"

"Yeah, yeah, dammit. *This* is what she figured would happen. I'd throw my damn back out."

"You didn't. Tell me you didn't." The last time his dad threw his back out he was crippled up and in pain for weeks. "Can you stand up?"

"I can stand. I didn't throw it out like last time."

"Are you sure?"

"I'm sure." He backed out of the closet and straightened slowly. "There. See? Nothing to it."

Adam frowned. "No more lifting."

"Now you sound like your mother. I tell you, son, getting old is a bitch. If it ain't one thing, it's another. Bad back, hair loss, arthritis, false teeth."

"Sure sounds like a bitch," Adam said, sympathizing.

"It's not for wimps, that's for sure." He looked back into the closet. "I'm afraid I've made a mess of it."

Adam glanced past his father to find the box on its side, papers spilling out onto the floor.

"That's nothing," he said. "I'll get it later. In fact, I can get all the rest of this later. We got the big stuff, the stuff I needed your help with. Why don't I take you home?"

"Son." Teddy placed a hand on Adam's shoulder. "There's such a thing as too much sympathy and concern."

Adam grimaced. "Sorry."

"There'll come a time when you'll probably have to take care of me, but that day's still a good many years off, praise the Lord. I drove over here; I can drive myself home. There's nothing wrong with my back that a heating pad won't take care of."

"And maybe a trip to the nearest chiropractor?" Adam asked.

"Maybe." Teddy's smile was slow and reluctant.

Adam saw his father off, and worried about him as he went back upstairs. Then he shook it off. This was his father, after all. The man who had always been larger than life to Adam. The man who could do anything, who knew everything. He was the strongest, smartest man alive. If that was a young boy's view of his father, so be it.

Adam knew his father was aging, but dwelling on it would help nothing.

He returned to the guest room and went to the closet. There he knelt, righted the box, and started returning the papers to their home.

And stopped dead in the act. The words on the top page in his hand leaped out at him as if magnified.

"What?" He read them again. "Oh, shit. Oh, shit."

There was no way in hell Whitney knew about these papers. No way. And he wished to God he didn't, either. He didn't want this knowledge, because it meant he had to tell her, or at the least, show her the papers.

It was going to kill her. It was going to break her heart and rip out her guts. And he had to be the one to tell her, because this was not something he could withhold from her. If she found out the truth on her own, then realized he'd already known and not told her, she would skewer him with the nearest sharp instrument, and he would deserve it.

But how did a man tell a woman something that

was going to change the very foundation of her world, of who she thought she was?

There was no place to sleep that night at Whitney's except the narrow bed in the sewing room, where they'd slept that first night they'd spent together. The mattress and box springs from the guest room were standing on end in the hall, waiting for the texture to dry overnight on the walls so Adam could paint tomorrow.

The other full-sized bed was Miz Henderson's. Adam didn't even suggest they spend the night in that bed. As far as he could tell, Whitney still wasn't ready to disturb that room.

"We could always drag the guest bed downstairs to the living room floor," Whitney suggested.

"Or we could sleep real close together on that skinny bed of yours."

"I'm sorry I can't . . . Aunt Claudia's room. I just . . ."

Adam cupped her cheeks and kissed the tip of her nose. "It's all right. I understand. You're not ready to tear that room apart yet. That's okay."

It never crossed either's mind that they could spend the night apart. From that Thursday night when she'd walked home in such high spirits, as it were, from Bridge Thursday, they had spent every night together.

"Let's go to bed." He led her to the room with the narrow bed. Slowly he undressed her, then she him. It seemed to Whitney that Adam was more gentle than usual with her. He'd never been what she considered rough. Aggressive, yes, but not rough.

Now he was more tender than he had been. Slower. Slow enough to drive a woman up and over the edge long before he joined his body to hers and took her up again.

They slept close together in that narrow bed, wrapped in each other's arms. And she wondered, as his breath warmed her cheek, if she had already fallen in love with him.

Did she love him? The question nagged at her the next day until she could think of nothing else. Between the idea that she might be in love, and the reminder that she now owned a local business, Whitney was as close to terrified as she had ever been.

Of course, owning Claudia's Attic didn't mean she had to live in Washita. Carla had been running the shop for years; she could continue doing so. Between the phone, fax, e-mail, and UPS, they could handle whatever came up without Whitney needing to be in Washita.

But if she never came to town, she would never get to see Carla, or Janey, or dear, dear Miss Ella. She wouldn't get to sit out on a shady patio with three older women one Thursday each month and sip potent Mexican beer and puff on a nasty cigar. No more lemonade and oatmeal cookies from Betty. No more listening to Franki and Ada bicker down at the café. No more scruffy cat sneaking up to her back porch for food.

No more Adam.

God help her, she had not only fallen in love with him, but with half the damn town. How had this happened?

A sense of panic rose in her throat. Going home to New York was going to be like ripping out her heart. The longer she stayed in Texas, the worse it was going to be, the closer she would feel to everyone, the more she would love Adam, the more it was going to hurt.

The panic in her throat began to flutter like a trapped bird.

She should leave now. Today. Before she got herself in any deeper. Before she was so tied to this town and these people—and one man in particular—that leaving would kill her.

But she couldn't leave today. She couldn't pack her bags and walk out the door without a backward look.

Why not? That's how you came here, isn't it?

It wasn't the same, and she knew it.

Her boss would be glad if she went home early. Carla would handle the shop. Adam could certainly finish the work on the house without her being underfoot all day. The Realtor could sell the house without Whitney's presence.

Her only excuse for staying this long had been to oversee Adam's work on the house. A flimsy excuse at best. She'd never seen such fine carpentry work. He had magical hands. So capable. So strong. So tender. Always knowing the precise place to touch, with just the right amount of pressure to bring her the utmost pleasure.

None of which had anything to do with working on her damn house, and everything to do with the ache in her heart and the strangling sensation of terror in her throat.

This would not do. It was time, past time, to pack and go home.

But she couldn't go today. She needed one more night. One last night in his arms.

How could she spend the night with him and not tell him she was leaving?

It would be all right, she decided. She didn't live here, after all. Texas wasn't her home. Everyone knew that. Adam certainly knew it. He'd known from the beginning that she would soon be leaving. Why should he care if it was a little sooner than planned?

He wouldn't care. She was almost sure of it. He would be able to have his life back, work for other customers, see other women.

Tonight he wanted to take her to a town called Canadian, the county seat, for Mexican food. He'd offered to take her somewhere fancier, but he figured he couldn't compete with New York's fancy restaurants. But New York, he assured her, could not compete with authentic Tex-Mex.

Adam was probably right about the local Tex-Mex food, but Whitney barely tasted the cheese-covered enchiladas, the refried beans, the rice. She was too filled with despair at the thought of leaving.

Each hour she spent with Adam increased her realization that leaving was the best, the only thing she could do. Staying would only prolong her pain.

"You all right?"

Whitney blinked and focused on Adam, across the dimly lit table from her. "I'm fine."

"You seem distracted."

"Come to think of it," she realized aloud, "so do you." He'd been at least as quiet as she since leaving the house, and that wasn't like the man she had come to know. "Is something wrong?"

"Nope." Was there a little too much effort at cheerfulness behind that word? "Not a thing."

"Oh, good."

"How's the food?"

"You were right." She smiled. "It's great."

As far as stilted conversations went, Whitney thought, this one might possibly take the grand prize.

The tiny flame on the fat candle on their table flickered, casting light and shadow across Adam's face, highlighting his strong cheekbones, the blade of his nose, the shape of his lips. Dancing in his eyes, turning the blue to fire.

One more night, Whitney thought. She had this one final night with him, and then she would leave.

She wouldn't run, wouldn't sneak away. In the morning she would tell him it was time for her to go, and she would pack her bags and be off.

She could lie and tell him there was some emergency at work that only she could handle.

That would be a good excuse, but she couldn't do it. She could not end their relationship on a lie.

"Are you sure you're all right?" Adam asked her again while they waited on the check. "You look a little sad."

The smile she gave him did, indeed, feel sad to her. "I guess I was just thinking about Aunt Claudia."

"Missing her?"

"I guess."

The waitress arrived with the check.

* * *

During the drive home from Canadian Adam tried to think of what to say to her, how to tell her about the papers he found.

He was also worried about whatever it was that was bothering her. She could deny that she was bothered by something, but he knew better. He could see some sort of deep conflict in her eyes.

Yet, with the secret he was withholding, it didn't seem fair to badger her to tell him what was wrong.

They arrived back at her house with each of them still locked in their own private thoughts.

For the first time since they had become intimate, they made love only once. The lovemaking was long and slow and filled with feelings that neither was willing to admit.

The next morning Whitney surprised them both by cooking breakfast, something she had never done for him.

"Hey, wow. What's the occasion?" Adam wondered aloud.

"I don't know." She cracked open one egg and reached for another. "How about . . . to celebrate my not selling the shop to Bobby Simms."

Adam raised the glass of orange juice she'd poured for him. "I'll drink to that."

"Your mother won't be upset, will she?"

"That you didn't sell to Simms?"

"That you ate breakfast before you came home this morning," she corrected with another crack of egg against bowl.

"I'll just tell her a generous woman took pity on me and fed my starving soul."

Whitney pursed her lips. "This is your mother, rolling her eyes." She rolled her eyes.

Adam laughed. "She's not going to ask or say anything. I eat at her table because she likes me to. It doesn't mean I owe her any explanations."

Whitney shook her head and cracked a final egg into the bowl. "I guess if I was really worried about it I wouldn't be fixing your breakfast."

"There is that." He chuckled.

If I wasn't desperate for one more hour with you, Whitney thought, *one more minute, I wouldn't take the chance on making you vulnerable to your mother's concern.*

But she was, so she did. And when he left thirty minutes later, she kissed him good-bye and said nothing about leaving for New York, thereby proving her total and complete cowardice.

Maybe she wouldn't leave today, Whitney thought frantically. Maybe she would wait until tomorrow. That would be better, wouldn't it? Tomorrow instead of today?

Oh, God. She pressed the heels of her hands hard against her temples. She was losing her mind. She was a normal, intelligent, logical person, and she was acting like a blithering idiot.

Because she felt like a blithering idiot.

She had to calm down, regain her perspective. Fresh air. Maybe that would help. She stepped out onto the back porch, for privacy. She wasn't interested in talking to anyone until she got her head on straight again.

Scruffy was there, on the porch, eating from the dish Adam had brought him. This was the first time the cat had not run off to hide behind the garage when Whitney came out.

"Hey, boy."

He looked up at her, blinked his eyes slowly, then settled back down to his eating, completely uninterested in her presence.

She had gone from being too scary to be around, to a good food source, to not important enough to notice.

"Going to take me for granted now, are you?"

He just kept eating.

She walked past him and sat on the top step, staring out across the yard toward the tree-lined creek beyond the field behind the yard.

A bee was buzzing in and out of the marigolds along the west fence. Out on the street a car went by, its radio blasting rap music. Directly behind her, Scruffy crunched his dry cat food.

Then the crunching stopped, and a low humming replaced it. Whitney looked over her shoulder to investigate, only then realizing the cat was purring.

Whitney smiled.

The cat further amazed and delighted her by walking up and rubbing himself from head to toe along her side.

"Well, well," she said. "I guess this means you like me?" A lump rose in her throat. This was the first animal to accept her, the first one she'd accepted, since childhood. Only now did she realize how totally empty her life had become.

Wasn't it odd that she thought she could actually feel one of those rooms Adam mentioned in her heart open up to let in a scruffy stray cat.

* * *

Whitney sat on the porch and petted the cat until Scruffy darted off to investigate a rustling in the grass near the back fence.

Instead of going back into the house, Whitney walked around the side and kept walking until she found herself standing before the nursing home. If she decided to leave town, she couldn't go without finishing the book she and Miss Ella were reading.

She pulled open the door and went inside.

"Is she awake?" she asked Edna.

"She was a few minutes ago when I gave her her meds. She was wondering if you'd be here today. She'll be glad to see you."

When Whitney stepped into Miss Ella's room a minute later, the elderly woman turned and smiled; her entire face brightened.

It was humbling, Whitney thought, to mean that much to someone, that a simple visit could please and excite that person so much.

Even as Whitney felt Miss Ella's presence in another of those rooms in her heart, she cursed Adam for pushing her to let people in. How was she ever supposed to leave?

God help her, how?

No answer came from on high to her question. She set it aside for now and concentrated on Miss Ella and the thriller they were reading. They would finish it today.

Whitney and Miss Ella did not finish their thriller that day. Miss Ella fell asleep with two chapters to go.

"It's the meds," Edna said. "She'll probably be out for an hour or more. If you want to come back . . ."

"I don't know if I'll make it back today or not," Whitney told the head nurse. In truth she wasn't sure she would make it back at all. The thought left her feeling empty and shaken. "Tell her . . . tell her I said good-bye."

"I'll do that."

Whitney went home. Adam was finished and gone for the day. She went inside and climbed the stairs to her room.

Aunt Claudia's journal caught her eye. The last thing Whitney had read had been about Aunt Claudia's weekend with Harry. She picked it up and began to read.

September 20:

God damn this war and whoever started it, who-ever keeps it going. They've killed him. Killed my Harry. How am I supposed to exist without his love, knowing he'll never return to me?

They say it happened two weeks ago. How have I lived this long? How could I not have known?

Nothing else was written for that day, and the next page was blank. But a worn letter on lined white paper turning yellow with age fell out.

My darling Claudia,

If you're reading this, then I am dead. I'm sorry. I tried my best to stay alive so I could come back to you. You must know that the one weekend we shared to-gether was the best time of my life. I love you so much.

I wanted so much for us. I wanted to take you

home to meet my mother. It's been just her and me
since Daddy died when I was ten, so we're pretty close,
Mama and me. She would have loved you. She
wouldn't have cared about our age difference any
more than I do.

Don't weep for me, Claudia. My pain and trials
are over. Go out and live your life. Live enough for
both of us and know that I am always with you.

                                    I love you forever,
                                    Harry

With tears streaming down her cheeks, Whitney
carefully refolded the worn letter and returned it to
the journal. In a careless motion, Whitney thumbed
the remaining pages. Words leaped out at her, words
like *pregnant* and *cancer* and *adopt.*

Shocked, Whitney turned back and read each
page, searching for a logical reason for such words
to appear in her aunt's journal.

The story that unfolded was one Whitney would
never have believed had it not been written in Aunt
Claudia's own handwriting.

She'd been pregnant. Aunt Claudia's weekend at
the motel had left her carrying Harry's child, but
she hadn't learned of her pregnancy until after re-
ceiving word of Harry's death.

Whitney had to read the information three times
for it to sink in. Aunt Claudia had been pregnant.

Whitney searched her memory for any hint from
her parents or Aunt Claudia that there had been a
baby, but she came up blank. Poor Aunt Claudia.
She must have miscarried, or given the baby up for
adoption. Whitney couldn't believe her aunt would

have had an abortion. Back then such a thing was even less acceptable than it was in this day and age.

Pregnant and unmarried. Whitney remembered that her grandfather, the father of her mother and Aunt Claudia, had been a strict Southern Baptist. Aunt Claudia must have been terrified to tell him. If she'd told him.

Whitney returned to the journal and learned that if being single and pregnant and learning the father of her child was dead was not enough of a trauma, Aunt Claudia found out, when she was barely three months pregnant, that she had breast cancer.

"Oh my God." Why had no one told her? Having breast cancer in a woman's family was a little on the important side. She should have been told, dammit.

Then it hit home. This was not about Whitney. It was about Aunt Claudia. Pregnant, unmarried, Harry was dead, and now breast cancer.

And—dear God—Aunt Claudia had refused treatment for fear of harming the baby she carried. She had been willing to trade her life for that of her child.

But she'd obviously survived, so what had happened?

Back then, more than thirty years ago, treatment options had been few. Radical mastectomies, if Whitney recalled correctly, had been the norm back then. Followed by radiation and chemotherapy, and more often than not—much more often—followed by death in a matter of some months to a few years.

The baby grows so fast within me, I feel it getting larger by the day, and I am reaffirmed in my decision to decline treatment.

Then, too, the cancer grows. The lump is larger. Yet that is the only indication I have that something is wrong, for I do not feel ill. In truth, I have never felt better. I feel new life growing in me, and it seems as if nothing can go wrong. Am I a fool? I think not. Even if it costs my life, I pray that Harry's baby has a chance in this world. If I can assure that part of him, and part of me, lives on, I will be satisfied.

What Whitney read in the journal both chilled and fired her with inspiration. She wanted to reach out through time and offer her strength and support to the aunt she'd only thought she'd known.

"Aunt Claudia, why didn't you ever say anything about this?"

But, of course, Whitney had been only a child the last time the two of them were truly close. By the time she'd been old enough to understand and appreciate what her aunt had gone through, Whitney had already put distance between them. Their visits in the years since had been few, brief, and far between. Confidences had not been invited.

Whitney touched the page before her with trembling fingers. "I'm so sorry, Aunt Claudia. So, so sorry. For so many things."

She didn't want to read any further. Aunt Claudia would survive the breast cancer, but the baby . . .

She said yes. My sister, God bless her, will raise my child as her own.

Whitney's world slammed to a halt and tilted on its axis.

The cancer is consuming me now, I can feel it. I am terrified for my baby. She's due any day. Please, God, keep her safe from this dread disease. My life for hers, if it please You, oh Lord.

The baby was a girl, and was adopted by Karen and Steven Sheridan, Claudia Henderson's sister and brother-in-law, who could not have children of their own.

Whitney pressed her fingers over her mouth and blinked to clear her vision. But no matter how many times she blinked, the world as she had always known it would not come aright.

They let me name her. I call her Whitney.

Chapter Fourteen

The words blurred before her eyes. She stopped short of rubbing them to clear her vision. She wasn't sure she wanted to read any more.

Her parents weren't her parents? Her aunt wasn't her aunt?

She went from sympathy and confusion to rage in an instant. They lied to her. For her entire life, they had lied to her. All of them. Even her grandfather.

How could they have done that?

Furious, she threw the journal at the nearest wall with a satisfying *thunk*.

Then, with a choking cry, she leapt off the bed and rescued the book from the floor.

"I'm sorry." She held it to her breast and wrapped her arms around it, stroking it with one hand. "I'm sorry."

How could she hate them, or even be angry, when all any of them had wanted was what was best for her?

Frantic now, she tore open the journal and continued to read.

After she was born, after Karen and Steven Sheridan adopted her, Claudia had decided, after much urging by her sister Karen and her father, to seek treatment for her breast cancer.

Whitney skipped over the pages detailing the grueling process of being stripped of her breast, her dignity, what little health she'd had left. One entire journal dealt with surviving from one day to the next, not knowing whether to hope or despair. Not knowing what to hope for, what to despair of.

Then, gradually, her health began to return. Her doctors were hopeful that she might beat the cancer.

And now came the pain of visiting her own daughter and not being able to claim her.

It's all right. I tell myself it must be all right. There is no way, during these past many months since her birth, that I could have cared for my darling Whitney. The sad truth is, I didn't have the strength. Even now, as healthy as I feel, I am still weak. I doubt I would be able to keep up with an active toddler. I can't even pick her up and hold her now, she's grown so much.

The light in the room waned. Irritated at having to squint, Whitney turned on the lamp and reached for the next journal. They entries were not as frequent now. Sometimes several months would pass without a notation.

Then came the day when the doctors declared her, at least for the time being, cancer-free.

I have prayed and worried and thought and rethought, and I have finally made up my mind. It is time for me to leave. I cannot continue to live in the same town with Whitney and not have her with me, not be able to claim her.

Karen and Steve are so good with her, they love her so much. And she adores them. At three years old, she knows no other parents. To her I am Aunt Claudia. That is how it must be.

Who would have thought I would live this long? Certainly not I. But there is no guarantee the cancer won't come back tomorrow or the next day. Or next month, or next year.

I'm going to Texas. Harry's mother is all alone since he was killed. She doesn't know he fathered a child. I hope she is a generous soul and will understand why I did what I thought best for Whitney. Surely a librarian is a reasonable person. Harry said his mother was the town librarian in a place called Washita, Texas. That is where I'm going. Perhaps they need a teacher there.

A tiny cry escaped Whitney's throat. Miss Ella? Miss Ella was . . . her grandmother?

"Oh, God."

"Whitney?"

With a gasp, Whitney whirled toward the door. "Adam. You scared the . . ." Her words trailed off.

Adam had gone suddenly pale. His troubled gaze darted from her face to the journal and back. And then she got it.

"You knew!" Here, then, was someone she could be angry with. "You knew she was my mother and you never said a word? Not a *word*?"

"Whitney, I—"

"How *dare* you!"

"Whitney, I was trying to find the right way—"

"How did you find out? How long have you known?"

Frustrated, Adam ran a hand through his hair. "A box of papers fell over. I was picking them up and ran across a copy of . . . your . . . adoption papers. Friday."

"Where are they?" she demanded.

"They were in the guest-room closet. I put them back in the box and set it in Miz Henderson's bedroom."

With fire in her eyes, she shoved him aside and marched out the door. "Show me."

Adam followed her to her aunt's—to the master bedroom—and showed her the box his father had dropped.

Whitney fell to her knees and grabbed the paperwork on top. Adoption papers. It was all there, in black and white, duly recorded by the state of Georgia.

"My mother," she whispered, still in shock. "She was my mother. And you didn't tell me."

"Christ, what do you want from me? I didn't know until yesterday. I'm sorry. I should have told you immediately, but I didn't. I couldn't. I knew it would upset you."

"Well, you figured that right." Her whisper was gone. She was very nearly shouting now. "It upset me."

She pushed herself to her feet and shoved past him. In her bedroom she pulled her suitcase from the closet and started throwing clothes into it.

"What are you doing?" Adam demanded.

"What's it look like?"

"It looks," he said tersely, "like you're running away."

"Oh, that's great. Running away. I suppose you think I should stick around and see just how many more ways a person can be torn apart."

"I think you should take it easy, and not make any rash decisions."

"Going home, where I belong, is not a rash decision. I should have gone home the day after I got here. You said so yourself at the time, if you'll remember."

"And you said you wanted to oversee the work on the house."

"Well, I've seen. You do fine. I don't need to baby-sit you."

"I don't want you to baby-sit me. Dammit, I want you to love me."

"Oh, well, pardon the hell out of me." She threw one hand in the air. "I've got a man who wants me to love him, a grandmother I've just now learned of who is dying by inches before my eyes every day."

"What? A grandmother? Who?"

"Miss Ella," she snapped. "Mrs. Ella Fields, who taught me at the age of five to enjoy reading, and I just found out a few minutes ago that she's my father's mother."

"Good God." Adam shook his head. "Then her son—what was his name?"

"Harry. My father. Harry Fields. He was killed in Viet Nam before he ever knew about me."

"My God, your father is buried here."

"I can't deal with that now. I'm having enough trouble with the fact that the man I thought all my life was my father was really my uncle, and my mother was my aunt, and my aunt was my mother."

"Whit—"

"I've got a mother who gave me away, no matter the reasons. A cat that has to be fed."

Adding insult to injury, her nose started to run, which made her realize she was crying. And that pissed her off. She grabbed a tissue, blew her nose, then tossed the tissue in the wastebasket.

"Now I have to worry if Bobby Simms will think up some new scheme to get his hands on the shop, or if Avis's granddaughter is going to end up pregnant, or if Janey's son will recover from his knee injury soon enough to play ball again before the season ends, of if your mother will take the blue ribbon at the county fair this year with her green-tomato relish or will that old biddy from over in the next town beat her out again. And you think I don't love you?"

"Do you?" he asked, his breath halting in his lungs. "Do you love me, Whitney?"

"It's too much," she cried. "It's too much. I can't deal with all these feelings, all these worries. All of this caring."

"There's nothing wrong with caring for other people," he said.

"I'm going home, where all I have to worry about is if we can get on the air fast enough with the news that the world is about to end before the world actually ends. *That* I can deal with. But love, and caring? One way or another, every person I've ever loved has abandoned me, either by choice or otherwise. Now I learn my own mother abandoned me, gave me away. And you want me to what, open my heart to you, to all these other people, to deliberately set myself up for more of the same?"

"It sounds to me as if it's too late to avoid it," he told her.

"I don't know where you got the idea that I'm strong enough to be ripped to pieces this way, but I'm not. I'm just . . . not."

"But you're strong enough to just walk out?" Adam cried. "Without a word to anyone? Even Miss Ella? What about your business? Can you just walk out on all of that?"

A muscle in her jaw ticked. She stared at him a moment, then slammed her suitcase shut. "Yes," she hissed.

Adam stood, stunned, and watched her grab her purse and haul her suitcase out the bedroom door.

"Whit, you can't just leave like this." He darted out into the hall after her.

"Oh, can't I?"

"No, you can't." He raced down the stairs behind her.

"You just stand back and watch me."

"Stand back?" He jumped around her and blocked her exit out the back door to where her car sat in front of the garage. "You expect me to stand back and let you walk out the damn door, out of my life, without a word? Dammit, Whitney, I love you, don't you know that?"

Whitney stopped just short of ramming into him. She stared at him warily. "You said that once before."

"And you said upstairs that you loved me."

"I did not. Why on earth would I say something like that?"

"You did say it, or meant it, because it's true. A woman doesn't give herself to a man the way you do me if you don't have some pretty damn deep feelings for him."

"A lot you know. Get out of my way."

She was, Adam had to admit, pretty damned convincing. Could he have read her wrong? There was an ache in his chest that told him not to let her go.

"You can't expect me to just step aside," he protested.

"I don't know why not." She hitched her purse onto her shoulder and dug out her car keys one-handed, never letting go of her suitcase with the other hand. "We both knew I'd be going home soon anyway. Now or a couple of weeks from now. What's the difference?"

How was he supposed to argue against that? "Maybe the difference is in the way you're leaving. Angry, without saying good-bye to anyone. Just walking out because feelings get a little intense and life isn't exactly what you thought it was."

"Not exactly—?" She made a squealing noise that alarmed him. "I find out my entire life has been a lie, and I'm supposed to, what, shrug my shoulders and carry on as if nothing has changed?"

"Of course not." He cupped her shoulders to keep her from getting past him. "You need to take your time and think through it all, decide how it affects you. Figure out how you feel about it."

"I'll tell you how I feel," she ground out. "I feel lied to and betrayed, by every member of my family. The people who were supposed to love me the most, look after me, take care of me. Every single one of them lied to me my entire life. And that makes me angry, and it *hurts*, Adam. It hurts so bad I can barely breathe. I have to get out of here. Let me go. If you care anything at all about me, please let me go, Adam."

Adam gripped her shoulders tightly. He wanted

most in the world to pull her close and never let her
go. But she was right. They'd both known from the
beginning that she would leave, that there was no
chance for them to build anything lasting.

If he'd forgotten that, it wasn't her fault. He
shouldn't be blaming her, heaping more heartache
on her when it was so obvious to him that she was
tearing herself apart over the new facts of her life.

"They loved you," he told her. "Remember that,
will you, while you're sorting it all out? I don't know
the why of any of it. I imagine you've got that in
those journals. But I'd stake my life that Claudia
Henderson only did what she did out of love for you.
I'd bet the same was true of your parents."

Whitney closed her eyes, afraid she would end up
in a blubbering puddle at his feet if she didn't get
out that door in the next instant.

"Let me go, Adam."

It took every ounce of strength Adam had to release her shoulders and step aside.

Yes, he'd known she would soon leave, that there
was no future for the two of them together. He just
hadn't known it would feel as if his guts were being
ripped out.

Whitney was disoriented, stepping out of the
house into the darkness. She'd forgotten that she'd
had to turn on the lamp to read the journals.

She half expected Adam to follow her outside.
Maybe even hoped he would?

No. Surely not. She surely was not that pathetic.
But maybe she was that hopeless.

Something brushed against her leg, making her drop her suitcase as she jumped back and shrieked.

Inside the house, Adam heard the commotion and leapt to the window to look out. It took everything he had not to run to the door and rush to her aid.

But it was only the cat, now scared off by all the racket Whitney made when she screamed and dropped her luggage. Whitney didn't need his help. She didn't need or want anyone messing up her private, solitary, independent life. Didn't want love or friendship or anything like that messing up her life.

Outside on the porch Whitney let out a shaky curse. "It would have served you right if I'd stepped on you, you mangy cat, sneaking up on a person that way."

She was angry. Damn cat could have caused her to fall down the stairs and break her neck.

So why did she feel like sitting down and crying her eyes out? Dammit, she'd cried more in the past two weeks than in the past five years.

She picked up the suitcase, hitched her purse higher on her shoulder, and started down the stairs. At the car, she took one final look around the dark backyard. She imagined she could see a pair of gleaming yellow eyes peering at her from beneath the shrubbery along the garage.

"Good-bye, Scruffy Boy." She glanced at the house. "Good-bye, Adam Burkett."

She tried. Whitney seriously tried to drive straight out of town without looking back. That was her intention when she backed out of the driveway. But rather than drive the length of Main and keep going, she turned south at the east end of the park and pulled up in the small parking lot in front of Shady Oaks Nursing Home.

It was too late to visit. She knew that. What would she say, anyway? Hi, Grandma?

But she couldn't simply drive out of town without a word. She climbed out of the car and went inside. The nurse at the front desk was unfamiliar to her.

"May I help you?" the nurse asked.

"Is Miss Ella still awake?"

"No, ma'am. It's past visiting hours anyway. I'm sorry."

Whitney tried to smile but wasn't sure how well she pulled it off. "So am I. I wonder if I could leave her a note? Someone might need to read it to her tomorrow when she wakes up."

"We could do that," the nurse said.

Whitney pulled a reporter's notepad and pen from her purse.

Dear Miss Ella, I'm sorry to have to leave town without saying good-bye to you personally. I have enjoyed and valued our time together. Please take care of yourself. If it's all right with you, I'd like to come back and see you someday. All my best, Whitney.

P.S. Any girl would be proud to call you Grandmother.

"Would you see that she gets this tomorrow?"

"Certainly."

"It's very important. She's expecting me to be here, and I won't be able to."

"I'll see that she gets your message."

That was as much as Whitney could hope for under the circumstances.

God, she hadn't realized how much it was going to hurt to leave knowing that the sad truth was that she would in all likelihood never see Miss Ella again.

She didn't even try to say good-bye to anyone else in town. She simply drove.

Three hours later she was checking into a motel in Amarillo because there were no flights out that late at night.

Okay, she told herself. It would be okay. She could stand to be in Texas one more night. Tomorrow, she would be home where she belonged. Where she didn't have to have her heart wrenched by every other person she ran into.

Who could live like this? With all these emotions boiling away inside?

Her mother. Aunt Claudia was her mother.

Her mother wasn't her mother, but her aunt.

Her father was her uncle. Her real father had died before she was born.

And if she thought about any of it for one more minute she would go stark raving mad.

Morning would not come soon enough.

Chapter Fifteen

If she didn't exactly slip back into the rhythm of the WNN control room like a hand in a glove, it was close enough to fool everyone around her, Whitney thought. No one else seemed to notice that she had to ask people to repeat themselves way too often. If they knew she was hearing a hammer or electric saw, or maybe the crack of a bat meeting a ball, or the meow of a cat, they would likely have her committed.

Hell, she should commit herself.

She felt as if she was slightly out of step with the rest of the world. Things were moving so fast around her, and she had trouble keeping up.

"You must have had a great trip, Whitney. You look really rested."

Whitney couldn't for the life of her remember the young woman's name who made that idiotic comment. The girl had been hired the week before Whitney had gone to Texas.

"Thanks," she said. "Funerals do that to me."

"Ouch," someone muttered from behind Whitney.

The girl who'd made the comment blanched. "I'm so sorry. I didn't know. I—"

"No," Whitney said with a sigh. "I'm sorry, There was no call for me to be rude. Let's just forget it, okay?"

The girl gulped. "Okay. Sure. Fine. Uh, can I get you a cup of coffee?"

Whitney didn't want any coffee, but the girl looked like she would cry if Whitney said no. "That'd be great. Black, no sugar. Thanks."

Didn't want any coffee? She really was out of step with the world, Whitney thought. At least, with her own world, pre-Texas.

Mary. That was the girl's name.

Shit. Her mind must have turned to mush while she'd been in Texas if she couldn't remember a name like Mary.

Mary brought her a cup of hot black coffee. Whitney thanked her, then, because it was in her hand, took a sip.

It was horrid. She used to drink it by the gallon, and now could barely stand it.

Frustrated, she tossed it in the trash. How many more ways had she changed since Texas?

What little coffee she had sipped now burned like acid in the pit of her stomach. She reached automatically into her pocket . . . and found it empty. She had actually come to work without antacids? She must be losing her mind.

A frantic search through her purse came up with half a roll of tablets. She thumbed one loose and popped it into her mouth. It was the first one she'd needed in well over a week.

Texas may have messed with her mind and destroyed her heart, but the rest of her body had done well.

* * *

Back in Texas, Adam was not doing well. He couldn't sleep, wouldn't eat, and looked, according to his mother, as if he'd just run over his own dog.

"You're acting like you've given up on her," his dad said with disgust.

"What's to give up on?" Adam said with equal disgust. "She's gone, and that's that."

"Well," his mother said as she passed the bowl of mashed potatoes his way. "It's not as if you don't have any practice at watching women whisk into town, steal your affections, then leave you flat. This one's no better than the last."

"What are you saying?" Adam cried, appalled. "You think Whitney's like Monica?"

"The similarities are obvious. Pass the butter, please, dear."

Her husband passed her the butter.

"What similarities?" Adam demanded. But he'd been thinking the same thing himself not long ago.

"Here's the gravy. They're both from a big city." she said.

"A Pinto and a Corvette both came out of Detroit, too, but that doesn't make them anything alike."

"Don't hog the gravy, son; pass it along to your father. They're not cars, they're women, sophisticated women who want nothing to do with small-town life."

Why did his mother always have to be right? Still, he felt the need to say, "There are millions of sophisticated women, from big cities and small towns alike, and Whitney made a lot of pretty good friends here. We all knew she wasn't staying when she came.

She doesn't hate small towns, she just happens to have a very important and probably high-paying job in New York. And nobody asked her to give that up and live here."

"And why," his mother asked, leaning across the table and pointing at him with her fork, "didn't some enterprising young man ask that very thing?"

"Get real, Mom. I've known her barely two weeks."

"And your point is?"

It was the first laugh Adam had had since Whitney left four days ago.

"Son," she said earnestly. "When Monica left, it tore you apart. You curled up in a ball and licked your wounds for weeks. Mostly I think you were kicking yourself for believing in her. She wasn't worth it. But this one . . . Whitney . . . isn't she worth a little effort?"

Adam didn't have to give the idea any thought. It was suddenly so clear to him. Whitney was, indeed, worth a little effort. She was worth a hell of an effort. She was worth fighting for, even if it meant he had to fight her.

She was worth going after.

"What does that look in your eyes mean?" his mother asked.

"I think," his father said, "it means he'll be taking a little trip east very soon."

Adam smiled. "When's the last time I told you two I love you?"

Thursday night Whitney popped another antacid into her mouth and rubbed at the ache in the back of her neck. The on-air monitor showed an ID, then a commercial.

She was through for the night. Thank God.

She used to feel a little lost at the end of her shift. If she couldn't work, what was she to do with herself? But now all she wanted to do was go home. There were a million other things to do besides work.

She stepped out of the control room and headed for her desk.

"Good job tonight, Whitney."

"Thanks, Ed. You, too."

She turned the corner to her desk and stumbled to a halt. Her heart gave a hard thud, then fluttered rapidly in her throat. Sweat broke out across her palms. Her mouth went dry. And her heart, that aching, dried-up collection of musty, dusty rooms, nearly burst with joy.

"Adam!"

Coming to where she worked had been a gamble, but he'd been unable to wait a minute longer to see her. From the look on her face, it appeared that his gamble had paid off.

He pushed away from her desk, where he'd been sitting, and swooped her up in his arms. "I missed you."

"Thank God, thank God. I missed you, too."

"Whitney, here's that—oh. Excuse me."

Adam felt Whitney stiffen and released her. With only a slight blush, she smoothed her hair and turned to face a fiftyish man with silver sideburns.

"Uh, sorry," the man said. "I was just dropping off this cassette you asked for."

"That's all right, Bob. Thanks."

She took the tape from Bob and placed it on her

desk. When Bob left, she turned back to Adam. "Please, sit down. What are you doing here? When did you get in? How long are you staying?"

Adam laughed, relieved by her response. Yes, this woman was worth fighting for. And she did love him, or his name wasn't Adam Burkett.

He waited for her to sit, then took the chair next to her desk. "I just got in. I came to see you. And how long I stay depends on you."

"On me?"

"On you." He leaned forward and took her hands in his. "Whit, I'm not ready to end whatever it was we started in Washita. I want more time with you. I want to be with you. If the only way that can happen is for me to move to New York, well, hell, they need carpenters here, too, don't they?"

Whitney's heart stopped. "You would do that? You would leave your home, your family? For me?"

"Whitney, I love you."

"Adam, I love you, too. I didn't realize how much until I left and came back here. But how long would you be happy living in New York. Before long you'll start to miss your friends, your family, the town, the wide-open countryside."

"I'm willing to give it a chance, Whit."

"You'll end up hating me," she protested. "I know how much you'll miss all those things."

"Whitney—"

"I know because I've been back in the city less than a week and already I miss those things fiercely. You've got family and friends who need you, and I have a grandmother to care for and a business to run and a cat to feed."

Adam's pulsed leaped. "What are you saying?"

"I'm saying, if you don't mind, can we go home to Washita?"

"Mind?" he cried. "Of course I wouldn't mind. But what about your job? Your life here?"

"It's a job, Adam, that's all. I might miss it. I probably will miss it. But do you realize that the whole time I was in Washita I didn't spend every day washing down antacid tablets with black coffee? I didn't eat out of vending machines. My hands didn't shake from too much caffeine. I felt *good*. You don't know how rare that is. So if you don't mind, I'd like us to go back to Texas."

"You know I don't mind," he told her.

Her smile was wide and brilliant. "That's good, because yesterday I turned in my two-week notice and started making plans to return to Texas."

"Do you mean it?"

"I mean it."

"Are you sure?"

"I've never been so sure of anything."

"What about all the other stuff? How are you doing with finding out about your aunt? Your mother?"

Her smile dimmed but didn't disappear. "I'm still coming to terms with all of it. It's hard to take in. I'll never stop thinking of my parents—my adoptive parents—as my true parents. They're the ones who raised me. I'll always think of Aunt Claudia as Aunt Claudia, because that's who she's been to me all my life. But knowing what she did, what she went through and gave up for me—my God, she nearly gave up her life just so I could be born."

"What are you talking about?"

"I'll tell you all the details later. For now just know

that I'm working things out in my head. And that I love you."

"You're sure about that last part?"

"I'm sure."

"Then, will you marry me?"

With a laugh, Whitney threw herself into his arms. "I guess since we've known each other all of, what, three weeks? That's plenty of time. Yes, let's get married."

Epilgoue

On a perfect fall afternoon, a Saturday that September, Mrs. Ella Fields turned eighty-two. Her granddaughter, Whitney Sheridan Burkett, threw a party for her in the small courtyard at the nursing home.

All the nursing home residents who could be moved were brought out to enjoy the day and have cake and punch. Adam's entire family came, and when word got out that the town's beloved former librarian was having a birthday, they had to send out for more snacks and punch, so many people showed up to wish her well.

The excitement of the day put new color in Miss Ella's cheeks.

Adam and Whitney were working on her, trying to get her to agree to move in with them. If she used an electric wheelchair she could maneuver her way around the house without much trouble.

The good news was, Miss Ella showed signs of changing her mind and giving in.

It didn't hurt their cause any when Adam and Whitney announced to her that in seven months, God willing, Miss Ella was going to become a great-grandmother.

The picture Nurse Freeberger took at that moment, which ended up on the front page of the local paper the next day, captured tears of joy on Miss Ella's cheeks.